THE LOST FOR WORDS BOOKSHOP

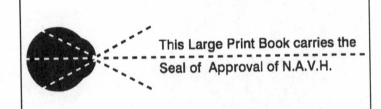

THE LOST FOR WORDS BOOKSHOP

STEPHANIE BUTLAND

THORNDIKE PRESS
A part of Gale, a Cengage Company

Farmington Hills, Mich • San Francisco • New York • Waterville, Maine
Meriden, Conn • Mason, Ohio • Chicago

Copyright © 2017 by Stephanie Butland.
The right of Stephanie Butland to be identified as Author of this work has been asserted by her in accordance with the Copyright, Designs and Patents Act, 1988.
Thorndike Press, a part of Gale, a Cengage Company.

Thorndike Press® Large Print Women's Fiction.
The text of this Large Print edition is unabridged.
Other aspects of the book may vary from the original edition.
Set in 16 pt. Plantin.

**LIBRARY OF CONGRESS CIP DATA ON FILE.
CATALOGUING IN PUBLICATION FOR THIS BOOK
IS AVAILABLE FROM THE LIBRARY OF CONGRESS**

ISBN-13: 978-1-4328-5351-8 (hardcover)

Published in 2018 by arrangement with Macmillan Publishing Group, LLC/St. Martin's Press

Printed in the United States of America
3 4 5 6 7 22 21 20 19 18

For Alan

POETRY

2016
UNLOOKED-FOR

A book is a match in the smoking second between strike and flame.

Archie says books are our best lovers and our most provoking friends. He's right, but I'm right, too. Books can really hurt you.

I thought I knew that, the day I picked up the Brian Patten. It turned out that I still had a lot to learn.

I usually get off my bike and wheel it on the last bit of my ride to work. Once you pass the bus stop, the cobbled road narrows and so does the pavement in this part of York, so it's a lot less hassle that way. That February morning, I was navigating around some it's-my-buggy-and-I'll-stop-if-I-want-to woman with her front wheels on the road and her back wheels on the pavement, when I saw the book.

It was lying on the ground next to a bin, as though someone had tried to throw it away, but didn't even care enough to pause to take proper aim. Anyway, I stopped. Of course. Who wouldn't rescue a book? The buggy-woman tutted, though I wasn't doing her any harm. She seemed the type who went through her days tutting, like a pneumatic disapproval machine. I've met plenty of those; they come with the nose-ring territory. They'd have a field day if they could see my tattoos.

I ignored her. I picked up the book, which was *Grinning Jack.* It was intact, if a little bit damp on the back cover where it had been lying on the pavement, but otherwise in good nick. It had a couple of corners folded down, neatly, making interested right-angled triangles. I wouldn't do that myself — I'm an honourer of books and, anyway, how hard is it to find a bookmark? There's always something to hand. Bus ticket, biscuit wrapper, corner off a bill. Still, I like that there are some words on a page that are important enough for someone to have earmarked them. (Earmarked, in the figurative sense, has been around since the 1570s. In case you're interested. When you work within five metres of four shelves of dictionaries, encyclopaedia and thesauri, it's just plain rude not to know shit like that.)

Anyway. As Archie says, I digress. Buggy-woman said, 'Excuse me, I can't see past you,' but she said it politely, so I shuffled the back wheel of my bike onto the pavement so she could get a better look at the traffic. And then I remembered not to make assumptions and judgements. Everyone is allowed to like poetry. Even people who tut at cyclists.

I said, 'Is this your book? It was on the ground.'

She looked at me. I saw her clock the piercing and the fact that my hair is black but my roots are brown, and waver, but, to give her credit, she apparently decided not to judge, or maybe my clean fingernails and teeth swung things in my favour. Her shoulders dropped a little bit.

'I can't remember the last time I picked up a book that didn't have lift-the-flaps,' she said, and I almost handed the book over to her, right then. But before I could offer it there was a break in the traffic and she launched herself across the road, trilling something about going swimming to her kid.

I looked around to see if there was someone close by who might have just dropped a Liverpool Poet, or be retracing their steps, searching, eyes to the ground. A woman standing outside the off-licence was going through her bag, urgently, and I was about to approach her when she pulled her ringing phone out and answered it. Not her, then. No sign of anyone in search of a lost book. I thought about leaving it on the off-licence windowsill, like you would with a dropped glove, but it doesn't take much in the way of weather to ruin a book, so I put it in the basket — yeah, I have a bike with a basket on the front, what of it? — and I kept on my way to the second-hand bookshop, where I've worked for ten years, since I was fifteen.

On Wednesdays I have a late start because I stay after hours on Tuesday for Book Group, which usually degenerates into something much less interesting after the second glass of wine. One of them is getting divorced. The rest are either envious or disapproving, though it's all hidden under sympathy. It's briefly amusing but ultimately unsavoury, like Swift.

One thing I do like about Book Group is that we host it rather than run it, so I drink tea and tidy up and listen in for the book-discussion bit, then zone out for the rest. It gives me the chance to do the things I can't do when the shop is open; it's amazing how much you get done when you're not interrupted. Archie says that if I had my way, bookshops would be set up like an old-fashioned grocery, with a counter and shelves behind it, so there were no pesky people messing up my beautifully ordered system. I say he's being unfair, but I don't think a Bookshop Proficiency Test would go amiss. Just some basic rules: put it back where you found it, treat it with respect, don't be an arse to the people who work here. It's not that hard. You'd think.

When I got in it was quiet. I was a bit late, partly because of the Brian Patten, but I was cutting it fine for an eleven o'clock start anyway. I stay after closing often enough for Archie to give me some leeway when I've got an urgent chapter to finish, though, so it's never a big deal. After I'd locked up my bike, I went to the cafe next door to get myself a tea and Archie a coffee before I made a start. If you ignore the silk flowers and the signs that say things like 'Arrive as a Stranger, Leave as a Friend', Cafe Ami is a pretty good neighbour.

I love stepping through the door of Lost For Words. The bookshop smells of paper and pipe-smoke. Archie doesn't smoke in the shop any more, officially at least. I suspect that he does when no one's around. All the years when he did go through the day puffing away non-stop have got into the

13

walls and the wood and the pages of the books. There's something about standing, surrounded by shelves, that makes me think of being in a forest, though I've never, come to think of it, been in a forest. And if I was, I'm guessing the smell of smoke might not be a good thing. Anyway. I gave Archie his coffee.

'Thank you, my ever-useful right hand,' he said. He's left-handed and he thinks that sort of thing is funny. I gave him a sarky smile and poked him in the waistcoat. There's a lot of Archie under that waistcoat. If you were going to stab him you would need a really long knife to get to any vital organs. He picked up his pipe. 'I'm going to take the air,' he said. 'Be excellent in my absence, Loveday.'

'As ever,' I said.

There are bay windows on either side of the shop door and one of them is filled by a huge oak pedestal desk. Archie says he won it from Burt Reynolds in a poker game in the late 1970s, but he's very hazy on the details. If all of Archie's stories are true, then he's about 300 years old — according to him he's had the bookshop for twenty-five years, been in the navy, lived in Australia, run a bar in Canada with 'the only woman who ever really understood him', worked as a croupier in Las Vegas and spent time in prison in Hong Kong. I believe the one about the bookshop and (maybe) the one about the bar.

It's a lovely desk, if you can find it under all of the papers. The letterbox is to the left of the shop door, and the end of the desk is underneath it; sometimes there are three days' worth of post and free newspapers on there before I clear them away. All Archie ever does is put more things on top of them.

The other bay window has a little window seat, which is about as comfortable as it looks — that is, not comfortable at all, although people who grew up on *Anne of Green Gables* can't help but sit in it. They never manage it for long. I think window seats are one of those things that are always better in books, like county shows held in fields on bank holiday Mondays, and sex and travel and basically anything you can think of.

There was plenty for me to do. I know you're supposed to appreciate a lie-in, but I always just feel as though I've let the day get away from me and I'll never catch up. The only benefit is that I don't have to bring in the bags of books people leave in the doorway because they can't differentiate between a secondhand bookshop and a charity shop.

My dad's mum always used to be up with the sun. I can still hear her saying, 'Best part of the day, little one,' with her voice burring and her eyes smiling. My dad's parents were the first people I knew who died. We went to Cornwall twice that year, once in spring when Granny died of stomach cancer, then again in autumn when Grandpa followed her, and everyone shook their heads and said 'broken heart'. I suppose I was four or five. I remember thinking it was strange that Dad's parents had died but Mum was the one crying. The beach we used to go to near Falmouth — where my dad was from — was like a beach from a story-book: in my memory, the sand is yellow, the sea felt-tip-pen blue. We lived near the sea at home in Whitby, but the Cornish beach was different. It was magical. After Grandpa died, we didn't go back. Dad always said that there was no love lost between him and Auntie Janey, so I suppose there was no reason to.

I started with a bit of a tidy-up and I went on to the customer enquiries. Archie's an unreliable computer-user — he can do it, but he's erratic — so I looked at the emails first, sitting at the desk while he puffed away at his pipe outside on the pavement. There was nothing significant: an enquiry about a book we didn't have, an online sale. Five minutes and they were done, and then I looked through the box of enquiry slips. I started leaving them out for customers to fill in themselves because Archie only passes on the queries he thinks are interesting.

There was only one new one, and it was for a book we had a copy of in the storeroom upstairs, so I dug it out and put it in a brown paper bag, wrote the customer's name on it, phoned the customer to say it was waiting, and put it on the shelf behind the desk. It was a Jean M. Auel, something Archie would definitely have considered below his notice. It might have only been a fiver but I'd bet good money that all of my fiver book sales add up to more than Archie's precious first editions. In fact, I don't need to bet. I see the figures. Archie takes me to the meetings with the accountant, so I can listen to the bits he misses. He starts by nodding and then nods off, double-chin to chest. It's funny, he looks small when he's sleeping. When he's awake, and he's talking, he seems too big for the shop, too big for York, although he says the city is perfect for him. I asked him once how he ended up with the shop and he said, 'It was time to be contained,' which is a ridiculous answer. Another time he told me that he came to York to see a friend, 'got overly merry', and bought the business on a whim. Also ridiculous, but more likely to be true.

Ben, who does house clearances and brings the books to us, had brought in a couple of boxes and, judging from the spines of the books I could see, they were going to be a welcome addition to the Music Biography (Classical) section: there was my work for the day. I like it when boxes like that come in, with a theme rather than a hotchpotch of collected living. It makes me feel as though I'm spending time with someone who had a bit of substance. Plus, there's always the possibility of what Archie calls buried treasure. A person with a passion is more likely to have bought and kept first editions and tracked down rare things for the sake of their content, but they won't have thought about financial value, because the value, for them, is all in the pages. Personally, I'm with them, but as Archie loves to point out, I'm not the one paying the rent.

Before I started on the box, I made a little notice — 'Found' — like the 'Lost' ones people make when their cats go missing. Like the cat hasn't just had a better offer and pissed off out of there. The notice said:

'Found: *Grinning Jack* by Brian Patten. If you are the (neglectful) owner, come in and ask for Loveday.' I stuck it in the window and tucked the book away, in the back, behind the door marked 'Private'. If no one else was going to appreciate it, then I would.

It takes Archie half an hour to smoke his pipe, gossip with everyone and anyone who's going past, and come back in again. He makes no concession to weather, and I kind of admire his commitment, though I'm well aware that if he was smoking cigarettes I might not be as sympathetic. The smell of cigarette smoke reminds me of my dad. My mother made him stop when money was tight. Even now, cigarette smoke makes me uneasy, and at the same time it smells something like home.

There was a biography of J. S. Bach in the box, and when I opened it up I found a piece of greaseproof paper, carefully folded to enclose a rose. The paper crackled as I unbent it, but didn't break; the rose seemed more brittle than the wrapping, and I held my breath over it, not wanting to touch it with anything at all, in case I broke it apart. The petals might have been pink, once, but they had become a dusty grey, tucked away from air and light. I refolded it in the paper and pinned it on the 'Found in a Book' noticeboard at the front of the shop, wondering who had saved it, and why; whether it had been pressed on an impulse and forgotten, or whether it was a symbol of something more significant. I find the fact that I'll never know quite comforting. It's good to be reminded that the world is full of stories that are, potentially, at least as painful as yours.

A week passed, and there were no takers for the Brian Patten. I was planning to take the sign down that afternoon. My plan was to tuck the book behind the counter and then give it to someone who was buying something that suggested they might appreciate it. I wasn't going to sell it; that didn't feel honest. Yeah, I sometimes over-think. There are worse faults.

I was having my lunch in the back of the shop, which is basically: a tiny loo and hand basin behind an ill-fitting wooden door that needs a yank to close it and a shove to open it; an armchair in front of the fire exit; a shelf; a bin and the hoover underneath the shelf. The armchair is big and comfy, jammed into the space: I can sit crosslegged in it. I have cereal and a banana for lunch — which is also what I have for breakfast, but I like breakfast best, so why the hell shouldn't I have it twice a day? — and I was halfway through it when I heard Archie calling my name.

When Archie calls it's usually because one of 'my' customers (i.e. one of the ones he doesn't like) comes in. It won't be a question about stock, because I swear he knows every single book in the shop, and where it is.

Archie and I are alike in that we have a low tolerance for people who annoy us — not an advantage in the customer service game, as he says — but the good thing is that different categories of people wind us up. I don't like people who giggle. He says there's nothing wrong with a little bit of *joie de vivre*. He doesn't like people who smell. I say you shouldn't penalise people for their circumstances and books don't care when you last washed. I don't like people who try to knock down the price or bang on about how they could get it cheaper on the internet. Those people don't realise that, for a lot of rare books, if they search the internet they'll end up at us anyway, but we'll charge them postage, too. I quite like it when that happens. A bit of schadenfreude really brightens up twenty minutes in a post office queue. I feel like Becky Sharp from *Vanity Fair.*

Archie doesn't like the people he calls superfans, but I like a bit of focus in my customers. There's nothing wrong with wanting to own every edition of every book by a particular writer, and most of the authors who are being pursued through our shelves are dead, so if they're not bothered by obsessive fans, I don't see why we should be.

I thought the visitor was probably a collector, who Archie would automatically pass to me, regardless of how far through my lunch I was. I overlook his minor infringements of employment law on the basis that his good points outweigh his flaws by a ratio of about three to one. The old lady gothic novel fan has a sixth sense for when she can ruin my lunch by interrupting me, so I was expecting it to be her, but as I rounded the end of the cookery section, I saw that Archie was talking to someone I had never met. I'd have remembered.

Leather coat and a crew cut, metallic-blue DMs laced up differently, a laugh — Archie looked as though he was on a charm offensive — like sea over gravel. Archie saw me coming and he caught my eye.

'Brace yourself,' he was saying, 'she doesn't approve of people who aren't good to books.'

'Fair enough,' said the stranger. 'I don't approve of them either.'

'Here she is,' Archie said. 'My straywaif.' I thought for a horrible moment that he was going to launch into his how-I-met-Loveday story, but he managed to resist.

'Can I help?'

'You certainly can,' said the stranger. 'You already have, I believe.' He smiled and his teeth were straight and even, middle-class teeth, braced into conformity at great expense, no doubt.

'Really?' He could work for it.

'Loveday,' Archie said, 'this gentleman is in search of a missing poet.'

'The sign in the window. The book.' The stranger's voice was clear and I couldn't find an accent in it, not that it was exactly posh, either.

'I found it on the pavement,' I said. I sounded accusatory. I didn't mind. Poetry has a difficult enough time without people throwing it away.

'I think it fell out of my pocket,' he said. 'It's quite deep but I was reading it on the bus, then I realised I'd nearly missed my stop, and I don't think I put it away properly.' He put his hand into the pocket of his coat and it disappeared up to the wrist. I noticed that his hands were long, even in proportion to the rest of him, his fingers tapering, the tip of his thumb arching away from his hand, as though it was going to do a runner.

'Uh-huh,' I said. I figured he could work a bit harder, though it amused me that he thought he had to make a case, as if he'd arrived late for a job interview.

'And I love the Liverpool Poets,' he said. 'I studied them. People don't realise they pretty much invented performance poetry. They invented The Beatles, come to that.'

I didn't need to hear his dissertation. 'I'll just go and get it,' I said. I had a spoonful of cereal when I went through to the back, but it had gone to mush.

'Our neglectful new friend is a poet himself,' Archie said when I returned.

'Then he should know better than to fold down the corners of poetry books,' I said, and gave him his Brian Patten back. I wasn't going to be impressed. I've got a couple of notebooks of my own poems at my place; I wouldn't tell people I'm a poet. I'd tell them I work in a bookshop. If I thought it was any of their business.

'I know, it's a terrible habit,' said the leather-coat-poet, and he smiled and I smiled back, even though I didn't really want to. Smiles give too much away. More than your teeth.

He tucked the book into his pocket and pulled the flap over the top, as if to show me that he'd learned his lesson. It was the beginning of March, cold still. I wondered what he wore in summer.

'Well, I'll be more careful in future.' He made a gesture — I thought he was saluting, but then I realised it was a sort of hat-tip, though he wasn't wearing a hat, so it came off slightly stupid, or it should have done. Then he held out his hand to me to shake, and I shook it. He said, 'Thank you, Loveday. Nathan Avebury.' His wrists were slim, straight.

'No problem,' I said. This is why I don't like talking to people. I never think of anything interesting to say. I need time to find words, and that's hard when people are looking at me. Also, I don't like people much. Well, some are okay. But not enough to make it a given.

He turned away and I realised there was something in my hand. A chocolate coin, wrapped in gold foil and thoughts of long-ago happy Christmas mornings. If he'd been looking at me when I realised, waiting for a reaction, I would have written him off as a stupid show-off. But the bell above the door had already jangled out the message that he'd gone, and when I looked up there was no sign of him outside.

'Well,' Archie said. 'Nathan Avebury.'

'Do you know him?' I asked.

There aren't a lot of people in this corner of York that Archie doesn't know. He's friends with the publicans, though they've started to change over the last few years now the pubs have become more like restaurants, run by foodies rather than drinkers. He makes a point of shopping in all the nearby places, buying cushions and paintings of the coast, artisan chocolates and lots and lots of cheese. His doctor is always talking to him about cholesterol and losing weight, but Archie says good relationships are more important than being able to see your feet.

'I only know him by reputation,' Archie says. 'Time was, he was the next big thing.'

I knew he was waiting for me to ask for details, so I didn't. I went back to the armchair and ate the rest of my banana, and when I came back into the shop I took the 'Found' notice down. Then I got stuck in to the box of music biographies again.

There were no more treasures among the pages, no pressed flowers or postcard bookmarks or names on the flyleaf that made me wonder. My favourite, ever: a 1912 edition of *Mansfield Park,* which had 'Edith Delaney, 1943' written in the careful, joined-up writing of a child on the inside front cover. The 'Delaney' was crossed through and 'Bishop' written underneath. Then 'Bishop' crossed out and another name, a longer, double-barrelled one, scored through so thoroughly that it's impossible to make out. 'Brompton-Smith' is my best guess. Then 'Humphrey' underneath that. All the same handwriting, but you can see she's getting older. I've got the book at home. Along with my wages I get a book allowance and this was one of the first ones I took. I look at it and I think, well, Edith Delaney-Bishop-Brompton-Smith-Humphrey, I hope you married them all because you liked them, even if Brompton-Smith turned out to be a bastard, by the looks of it. Good for you for taking no shit off anyone.

Wednesday is Archie's bridge night so he left early, putting on his Crombie coat with the moss-green velvet collar and shouting, 'Toodle-oo, Loveday' as he went. I stayed a bit late, getting through the box, putting aside the books that I thought were worthy of Archie's attention. I always lock myself in at five, because late afternoon is Rob's favourite time for coming in and talking about how I should go out with him again as we got off on the wrong foot. He wouldn't try anything nasty — he wouldn't dare — but I can't be bothered with him. Well, I can't be bothered with men in general, so if I'm not getting any of the alleged thrills, I'm sure as hell going to do without the aggro.

At five fifteen, there was a tap on the door, and there was Rob's grinning face, making a 'let-me-in' gesture. I shook my head, pointed at the 'closed' sign, and went back to what I was doing. He knocked a couple more times but I ignored him. Then there was a sort of crunching, rattling sound and I realised he was pushing a rose through the letterbox. It's one of his regular tricks. He also brings in chocolates for me and leaves them with Archie because he knows I won't take them from him. I don't eat them; I put them on the big table with a 'help yourself' sign and they're gone within an hour. I'd like to think that Rob would read the sign as a bit of advice for him — as in, 'please get yourself some help' — but if he comes in when the chocolates are out he just looks pissed off.

Rob stood there for a bit longer waiting for me to go and get the rose, but I didn't, so he went away, giving the door handle a last, vicious rattle as he went. I picked up the stem and crushed petals from the desk and was taking them through to the bin when the letterbox rattled again and I jumped. I turned around and saw the back of a leather coat swirling away, and there was a leaflet sticking through the letterbox.

Poetry Night at the George and Dragon Wednesdays from 8 p.m. £3 entry. Open mike.

There were Facebook details at the bottom. I put it on the community noticeboard, which is next to my noticeboard of things we've found in books, and I locked up and left. I pass the George on the way home; it's on the corner before the cycle lane starts.

I didn't go in.

I wondered if that twirling-away of leather was the last I'd see of Nathan Avebury. But no. He came back the next week.

'Hello, Loveday,' he said.

I turned around and nodded, then went back to what I was doing. I'm not paid to pass the time of day with any old poet who wanders in. That's Archie's job.

I was tidying up the Sci-fi section — it never stays neat for more than half a day —

and had my back to the door when he came in, though I'd heard Archie greeting someone. I hadn't bothered to look; Archie greets most people as though they are a visiting foreign dignitary, a lover, or someone recently returned from the dead.

Nathan didn't move away. He was still there when I got to Wilder, Wyndall and Zindell. I stood up. He was looking at the shelves, idly, as though he was killing time waiting for something. A bookseller, for example.

His boots were still laced up differently, one criss-crossing on the front, one straight across. I wondered if he noticed, or cared. He noticed me looking.

'Magician's trick,' he said. 'If people notice the lacing it distracts them. Also, if people notice that, I know they're the noticing sort, and I have to be careful.'

I nodded. I could see the sense in that. I liked it better than carelessness, or affectation. If I cared, which I didn't.

'Magician?' I asked, and then remembered. 'The chocolate coin.'

'Close-up magic,' he said. 'It's sort of my day job, though it's quite a lot of evenings. Afternoons are kids' parties; evenings are corporate events. Poetry doesn't really pay the rent.'

I laughed. I'm not sure why. I think I was amused by the idea of being a magician as a day job. Most people with a day job work in a shop or a call centre, or serve cream teas to tourists while wearing a mob cap, around here at least.

'I thought I'd come and take a look at the poetry section,' he said.

'I'll show you,' I said. The shop isn't huge but it's twisty, and it's easier to take people than to explain where to find things. The poetry books live along the back wall, with the plays and the old maps. Archie isn't a fan of poetry and plays because he says they shouldn't be written down, so he's put them in the darkest corner he can find. The walls all have shelves built along them, in a mishmash of a way, different heights and depths in different places. Fiction goes all around the walls, and then the middle of the shop is filled with freestanding book-cases, back to back and at right angles with each other around a central table. They're all different, but what they have in common is that they are all some kind of old, solid wood, uncomplaining, doing the heavy lift-ing of non-fiction in all of its glorious forms. Although, give me a novel any day.

I led Nathan to the back wall. His boots squeak-squeaked behind me, and I was suddenly aware of my spine, my arse, the back of my neck where I'd bunched my hair in an elastic band to keep it out of my face. I stood straighter, and turned when we got there.

'Poetry,' I said.

'Thanks,' Nathan said. He smiled. He seemed to smile a lot.

'All part of the service,' I said.

Then Melodie appeared. When we're swamped, Archie pays her to do a bit of shelving, and she does a good job, but she witters on the whole time, like a trapped chaffinch, and it drives me demented. When she's not doing her main job — leading tourist walking tours — she treats the shop like her living room, sitting at the table with a coffee, making impossible-to-ignore phone calls, using the Wi-Fi. You couldn't pay me enough to be herded around York and yammered at by Melodie, but I think she probably does quite well. She's big-eyed and big-mouthed and tiny, a pert kitten of a thing. I think her mother's Malaysian, though I have no idea why I've remembered that. When she's in the shop she keeps up a constant monologue, which I try to drown out by turning my own mental chatter up, but some things must permeate. She's not backward in coming forward, as my dad

32

used to say.

'Loveday showing you the poetry section?' Melodie asked.

'That's right,' Nathan said.

'Alphabetical order,' Melodie said. 'I did it last week. I like my poets stay in line.' She talks in this pirate patois that I think she must have picked up from a film, because I know for a fact that she grew up in Pickering.

'Noted,' Nathan said. 'I won't disturb the line.'

'Hello.' She held out a little hand, palm-down, fingers draping, as though she thought he should kiss it.

He shook it and smiled. 'I'm Nathan Avebury,' he said.

'Nathan Avebury,' Melodie said, 'it lovely to meet you. I am Melodie. Like in music.' She held the chocolate coin up to the light, turning it slowly, cool as you like, as though its appearance in her palm was exactly what she had expected.

'Melodie works here sometimes, when we're busy,' I said.

'Loveday work here all the time,' Melodie supplemented, 'every day. This her world. I come and go, as I please.' She turned away, with a cat-eye look, and I found myself looking at Nathan to see what he was making of it all. He watched her go — she was wearing denim shorts over black tights, plimsolls, a striped jacket — and then he looked at me and he smiled.

'It's a great world to spend every day in,' he said. His eyes were the kind of blue you find on self-help book covers, to suggest clarity and calm.

'Yes,' I said. I liked that he didn't bitch about Melodie. I don't like her but I don't like people who are nasty either, especially about easy targets. Like women with tattoos and a nose-ring, for example. Still, if I take a bus, I mostly get a seat.

We looked at each other for a minute and I wished I was like Archie, who can start a conversation with anyone, about anything. Half the people who come into the shop are people he's got talking to at art gallery openings or while buying sausages at a farmers' market. He's just at ease. I'm not. Well, not with new people. It takes me a while to get comfortable with them, and in the bit when I'm getting comfortable I don't say much, and what I do say is pretty everyday. Archie says I keep all my interesting bits well hidden and getting to know me is an exercise in faith rewarded. I think he thinks he's being nice.

I couldn't think of anything else to say, so

I said, 'I'll leave you to it.'

'Great,' Nathan said.

Another box had come in. It was full of run-of-the-mill 1990s mid-range paperbacks, Penguin Classics, the ones with the black covers and the National Gallery chocolate-box paintings on the front, hardly touched. Nothing special, or at least, nothing remarkable: Eliot, Trollope, Dickens.

We have what Archie calls the 'breakfast bar' at the back of the shop. It's basically a deep shelf fixed halfway up the wall, and a high stool to sit on while you work there. There's a couple of old mugs, filled with pens and bits of paper for notes. The breakfast bar is where we sit to sort the books that come in. I say 'we' but Archie's not a fan of this part of the business. We (I) can work as well as keep an eye on the shop: there's a convex mirror fixed over the top so we can see who's coming and going, if there's only one of us here. He lets me do the first sift and look over anything interesting that comes in. I was eighteen and I'd worked here for three years before I was allowed to do it on my own. 'Off you go, Loveday,' Archie said that day, 'consider yourself qualified'. It felt better than my A Level results did, better than the applause at the end of the school play when I was a kid. I didn't go straight back to my flat that night. I went to the river and I sat by the water and I thought; *Loveday, it might be okay.*

As I started to take the Penguin Classics out of the box, 1 felt a bit odd. I was free-floating above myself, as though something important was happening. It was like the feeling I had when I checked inside the dust jacket of a recently delivered and ordinary-looking 1930s hardback to find that it was actually a copy of *Lady Chatterley's Lover,* disguised to get through customs. They're really rare, because once they got into the country, the spurious dust jackets were thrown away. I knew it was worth hundreds of pounds and at the same time I couldn't believe it was in my hands. But there was nothing in this box that was anything special for a collector, so the looking-down-at-the-sea-from-a-cliff feeling it was giving me didn't make any sense.

Then I realised what it was. They were all books that my mother had owned. Every single one. She knew books were important, my mother, and she liked that I liked read-ing, and she encouraged me to do it. She had a little set of bookshelves in the living room under the stairs — we lived in a tiny new build on the outskirts of Whitby, which probably looked quite big before the furniture went in, but felt squished even to little me.

The top shelf was for the black-bound Penguin Classics, the middle shelf, for the books I didn't keep in my bedroom — ponies, fairies, picture-books I refused to get rid of, even though I thought I was too old to read them — and the bottom was puzzle magazines and copies of women's magazines that my mum's friend Amanda passed on to her, though I don't know that she ever read those either. On the top of the shelf unit were photos in frames, all permutations of twos — me and Mum, me and Dad, Mum and Dad — because Dad was very precious about his camera, so we only took photos when he was around, and when he was around he wanted us to spend time, just the three of us, no one else, so we could make the most of things. He was precious about us, too. Or was it that we were precious to him? God, I don't love much but I love words. We all looked happy enough in the photos, I think. After the frames got broken there was nothing on top of the shelf unit any more.

Like I say, the books weren't unusual. You could get them in any bookshop, anywhere. But the fact that they were all ones we'd had at home made me feel . . . well, something. A pricking of my thumbs.

I took the Penguin Classics and I stood them, spines facing out, against the wall at the back of the breakfast bar shelf. I wanted to see how they looked. Could they really be the ones I remembered, or was I trying to make something that wasn't there?

I wasn't sure, at first.

Then I remembered that my mother used to put things in alphabetical order by the first word of the title. I've sometimes wondered if we should do that here. Most people remember titles more than authors, so it might make sense. At home, I just go with 'read' and 'unread', and move books from one shelf to another. Why waste precious reading time on sorting, that's what I say.

But my mother started at *Anna Karenina* and ended at *Wuthering Heights.* She said her books looked tidier that way. She also organised clothes by colour, which was great if you wanted your vest and your tights to match, less helpful if you wanted to find one of everything. My dad used to tease her about it. 'What's your mother like, Loveday?' he used to say, and I knew that was my cue to roll my eyes.

When I rearranged the books by title, I

felt dizzy. As though I'd stepped too close to the cliff edge, and the land was slipping away from the soles of my feet. Because they seemed right. As though they could really be the actual books that sat on the bookshelf in our house.

I could smell the smells of that first home: salt from the sea, and the damp earth of my mother's endless (endlessly dying, she never learned) potted plants. The house was rented and Mum was always saying how, when we had a place that was really ours, she would paint everything green. 'There's an upside to living like this, then,' my dad would say, and sometimes he made it sound funny and sometimes he said it in a way that made Mum say, 'Oh, Patrick,' and reach out to touch his arm or his cheek.

There were even twenty-six books on the bench in front of me. I counted them. And then I counted them again, like a man with a metal-detector who can't believe he's seeing the coins in his palm.

Twenty-six books. The ones my mother bought, once a fortnight, for a year, beginning with a bright New Year resolution and ending with a cold New Year's Eve, the year I was eight.

We used to go to the bookshop near the bridge in the centre of Whitby, every other

Friday after school. It was a little shop, cramped, with just a shelf or two for everything, but the lady in charge always smiled and said she could order anything we wanted. It was a warm place. I could choose a book for me, and Mum would have a long chat with the bookshop owner about what she was going to add to her collection. I don't think she ever told her that she didn't read them, but then again, I know she wouldn't have lied. And she meant to read them, I'm sure, she just never did. After a year she stopped buying them. Her resolution the next year was to learn to dance. She didn't do that either. She found a class but my dad didn't like the idea of her dancing with other people.

Anyone who's worked in a bookshop for longer than an afternoon will tell you that people buy books for all sorts of reasons. There's the simple love of books, of course: the knowledge that here is an escape, a chance to learn, a place for your heart and mind to romp and play. Recommendations, TV shows, desire for self-improvement, the need to impress or the hope of a better self. All valid reasons, none of them guaranteeing that the book will be opened at all. I think my mother liked the covers, the word 'classics', and the possibility of other worlds.

Of course, I have no one to talk about these things with. No one would remember the bookshelf, or if they did, they wouldn't remember which books and which order.

Sitting there at the back of the shop I also felt my world overlap with my only real childhood home, smelling the vanilla pot pourri that was supposed to disguise the cigarette smoke, listening to my mother pottering in the kitchen. I would pull out the books and look at the covers, spell out the titles. *The Mill on the Floss* sounded strange, because I didn't know that the Floss was a river. 'You're a little young yet, angel,' my mother said when she looked through the doorway and saw me turning the pages. I remember the words were crammed on to the pages like sweets in a jar.

'Loveday,' Nathan said, behind me.

I jumped. I mean, really, physically, arse off the stool for a nanosecond.

'Sorry,' he said.

'No problem,' I said. 'I'm just . . . I was busy.'

'My parents have Penguin Classics,' Nathan said. 'There are hundreds, aren't there?'

'Yes.' I could have added, 'My mother had some' — the words were almost in my mouth — but I don't talk about myself. So

41

I just sat there, doing a fair impression of the sulky emo-goth I look like.

'Well,' Nathan said, 'I found this.' He held up a copy of *Penny Arcade* by Adrian Henri. The slender spine was cracked, and there was a brown ring left by a coffee mug on the cover. 'I don't have it. I should. Unless I dropped it getting off a bus.'

I smiled. Yes I did. 'It's got "At Your Window" in it.' Anyone who likes Henri likes 'At Your Window'. I can talk about what's in books.

'I saw,' he said. 'Genius.'

'Over-used term,' I said.

'Couldn't agree more,' he said — he can smile and talk at the same time — 'but in this case, justified.'

I didn't agree, but I didn't say so. 'At Your Window' is about a cat who can't see why anyone wouldn't want a dead mouse. It made me think of Rob and his roses.

Nathan did the hat-tip-without-a-hat and turned away, but then swung back. 'I left a leaflet last week, about a poetry night. It's on Wednesdays at the George and Dragon. It's tonight.'

'I found it,' I said. 'I put it on the notice-board at the front, next to the one with the book finds.' I pointed, helpfully, in case he didn't know where the front of the shop was, or what a noticeboard looked like. I despair of myself sometimes. I'd like to blame the shock I felt at seeing those twenty-six books. But I don't know that I need an excuse to be incapable of sensible human interaction.

'I know,' he said, and he stopped smiling. 'Thanks, but I meant it as an invitation for you.'

'Me?' I thought for a horrible minute that he knew I wrote poetry, that I'd transmitted my dream/nightmare: me on a stage, me reciting my poems, the lights coming up and all the faces — my mother's and my father's, half of the auditorium him, half of it her, not knowing where to look . . .

'Well, you obviously have a fine appreciation for poetry,' he said, 'rescuing books dropped by feckless poets, so I thought you might enjoy it.'

'Thanks, but I'm not very sociable,' I said. I've found this is the best way to stop people asking me to do things, because there's not really a response, in the way that there is when you say that you're busy ('It's only a couple of hours!'), you're skint ('It's only a fiver! I'll treat you!') or you don't think you'll like it ('You never know! Give it a try!').

'Okay,' Nathan said, with a shrug (see?),

43

'but if you change your mind, come along. We've got a Facebook page. Message me or text and I'll keep you a seat.'

'I don't do Facebook.' There are enough people to contend with in real life without adding virtual ones. Or ones who might remember you from way back.

'Okay, text then,' he said. I didn't point out that I didn't have his number. I thought about how that just went to show how much he meant it.

When I turned back to the row of books, I saw that there was a business card sticking out of the top of *Jane Eyre*. 'Nathan Avebury: close-up magic', it said; there was a picture of a top hat and a mobile number. I swear he never moved his hands. One was holding the Adrian Henri, the other was in his pocket the whole time.

There were probably eight hundred Penguin Classics in print the year Mum was buying them. But small booksellers would have carried maybe the hundred most popular ones, so actually, anyone buying twenty-six Penguin Classics in Yorkshire in the 1990s would have had a limited choice. My mother hadn't gone far away from the mainstream — there had been at least one television adaptation of every single book on the shelf in front of me — and so probably anyone buying the books would have had much the same selection. And that was assuming I'd remembered all the titles correctly as hers.

I sat there for a while, looking at the unbroken black spines, and first I convinced myself that there was no way they could be her books, and then I decided there was no possibility that they weren't. I didn't like either answer. I put the twenty-six books into the classics section.

I didn't go to the poetry night. Obviously.

The next week, I locked up the shop later than usual because we'd had a couple of big online orders. Selling online was my idea, which means I'm not really entitled to complain about what a massive pain in the backside it is. It's mildly thrilling to package up a book that's two hundred years old and send it off across the world on the next part of its journey. Except that you don't know where it's going, whether it's going to be pored over and treasured, or put in a temperature-and humidity-controlled cabinet as part of a collection, added to the insurance documents, and ignored. What's the point of a book that isn't read? You wouldn't buy a pear and then just look at the outside forever, would you? Presumably the person who finds a book they've been searching for online does a happy little dance or an air-punch or, at least, grins like an idiot. I get to see that when they come into the shop. I can't get that from an email.

But, I'm not complaining. Really not. Just bored, because packaging and addressing is . . . boring. It's not bookish. I could just as well be wrapping up candles, or toolkits, or wooden spoons. I put some music on, loud (I like folk music, so what?), and I stood at the breakfast bar and wrapped and taped until there was a pile of packaged books. Archie would take them to the post office the next day. He likes that job more than I do. He would come back trailing more customers, no doubt, tourists he'd charmed in the queue. He wears a lot of tweed, and I suspect he was born with his moustache. He sometimes gets asked for his autograph — which he always gives, graciously, with a flourish to his signature — and I wonder who people think he could possibly be.

Rob had put another rose through the door. I couldn't be bothered to bin it so I left its bits on the desk where they had fallen, locked the door from the outside and went around the back to get my bike. There's a shed that all six shops in the parade share, and I leave it in there, with the cafe's summer pavement-tables. When I came back around to the main street, there was the man himself, leaning on the corner.

'Did you like the rose?'

'Hello, Rob,' I said. I went to self-defence classes when I was in sixth form. One of the main things I learned was: avoid getting yourself into a position where you'll need to defend yourself. Although that particular horse had bolted as far as Rob was concerned, I wasn't going to make things any worse.

Before The Incident, I wouldn't have thought I'd ever need to worry about Rob — he's tall, but he's got the physique of a wet teddy bear and is about as scary — but something I had learned without the aid of a self-defence instructor is that you never really know who's a threat and who isn't. I was on a darkening, quietish street with a man who thinks it's normal to repeatedly push unwanted roses through letterboxes, and that's on one of his good days. Not ideal. The next thing was to not piss him off. So I wasn't going to talk about the rose.

'Do you want to come out for a drink with me sometime, Loveday?'

'No thank you, Rob. I'm not very sociable.'

'I think we should try again.'

'Rob,' I said, 'I don't want to. I'm sorry. I've . . . I've moved on.' I looked at him for a second.

'You're seeing someone else?' He has nice eyes, but they were tired. I hoped he was sleeping, taking his medication. I like to think I'm not a monster. And I don't think he is, either.

I laughed at the idea of me seeing someone else. 'No,' I said. 'I'm just . . . I'm okay on my own.'

I tried to do the face Archie does, when someone comes in selling something he's not buying. He listens to the patter, says no thank you, then if whoever's selling tries again, he presses his mouth into a line and shakes his head, just a tiny bit. People pack up their wares and go. But it did't work. So I started wheeling my bike between us but he just swapped sides so he was walking next to me.

'Please, Loveday. I'm a nice bloke.'

'How's work?' I asked. I thought if I could get him talking about himself I might avoid an argument. Rob is one of those people who hang around in academia because it's safer than the world. I know, I know, as opposed to those people who hang around in second-hand bookshops because it's safer than the world.

'Busy,' he said. 'Exams coming up. My students are going to do well, I think. They're a bright lot.'

'Good,' I said, and I meant it. Rob's a clever guy. When he's not being a knob — when he's talking about the stuff he knows about, the Renaissance and Italy — he's worth listening to.

'But I don't want to talk about work,' he said. 'I want to talk about us.'

He put his hand on my back. He doesn't usually touch me. I could feel myself getting rattled. Next line of defence was to get on my bike and ride away, but I was just about to hit a bit of busy pavement, so I didn't fancy it. I was starting to feel like telling him what I thought of him, but confrontation freaks me out. My palms were getting damp and my feet were scuffing the ground, as though they were so busy getting ready to run that they'd forgotten how to walk properly.

And then I saw the George and Dragon. I checked my watch: 7.45. Wednesday.

I chained my bike up at the railings outside.

'I'm meeting a friend,' I said.

'I could join you,' he said.

'I don't think so,' I said. 'Goodnight.'

He put out his arm, as though he was going to touch me again, take hold, but I flinched away, turned, and went up the steps and into the bar without looking behind me to see whether he was following.

It was so fashionable I almost went back outside to run Rob's nasty little gauntlet — it would have been slightly less uncomfortable. Stripped floorboards, mismatched chairs, dark-grey paint, glittering black glass chandeliers, mirrors with unnecessarily camp frames. I had a horrible feeling that my drink would be served in a jam jar.

I remembered from the leaflet that the poetry slam was upstairs. There were twin metal spiral staircases, one for up and one for down. The function room was fairly small, a bar in the corner and half a dozen tables, a couple of sofas covered in cracked black leather. Smaller chandelier, less camp mirrors, as if to say: allow yourself to relax, traveller, we are fractionally less judgemental up here than we were downstairs.

I went over to the bar. I didn't think Rob had followed me. If he had, of course, I'd just made things worse because there was no reason why he wouldn't buy a drink and join the audience. I realised the windows overlooked the entrance. I could see if Rob had gone. If he had, I could just duck out again —

'Loveday,' said Nathan. 'Good to see you. I thought you were going to text me if you were coming.'

'I just . . .' The prospect of explaining was too much, as was, by then, the possibility of leaving, so I said the only other thing that was in my head: 'You haven't got your coat on.'

'No,' he said. 'I'm indoors.'

Did I mention that I love a cocky sod? No? Well, there's a reason for that. He was wearing navy trousers, pointed shoes, a striped shirt and — heaven help us — a cravat. I'm not chatty, but the cravat made me speechless. He was probably thirty. My mind was actually boggling. I don't think he noticed.

'Let me get you a drink,' he said.

'I'll get my own, thanks,' I said. Don't create obligation.

'Okay,' Nathan said. 'Do you mind if I keep you a seat?'

'That would be good,' I said. No sign of Rob yet, but if he did show I didn't want to be sitting at a table on my own.

The first time Archie took me for a drink after work — I might have been seventeen — I panicked and asked for a dry sherry, because that's what Annabel, my foster-carer, drank at Christmas and I couldn't think of anything else. Archie came back from the bar with a glass with something pale green in it. 'Gimlet,' he'd said. I didn't realise he was saying the name of the drink, but I liked the taste. The next time I was at the shop he gave me a copy of *The Long Good-bye* by Raymond Chandler, because the hero drinks gimlets. I only read as far as the bit where the woman is killed and her face is beaten to a pulp, but I would have liked it without the violence. Famous last words, I know. Anyway, Philip Marlowe and I drink gimlets, though he puts a lot more of them away than I do. Pubs always have gin and lime cordial.

I turned and looked for Nathan, and for Rob. Still no Rob. I let myself breathe a bit more deeply. Nathan was sitting at the table nearest the 'stage' — a little platform built out from in front of the fireplace. He raised his hand in an 'over here' gesture; I made my way to him. The room had done that thing that rooms do when you're not looking, half empty to full-to-bursting in the time it takes to buy a drink. Nathan was sitting on his own, though there were two empty glasses at his table, so I guessed he had mates at the bar.

Nathan Avebury was not afraid. He was

one of those people who made his way effortlessly through life. You could see it in his eyes, his ease, the way he dressed. (Nathan's possible middle names: Oliver, Stanton, Bartholomew.) Scared people don't invite strangers to poetry slams. They write poems in notebooks that they keep under the bed.

He nodded as I sat down next to him. 'I just have to go through this,' he said, tapping the piece of paper in front of him: a list of names. I drank some of my drink — it had a stupid, too-short straw in it — and looked at the stage, as it was better than looking at the people. Crowds make me nervous, even crowds of poets. There was a single microphone on a stand on the stage.

I'd never been to a real poetry gig, if that was what this was, but I spent a lot of time on YouTube, the dreamer's friend, watching the likes of Kate Tempest, Lemn Sissay, Joelle Taylor, and wondering if, in a parallel universe, that could have been me. I know what you're thinking, but there was a time when I was the first to volunteer for anything vaguely showy-offy, and my mother used to joke about saving up for drama school.

I started to feel a little bit excited.

'I was doing the running order,' he said. 'I

like to try and mix things up so that everyone gets a fair crack of the whip.' He held
up the sheet, and I saw that the names now
had numbers next to them, but the person
at the top of the list was number three, the
second; six, the third; four. There were
twelve names.

'There's no number one,' I pointed out.
Which was a great thing to do because
there's nothing I like more than someone
coming into the bookshop and trying to tell
me that the Macs should come before the
Mcs. You can see why I don't have a lot of
friends.

'I go first,' Nathan said. 'I'm sort of the
warm-up act. No one takes a lot of notice.
So seeing as I organise it, it seems only fair.'

I nodded. I couldn't think of anything to
say. He reminded me of Elspeth Phipps,
who was my foster-mother for a little bit,
while we all waited to see if my mother was
coming home. Well, I was waiting. Everyone
else knew that the only real question was:
how long will she be away for? What was
actually happening was social services trying to find someone well equipped to cope
with the person they'd already decided I
would become.

You could never properly get a rise out of
Elspeth. I wouldn't have tried, because I

was too locked in my own head at that point to fight with anyone, too homesick for my old life to really bother to engage with the new one that had been forced on me. But some of the others, the scary-angry ones, took everything out on her. There was a kid who tried to set fire to the sofa once. It didn't catch, but it did leave a black, smouldering hole. She just said, 'Well, that's a shame, we're all going to have to take turns to sit on the floor, now, because we've one seat too few.' Nathan seemed to have the same sort of niceness, underneath his swagger and his purchases from the last remaining Dandy Gentleman's Outfitters in York.

So I tried to make amends. 'How does it work?' I said.

Nathan smiled, as if he knew I was saying sorry. 'Any poetry goes. Everyone has a three-minute slot, then we vote on paper slips, and the top two go again, with a different poem, and we vote by applause. The prize is the money from the door minus the room hire. Which tonight looks like about —' he looked around the room, getting a sense of the people there '— a princely thirty quid.'

'That's not bad,' I said. That's two brand-new hardbacks, or a month's electricity, in summer.

'Better than a poke in the eye with a sharp stick,' he agreed.

'Yes,' I said. My dad used to say that. He also used to talk about getting the shitty end of the stick, although if I was in the room and my mother caught his eye before he said it, he would swap out the 'shitty' for 'stagged'. I asked him what it meant, once, and he said it meant that the other guy always wins. I had meant that I didn't know what 'stagged' meant — it wasn't in the dictionary at school, and Miss Buckley always encouraged us to look up words we didn't know. It was years later, reading Daphne du Maurier, that I came across it again, and I realised it was a Cornish word. It gave me a funny little stab of remembering, one of those that isn't entirely painful.

It seemed unlikely that Rob was going to show up now. I thought about leaving but I had my drink and, anyway, I might be antisocial, but I'm not rude. My mother had manners and so did Annabel, the long-term foster-carer I lived with for almost eight years. I remembered that I hadn't paid, and put three pounds on the table in front of him.

'It's okay,' he said. 'I've paid yours.'

I hate that sort of thing. 'I didn't ask you to,' I said.

'I always pay for people's first times,' he said. 'It's nothing personal, Loveday.' He smiled and got up, stepped onto the stage, and clapped his hands together, five times, perfectly spaced claps, fingertip-matched, that made everyone in the room look around.

'Take your seats, please, ladies, gentlemen and poets. This is your five-minute call.' Then he went around the room and spoke to, I guessed, everyone who was going to perform. No one came back to the table I was sitting at, but someone did take one of the extra stools away so they could add themselves to the group at the next table. My drink was almost gone. I was sitting with my back to the wall. I looked around the room to see who I recognised. Melodie was at the back with a group of people who I thought I knew from the tourist-tour crowd: they sometimes stop outside the shop, with some semi-factual yatter about how old the buildings are.

And five minutes later — it was exactly five minutes, I checked — there was Nathan, three sharp claps this time. 'Ladies, gentlemen and poets, allow me to start by reminding you of the rules . . .'

I realised I didn't dislike him. Which is quite a big deal, for me. I don't really do 'nice until you prove you're not' — I find it saves time to work it the other way around, in the normal way of things.

I quite liked his poem, too, though the way he did it was a bit cocky. There was a lot of winking and pointing at people: he came across as insanely over-confident. Which made me like him a bit less again. So he was, basically, on the exact neutral point between 'liked by Loveday' and 'disliked by Loveday'. Not that he'd have cared. Not that I did.

The whole thing was nothing like I imagined it would have been, if I'd spent any time planning to come rather than using it as a Rob escape hatch. Nathan was the most 'poetical' person there, in terms of dress sense, at least. Everyone else was relatively normal, except in the sense that poetry attracts people with some difficult shit to say, sometimes.

An older woman recited a poem about the birds in her garden, standing with her eyes closed, as though she was reading from the back of her eyelids. The audience applauded too loudly and enthusiastically for the quality of the poem, I thought. Nathan leaned over and whispered to me that she was deaf and she always brought the same poem. There was a guy who did something closer to comedy than poetry, hopping from foot to foot as he spoke; there was some whimsy about clouds from a girl who didn't look old enough to be in a pub, something about buying coffee that made me really properly laugh out loud; someone quite spitty and finger-snappy who needed to learn how to edit. It was weird, in that I didn't feel completely uncomfortable, and I should have, because I don't like being in big groups of people and I don't tend to go anywhere near anyone saying how they feel.

I voted for Nathan. During the break while the votes were being counted he asked if he could buy me a drink, but I said no thank you and bought my own. Then he asked if I wanted him to introduce me to some people, and I said no thank you again, so he left me to it. I was thinking of what I would have been doing at home. Reading, writing, thinking about tidying up but not bothering. (I hope you're not feeling sorry for me, because I just described my ideal evening.) He didn't win, but he didn't seem to mind. I left after the winner was announced, when everyone was going back to the bar.

There was no sign of Rob. But my front tyre had been let down. I walked my bike home instead of riding it, and I was cold and really pissed off by the time I got into bed. March looks like spring but it isn't really, not once the sun has gone down.

The more I thought about Nathan's poem, though, the more I thought how clever it was.

Book
As performed by Nathan Avebury at the George and Dragon York, March 2016

I sometimes think I want to write a book of
    my life
So that when I meet you — or anyone new
    — I can hand it over and you can read it
Instead of trying to read me.
You can take it away and decide whether
    it's worth giving me your time.
You can think about if, the next time we are
    walking towards each other, you'll smile
    without slowing down
Or cross the street and pretend you haven't
    seen me
Or stop and put an arm round my shoulder,
    steer me into the nearest pub, and buy
    me a pint of stout.
Because you'll know, having read the book,
    that stout is what I drink.
You see the elegance of my proposal.

But every time I sit down to write the book,
I hit a snag.
I could tell so many stories.
I could be a poet or a magician or a failed
mathematician.
I could be happy or soul-sore or lonely.
I could start when I was born, when I was
twelve, when I left university.
And the book would be different for each
story I choose.
And the book would be true, and untrue, for
each.
Our pasts are as unfixed as our futures, if
you think about it.
And I like the freedom I have to tell a
different story.

HISTORY

2013
YOU DO NOT YET KNOW

Rob didn't look like an academic. He looked like a young Mr Rochester, handsome enough to make Bertha leave her world behind. The first time we met, I was summoned by Archie's cry — 'Love-DEEE!' — from the front of the shop, loud enough to reach through to the back. Actually, I was only two yards away, trying to bring some semblance of order to the sagas section, which makes me feel like Dorothea in *Middlemarch,* but without the sense of divine purpose. Every time you think those fat, worn tomes are under control, another boxful comes in, the covers all fishing nets and grubby urchins holding hands. Archie won't turn them down because he likes nothing more than being flirted with by a saga-loving old dear.

'I'm here,' I said. 'No need to shout.' They both laughed when they saw me — I was on my knees, and I looked around the bottom of the shelf unit. Rob's laugh was actually a pixie giggle, which made me laugh too, just because it wasn't a sound you expected to come out of a grown man. Especially one that looked the way he did. The giggle didn't go with the stubbled chin. I didn't fancy him, or anything, but there was definitely something about him. The bright-brown eyes, maybe.

I was twenty-two, and I'd been working at Lost For Words full time for four years. It was early September. The city was still hot and busy but the shop was a dark, cool sanctuary. I think I was starting to feel safe for the first time in a long time. Maybe that's why I let my guard down.

I'd been decorating my flat. The landlord had offered to pay to have it done; I'd taken the money for materials but done it myself, because I didn't like the idea of strangers being in my place. The only person who had been over the threshold except me was Archie, and that was how I liked it. Not that the flat was anything special. It was basically a square, where one corner was a tiny bathroom and the rest open-plan, with a galley kitchen and a bed-settee that I didn't always bother to open out to sleep on. It was full of books (it's fuller now), some on an old bookcase Archie gave me, most of them piled up against the wall. It might look like chaos but I know where everything is. I have a really good reading lamp and a little table with two chairs that I hardly ever use, but the table has a plant on it. It's a weeping fig. I bought it in a fit of reminiscence when I moved in, because my mother liked them, and I confidently expected it to die within weeks, but no, it soldiered on.

For the two weeks before Rob's first appearance I'd been sanding and painting. The walls were now the blue-green of seaglass, the woodwork bright white.

I'd been in the flat for as long as I'd had my full-time job. When I'd finished my A Levels, I fought my way out of the care system, even though they try to hold on to you until you're twenty-five, if they can. I was done. I was an adult. Archie had claimed he'd been under-paying me while I'd been working part-time for the three previous years, and he gave me a lump sum. I'm not sure I believed him, but I've been a beggar, not a chooser, since I was ten years old, and when I found a flat, the money paid my deposit and my first month's rent. I'd saved most of my wages and all of the allowances Annabel had been scrupulous about giving me. The local authority gave me £2500, too. So I bought a sofa bed, towels and pans, a TV, a second-hand hoover and a charity-shop bike, and I still had money in the bank.

I was happy in the flat, and working in a bookshop was, I suppose, my dream job, once the other dreams had realised they were on a hiding to nothing and found someone else to bother. Rob chose a good moment to come in to my life. I was ready for something new.

I got to my feet. 'Hi,' I said.

'I'm Rob,' he said.

'Loveday,' I got ready to go in to the explanation.

'Ah, a good Cornish name,'

'Yes,' I said, and I thought, *there's a turn-up.* The usual response is a question-mark look or a crack about my parents being hippies, which is so far from the truth it would be funny, if it wasn't. Still, an unusual name is handy in that it stops people from asking other questions about you. 'How can I help?'

Rob smiled, with a sorry-this-may-take-some-time expression. 'I'm starting on a PhD,' he said. 'I've got the academic papers more or less tracked down and the university libraries are good, but I wouldn't mind trying to find my own copies of some others. And I do need some books that are more . . .'

I thought he was trying to be tactful. 'Mainstream?' I asked.

He laughed, that funny giggle again. 'I wish,' he said. 'I'm going to say . . . niche.'

Usually when people use the word 'niche', it's their way in to a request for erotica and I had a vision of spending months trying to track down some bit of Victorian porn or other. I think my sigh was audible.

'I'm researching Renaissance Engineering,' he said.

'Oh, okay,' I said. It was on the tip of my tongue to say, 'Is that a thing?' but then I thought that Rob probably heard that as often as I heard the hippy parent gag, so I didn't. Instead I said, 'That's interesting.'

'It is,' he said, and his eyes got brighter. 'The maths is fascinating and so is the political context. It's . . .' He stopped. 'Sorry.'

'No, no,' I said, 'don't apologise. Do you know what you're looking for?'

'I've brought a list,' he said, handing over a sheet of paper in a clear plastic folder. 'I found you online and I thought it was worth having a walk down, as I'm not too far away.'

'Sure,' I said. 'Can you leave this with me for a few days? I'll have to root around in the storeroom upstairs.' We'd had a few boxes come in from a da Vinci enthusiast a couple of years previously. The big, shiny Leonardo-the-genius type books had gone quickly. We knock coffee-table books out for a fiver because, second-hand, they're an impulse purchase at best: there's not enough substance for anyone who's really interested and most people don't want to give a second-hand gift, but they might blow a few quid on something big and shiny. It's insane. You could get the complete works of Rupert Brooke for that money. I'd choose poetry over glossy paper and big photographs any day.

I thought there was a good chance the other books that had come in in the Renaissance boxes were still around, though.

'Thanks,' Rob said, and he touched my elbow. 'I appreciate it.'

I don't like it when people touch me without being invited. I nodded. He was heading out of the door when I thought to ask the obvious question. I caught up with him in the street, outside the cafe.

'Sorry,' I said, 'would you mind telling me a bit more about your research topic? I know you said Renaissance Engineering but I'm guessing that there will be a lot of things that touch on that, so . . .'

He smiled and turned to me, squinting

into the early autumn sun. 'It's about the links between Brunelleschi, who built the dome on Florence Cathedral, and Leonardo da Vinci. None of Brunelleschi's own writings survive and popular history has sort of written him out. I'm looking at his influence. People treat da Vinci as though he's a genius in isolation, or some kind of god. I think he was a bit of a magpie, picking shiny bits from others.' As he talked his hands made shapes in the air between us — steeples, prayers, books — and he looked at me and then up, and then back again, as he explained. His hair was brown, the same colour as the darkest parts of his eyes.

'So it's a bit like, if you didn't have the Beat poets, you wouldn't have Bob Dylan,' I said. Not that we need Bob Dylan.

'Exactly.' Rob smiled again. 'I like you.'

Idiot that I was, I liked that he liked me. I should have known better. In retrospect, I think that maybe he didn't like me much beyond the fact that I was talking to him about him and what he was interested in. I didn't clock that until later, though. And it could be that that's normal for relationships. My parents weren't exactly run-of-the-mill. I'd gone on a few dates in sixth form. I felt like I needed to get my virginity out of the way, so I could think about more

71

important things. A bit like, if you like books, you have to read *Great Expectations* at some point, and then it's done and you can move on. I hadn't really bothered with men since I got rid of my hymen. I'd read enough fiction to know that relationships were:

— well disguised as the best thing ever
— complicated
— doomed to failure, most of the time
— usually comprised of a winner and a
  loser

I'd pretty much decided that I could live without them, even before you added the 'do you love me for me or for my novelty value' complication. So by the time I was back on my knees in front of the sagas, my head was brim-full of Brunelleschi. I was hardly thinking about Mr Rochester at all.

I got a little bit obsessive about the books on the list. I like a different sort of challenge. Book enquiries tend to fall into four categories. The first is the misremembered/ inaccurate. ('I'd like a copy of *Any Which Way But Loose* by William Shakespeare, please.' 'Could you mean *Much Ado About Nothing*?' 'No, I don't think so. It's a play. Could you look in the drama section?') The

72

second is the you've-got-to-be-kidding-me. ('There was a book I read in 1974, or '75. It was a love story, set in America, I think, or Australia. Do you have it?') The third is book-request-of-the-week. ('I heard this programme on Radio 4, and it mentioned a book about Pythagoras, or maybe Prometheus . . .') And the fourth is the sort of enquiry you can really get your teeth stuck into because it means tracking down something that's hard to find. We don't get many of those because people who need something really specific tend to use the internet, and a lot of our specialist stuff is online, so people don't ring up and ask; they just look at our catalogue and pay online and my role is, basically, bubble-wrapping. So Rob's list was a bit of a gift.

I think I felt empty, then. I'd decorated the flat and it was exactly as I wanted it. I had a long-term lease on my home and a job that was just right for me. My life was sorted. I was twenty-two. I liked everything I'd found, or made, and I was comfortable; but I didn't need to think about another fifty years of the same.

It was better to think about Florence. I looked up the cathedral on the internet and it's one of the only times I've wondered about getting a passport and going somewhere on a plane.

CRIME

1999

A BRASSY, JANGLING CLANG

I was nine when it all changed. I came home
from school an hour and a half later than
usual that Thursday, because of *Bugsy Malone,* our junior school play. My teacher,
who was kind and encouraging most of the
time, had started saying, 'No, No, NO, Year
4,' and shaking her head, and had arranged
an extra rehearsal with what she called 'the
principals' because, she said, if she could
knock us into shape then the rest would follow. I loved performing and I knew all of
my lines so I dodged most of the wrath,
although I got told off for looking sulky
when I should have been looking angry.
From the mouths of primary school teachers.

Mum let me walk to and from school with
my friend Emma, who was also in the play,
because there were no roads for us to cross.
It felt like a huge adventure at the time,
although I think the walk was less than two

minutes.

Thursday night meant it was pasta night. I liked spaghetti bolognese and Mum liked the spirally shapes with tuna and peas, so when Dad was away we took it in turns. I liked Thursdays because pasta was quick to make and quick to wash up, so there was extra time for reading, or sometimes Mum would let me come downstairs in my pyjamas and read a book on the sofa, tucked under a blanket, while she watched *East-Enders* or a cooking programme. And pasta night meant that it was almost the weekend. I liked school but I liked home better, and the weekends were fun, whatever we did. This was going to be one of Dad's weekends. They were the best kind.

So I was surprised to get home from school and smell something cooking already. The aroma, rich and thick, was seeping out of the kitchen and waiting in the air around the door. Beef in beer, Dad's favourite. And Dad's boots were on the step. They were cracked around the toes, worn and warped and telling me that my suspicions were correct. (I may have been reading mystery stories at the time.) He was home, all right. His boots, which smelled of salt and oil, rubber and leather, lived outside, because my mother said they made the whole house stink. If it looked like rain she put them under a tarpaulin and weighed it down with stones, and he laughed at her and said it was a miracle that he was allowed into the house as he must smell worse than the boots.

I went in and saw that the big cast-iron pot was out on the stove, a tiny flame under it. I knew I had to be careful with the cooker, and I knew the pot lid was heavy, so I didn't peek. Not that I needed to. The smell of it was unmistakeable.

Dad didn't usually come home on a Thursday — the oil rigs were three weeks on, a week off, changeover on Fridays, and he went to work on a train then a plane then a helicopter, something that made me feel proud. No bus or car for my dad. But there were no other boots like these boots. I looked at the laces, fraying at the end. I loved it when Dad came home. Although Mum and I were happy when it was the two of us, when Dad was back it was as though someone had closed a door that had been standing ajar and letting the wind come in. With Dad home we were complete, contained. I wondered if I might get the day off school tomorrow.

I heard steps from above and then my mother came down the stairs. Her dark hair, the same brown as mine, was loose, freed from its usual ponytail. She was wearing the jade-green satin dressing gown that Dad and I had chosen for her at Christmas. Her eyes were bright, and she was smiling.

'LJ,' she said, and she held out her arms. She cuddled me. She would always touch you if she could, my mum, hold your hand or stroke your hair. She was plump and soft, lovely to squeeze. Dad called her 'butterball' and now that I was growing, stringy and tall, he said we looked like the dish and the spoon who ran away together. My mother would laugh and he would grab at her, great handfuls of thigh and bum, and say: 'I could eat you up.'

Mum said, 'I thought that sounded like you. Have you worked it out, love?' She smelled of Dad: cedar and cigarette smoke and a tang of oil that never seemed to go away.

I thought of how many stories started like this, something unexpected on an ordinary day. I felt a tumble of excitement as I pressed my face into the satin.

'Dad's home!' I said, 'I saw the boots.' I pulled away and looked up at her, wrinkling my nose, because that's what we did when we talked about the boots. Mum wrinkled her nose back and we laughed.

'Clever girl,' she said. 'He's asleep so we'll leave him for a little while. I'm going to have a shower.'

'It's not the morning,' I pointed out, 'and it's Thursday. Dad doesn't usually come home on a Thursday. This is an intriguing day.' I liked collecting words.

Mum looked at me for a moment, puzzled, and then said, 'Oh! Yes, it is! But you say it "in-TREE-ging", LJ, not "in-trig-you-ing".'

I said it back to her, 'In-TREE-ging.' (Okay, this is a problem with books. But the only one.)

'Lovely!' Mum smiled, but then her face went serious; I know she was deciding something. 'Dad's not going to work on the oil rigs any more,' she said, 'so he'll get a different job. That's why he's come home early. I thought we should have beef stew, to cheer him up.' She smiled again, and touched my hair. 'When I come down, we'll make the parkin.' Mum and I always made that on the afternoons when we knew Dad was coming home, and we'd eat it warm, with cups of tea for them and a glass of milk for me, when he arrived. He said that if he came home blindfolded he could find us by the smell of that cake. Then she was gone, back up the stairs, and I heard the shower running.

I sat on the step and waited for her. At first I had been excited about Dad coming home early. The prospect of baking was always good. But I also felt upset. I knew what unemployment was, because my friend Lara's dad was unemployed, and now she got free school meals and her birthday party was at home, instead of at the pottery cafe where she had said it was going to be.

I had no real grasp of what was coming; I think I was tearful because of the simple confusion brought by the sudden changing of a rule that I didn't actually know was changeable. If anyone asked me about my dad, I said, 'He works on the oil rigs,' because that was the easiest thing to say about him. My weeks were marked by his comings and goings, Fridays the brackets in my little life. Dad's presence or absence dictated everything: what was on TV, what we ate (we ate more meat when he was home), when we ate it (we ate earlier when he was away), how we spent our time. Dad made the house feel smaller and smell different and I loved him being home, coming in and closing the door. But when he left, to take the train to Leeds airport, then the flight to Aberdeen to get on his helicopter back to work, it was good to be back with just my mother.

All of these things had brought tears to my eyes. I was crying, quietly, when mum came downstairs again, smelling of shampoo and lemon shower gel, wearing a long, dark pink dress that he liked, feet bare. She used to paint her toenails, then. That day they were raspberry. It was my favourite of her colours and sometimes she did mine in the same shade, at the weekends, and said we were toe-twins. 'Don't worry, sweet,' she said, 'he'll find another job. It will all be alright.'

Wrong on both counts, as it happened.

When it was just me and Mum on weekends, we used to go to the beach if it was sunny (or just not raining), weaving through the Whitby weekend crowds, my hand always tight in hers. We'd laugh because we knew this place was our place; everyone else had to go back inland, away from the sea, while we got to live within the sound of its crashing and watery burr all the time. Mum would look over the water as though it might disappear if she didn't keep an eye on it. I didn't understand that, then. It's almost tempting to look back and see her storing up those seascapes for the days that were coming. Almost.

Mum would say, 'See the sea, LJ!' and I

would say, 'Yes!', although I'd never lived anywhere else, and hadn't yet learned what it was like to be anywhere where you couldn't easily go and look at the sky touching a flat blue-grey horizon.

My mother had grown up in Nottingham, and studied there too. She was working in a supermarket after she graduated when she met my dad. She came to Whitby for a university friend's wedding. Dad was a friend of the groom; he'd not long since left the army and was sleeping in his soon-to-be-married mate's spare room. So Mum used to come to Whitby to see Dad, on her days off, and they walked beside the sea and that's where they fell in love. The sea was a part of their story. That, plus the fact that she'd grown up inland, meant that she was always full of happiness when we went to the shore, excited about the size of the sky, and the reach of the water.

When we went to the beach we added to our collections. I collected shells but I was fussy, only taking the intact ones home, rejecting anything that had broken edges. My favourite thing was to find a pair of egg cockle shells, still joined. Every now and then, after a high tide, they'd lie like small, silent butterflies on the shore. There were hundreds of them, white with curving blue-grey lines along their shell-wings. I'd walk among them looking for the best, tiptoeing sometimes so as to make sure that I didn't accidentally put my foot on perfection and shatter it.

Mum collected stones, and her criteria were different to mine. Perfect wasn't her bag; she liked things that were out of the ordinary, but what interested her wasn't predictable. Sometimes it was colour, a flash of pink in a black pebble. Sometimes it was smoothness, sometimes shape — points and jags in which she saw faces that I couldn't make out. Mum said we should only ever take two things home. She said that we had to leave enough for other people with collections, and I never looked beyond that to the tininess of our house, Dad's complaining that he couldn't move for clutter. My collection lived in a wooden jewellery box that had belonged to my Grandma Walker — Mum's mum. It was full of trays and drawers and was perfect for nestling my shoreline finds in. Mum's stones lived on the bathroom windowsill in a line that she rearranged every time she added another. I still have the jewellery box. I never look at it.

When we had chosen our two treasures we'd buy chips from the cafe near the stone steps, and sit on the pier or on the beach to eat them, depending on how busy it was, and how windy. I used the chip fork but my mother ate with her fingers. She said she was a tough cookie but sometimes they were so hot that she dropped them back in the polystyrene tray and blew on her fingertips. The smell of hot vinegar made the seagulls circle us but we ignored them. In our last good year, I would practise my lines as we ate, explaining the action as I went along, and although I'm sure my mother must have seen *Bugsy Malone,* she never let on, paying attention and asking questions and saying my lines back to me, as though she'd just heard the cleverest thing anyone had ever said.

On the weekends when Dad was home, we'd get into our old Ford estate car and go further. At Robin Hood's Bay, Dad chased me up sand dunes while my mother stood at the bottom and watched and laughed. On those days we'd have pub lunches and play games that Dad would cheat at. I thought he was joking, but sometimes, half sleeping in the back seat on the drive home, I'd hear them talking, my mother saying, 'Pat, it wouldn't actually kill you to lose once in a while, you know. She's a child.' And sometimes my dad wouldn't say anything, and at other times he'd say, firmly, 'Sarah-Jane, I wasn't cheating', and my mother would snort and say, 'Come off it, even your daughter could see that you were, and she's only nine. If you were fitter you'd have made sure you beat her to the top of the sand dune, as well.'

I didn't mind the cheating; it was part of the fun. Dad was generous with cream teas and comics, so I didn't mind that he was stricter about bedtimes than Mum was. I'd get into bed and fall asleep in no time at all, listening to the murmur of their voices coming up through the floor.

So that Thursday when he came home unexpectedly and I cried, I suppose it was because I knew that things were going to change.

When Dad woke, Mum and I were downstairs. We'd made the parkin and there had been time to do brownies, too. I loved baking with Mum, because she let me do everything, and she never fussed about mess, and if things didn't look the way they did when Delia Smith baked them, she just laughed and said it looked as though Delia could learn a thing or two from us. I'd already had my beef stew, and was allowed to wait up to see Dad, but Mum had laid the little table in the corner of the living room for two, and put a candle in a candle-stick in the middle, folded red paper napkins into shapes that she said were swans, although they looked more like ducks to me: their necks weren't long enough for swans. I was lying against Mum, reading my book, and I could hear her stomach rumbling. At the sound of his bear-stretch and his feet hitting the floor above us, she sat up straight and said, 'Your dad's had a bit of an accident, love, but it looks worse than it is. These things usually do.'

His smile was the same, but a tooth was missing. His hug was the same, but he held his face away from mine, a bit, because it was swollen. The way he roared my name, all three parts of it, with exclamation marks ('Loveday! Jenna! Cardew!') was exactly the same, and that was what gave me the courage to sit next to him, take a good look. If I couldn't be an actor or a detective when I grew up, I was considering being a vet. This looked like good practice.

'Smile,' I said. There was blood crusting around the place where his front tooth used to be. I put my finger in the space, not touching the edges. 'What happened?' I felt my voice wobble. His breath smelled terrible; blood and something worse.

He laughed. 'You should see the other

guy,' he said.

My mother said, 'Pat!' and sort of laughed, and told me I should be thinking about bed. She went off into the kitchen and I waited for Dad to send me upstairs, but he just sat there and looked at me while I examined him, first by looking and then with tentative touch. His smile looked wrong — it was the missing tooth — and his eyes weren't right, either, one of them half swollen shut. The black eye, being fairly fresh, I suppose, wasn't too bad, though over the next two weeks it would become a spectacular thing: indigo-black, his skin shiny and stretched to almost-bursting. It shifted and faded to purple, blue and then, worst of all, a bilious green-yellow. I tried to draw it but a nine-year-old's pencil case doesn't really have that palette. My dad laughed at the drawing when I showed him but it had disappeared when I looked for it the next morning.

That was later. That first evening, he winced when I put my hand against him. I pulled up his T-shirt, and was hit by the comforting, unchanging smell of our washing-powder; my mother was loyal in everything. I saw another bruise, along the side and front of his ribcage, the blues and blacks of it blending at the edges with the tattoo in the middle of his chest. I knew the tattoo was a 'regimental', although I think I probably thought that that was the word for the image, a crown above a bugle that was wider than my hand's span.

The first time I set foot in Lost For Words I found a book about insignia, put two and two together, and made the connection with the Somerset and Cornwall Light Infantry. I suppose he would have told me that, if I'd asked, but when you're a child you don't always know the right questions, and you don't know that you don't have forever to ask them.

I was close to tears. Once I had tripped on stage, a trivial fall, except that I caught my arm on the edge of a table as I fell and the bruise there was painful enough to wake me if I lay on my left side when I was asleep. So I knew that my dad's bruise and black eye would really hurt, and dads are not (were not, then, in my world) for being hurt; dads were for being protective and unbreakable, for shoulder-carries that your mother said you were too old and too heavy for, for helping neighbours to carry furniture or pushing strangers' cars when they wouldn't start.

'It's fine,' he said gently. 'Your dad got into a silly fight, that's all. I've learned my lesson and I'll be right as rain before you know it.'

'Did you tell the police?' I asked.

He laughed. 'No. I can't go back to work, and neither can the man who hit me. We've had our justice.'

I couldn't work out whether that was a good thing or a bad thing. My mother called from the kitchen: 'I think it's time you were in bed, sweetheart. It's getting awfully late.'

I asked my next question as I started climbing the stairs — I was tired, it felt like a climb — 'Will you be able to see me in the play? It's in two weeks.' Mum had already arranged to borrow the video that Emma's dad would make, her usual procedure when Dad missed things, but his being in the audience would be so much better.

'I'll put it in my diary,' he said. 'Now, do as your ma says, or you'll get me in even more trouble.'

I didn't get the next day off. It was clear from the get-go that this homecoming was different to the others. Before I went to school the next morning, my mother told me not to tell anyone that Dad had been fighting. People might get the wrong idea about him, she said. From what I remember — and yes, I know a nine-year-old girl isn't a reliable witness — she said this entirely without irony.

He came to the play with my mother, and he sat in the front row, even though his great height and broadness must have ruined quite a lot of views and videos. I still remember the thrill of peeping through the curtain and seeing them both there. It was a chocolate-for-breakfast feeling. Dad laughed in all the right places (some of the parents laughed in the wrong ones) and he applauded solidly, loudly, great slabs of noise. At the end, after the headmistress had said how hard we'd all worked and we deserved an extra round of applause, he stood up and shouted 'Bravo!' and clapped with his hands above his head and everyone else in the audience laughed and did the same.

The skin on his face was still yellow along the cheekbone and there was a dark purple bit on his chest, and sometimes when he laughed he put his hand there and his face went a bit pale. But to the casual eye, he looked like himself again. And I suppose he was, in most respects, except that he didn't have a job, which turned out to be more important than a nine-year-old knew.

When I came home from school one afternoon I heard shouting coming from upstairs as I made my way down the alley between the pavement and the back gate, where I could let myself in the back door. The days were warmer and I was in my gingham dress. I suppose it was May.

'It's not that simple.' My father's voice was low, but it was furious, like a growl from Ricky, the little Jack Russell on the corner who terrified me. I crossed the road every time I walked past and saw he was in the garden.

My mother's voice in response was quieter. I couldn't hear the words but I could sense that she was upset. As my ear tuned, I picked out my name, 'holiday', 'shoes'.

I didn't know what to do. If I went into the house I might be able to hear more than I wanted to, and it might be considered 'snooping' — another new word — which I knew was a bad thing to do. So I closed the gate loudly — the metal latch rattled — and I sat on the step. I could pretend that I was enjoying the sun, which was something that adults seemed to consider a worthwhile use of time. I took *The Famous Five* book I was reading from my blue school backpack. Dad had given it to me because he said *The Famous Five* were the best thing about his childhood. His name was in careful capitals on the inside front cover. I opened it, but I wasn't reading. I was listening, despite myself.

It had gone quiet upstairs. I can remember the feeling still, painful, unnatural, as though my stomach was consuming itself. The world I was living in was becoming different to the one I'd always known, and I didn't like it a bit.

Before he lost his job, when my dad went off to work I used to get upset that he was going away, sometimes, and he would scoop me up and say, 'You see, LJ, if I don't work, then there's no money, so I have to go.' No money then had seemed an abstract concept. I was just starting to see why it mattered. We had gone to the beach at the weekend, like we used to, except that we had taken sandwiches with us for lunch, come home in time for oven chips for tea; pub lunches and fish suppers, it seemed, were no more. I didn't mind that, but there had been something in the way my mother laid out the picnic lunch — 'Isn't this lovely!' — and my father's response — 'Don't rub it in, love, this won't last forever' — that made it feel like a strange sort of meal. It was a bit like going to a friend's house for the first time, and finding that you had to have different manners but you weren't quite sure what they were and you spent the whole mealtime watching and hoping that you didn't do anything wrong, and nothing felt comfortable.

It was still quiet upstairs. I was hungry. I was just starting to think about going inside when I heard the sound of my dad's footsteps, down the stairs, through the kitchen. Mum's footsteps always sort of bounced, as though she was doing a little jump between each step, but Dad's were a solid sound, one step overlapping the other. My mum said he had elephant feet. He said that she was spring-loaded. I didn't understand what that meant.

The door opened at my back and I lost my balance for a second. Dad reached to steady me and then he said, 'Budge up, Whitby Girl.'

He sat on the step beside me, and there wasn't quite enough space, so my leg and shoulder were squashed against the brick of the doorway.

'Have you got enough room?'

'Yes,' I said. I was like that, then. And the warmth and solidity of him on one side sort of made up for the scratching of masonry against my bare arm on the other.

He felt in his shirt pocket and brought out cigarettes and matches. He smoked Marlboro and I liked the red on the top of the packet. He put a cigarette between his teeth and then passed the matchbox to me.

He knew I liked to strike them. Mum always told him off when she saw me lighting his cigarettes, so we did it when she wasn't looking.

'Good day?' he asked.

'Yes,' I said. I knew that that was all he wanted me to say. Mum sat me down when I got in, and said, 'Okay, I'm ready. Daily report!' but Dad only needed a headline.

He inhaled, exhaled, and the smoke and the smell mingled with the warm air. 'Your mother says I should stop smoking,' he said.

'She's always said that,' I said. 'She doesn't like the smell.' He mostly smoked on the back step, but the smell still got into the house.

'She doesn't like that I'm burning money, either,' he said, 'and she's got a point.'

'We did about smoking at school,' I said. 'You know you could die?' Everyone who knew someone who smoked had had to raise their hand. I had felt as though I was confessing a crime.

Dad sighed. 'I know,' he said. I didn't like it when he was sad — when either of them were — so I tried to change the subject.

'Sam in my class has a new baby sister,' I said, 'and he says his mum says it was an accident. But I don't understand.' I knew the basics. Having a baby seemed anything but accidental.

I'd cheered him up. He smiled. 'Sometimes you get the chance to plan for a child and sometimes they just come along by themselves.'

'Was I an accident?' I asked.

'No,' he said, 'we always would have had you. You were sooner rather than later, is all.' Before I had the chance to work out what this meant he took another draw from his cigarette and asked, 'Did you hear me shouting, just now?'

'Yes,' I said.

He sighed and his free arm came around me, gathered me in, solid and strong. I could hear his skin rasping against the brick. If it hurt he didn't let it show.

'There's nothing for you to worry about,' he said. 'Your old dad's in a bad temper because he hasn't found a new job. That's all.'

'Are the oil rigs finished?' I asked. I knew about jobs finishing from Emma's dad, who was a builder. I liked using grown-up words, if I could.

He laughed. 'When the oil rigs are finished, we'll all be finished,' he said. 'But that's a while away yet. No, I've blotted my copy-book there, that's all. You're not supposed to fight. If you do, they send you home, and get someone else instead. There's always someone waiting to take your place.'

'Miss Buckley says fighting's always wrong,' I said. Some of the children in my class didn't like Miss Buckley but I did. You knew where you stood with her, and she was generous with her praise, as well as her rules.

'Well, maybe Miss Buckley should be in charge of an oil rig, then. She'd get on okay.'

I was going to ask what the copy-book thing meant but in the silence while I tried to remember the words came the sound of my mother crying. I looked at Dad. I could tell he was listening too. The tears were the sort that get even louder when you try to stop them. He looked back at me and his eyes were sad, as though he was the one who should be crying.

'I need to go and say sorry,' he said. 'I didn't mean to make her cry.'

'Why did you?' I asked. My teacher was very firm on this. 'It doesn't matter whether you meant to or not', she would say about spilled water for painting, books caught with an elbow and crashed to the floor, 'someone is still going to need to clear that up'.

He stood up and for a moment I thought he wasn't going to answer. 'I let my temper get hold of me,' he said, 'and I shouldn't have.'

'Like when you hit the man who gave you the black eye?' I said.

His face went dark for a moment and then he laughed. 'No,' he said, 'he hit me first. He deserved what he got.' He bent down to me, touched my hair. 'But I don't always think before I speak, and I've upset your mother. Are you all right here, if I go and say sorry? Then we could get the Lego out.'

I nodded. I was getting too old for Lego, but Dad really liked playing with it. 'I could have free school dinners,' I said. I knew that if there was no work then that meant there was no money coming in, and I'd been watching, seeing how often it was spent.

I thought about the glass jar that came out at Christmas, and how the sweets from my stocking and the contents of my selection box went into it. I would choose one thing a day until it was empty, usually around the middle of February. By the end I was stretching out my hand for the bottom of the jar, my fingers chasing the final blackjacks and drumsticks.

He made a funny noise, a wet cough. 'It won't come to that,' he said. 'I'll find something.'

■ ■ ■ ■

POETRY

■ ■ ■

2016
THERE SHOULD NOT
BE SILENCE

I came down with a bug after that night at the George and Dragon. No, not the poetry bug, smartarse, I already had that.

By Friday afternoon I felt like death warmed up. I knew it was bad because Melodie, whose sphere of interest usually begins and ends entirely with Melodie, pointed out that 'Loveday have a not-well look on her today'. I'm not ill very often, but when I am, I really go for it. I was tempted to blame walking home with my bike, but it was March, so not exactly freezing, driving rain. Plus, I read in one of the many hundreds of half-read popular science books that come into the shop that being cold and catching a cold has no relationship, so I'll let Rob off, though next time I see him I might tell him exactly what a shitty thing it was to let my tyre down.

Archie sent me home early on Saturday. I slept all of Sunday and most of Monday, which is my day off, so I thought by Tuesday I would be okay, but I felt worse.

I practically crawled to my bag to get my phone out, and rang Archie. He offered to come and pick me up and take me back to his place so he could look after me. It pisses me off when he does things like that. Just because he wouldn't live in a bedsit doesn't mean I'm not happy here. I sleep. I read. I write, a bit. I watch TV and I heat up stuff I buy in the Tesco Metro downstairs. It's peachy, thank you very much.

I thought about going to the doctor on Wednesday morning, but if I'm going to get something, it's this: rasping throat, sore ears, high temperature, and coughing up luminous phlegm. I knew what to expect and I waited it out. Archie turned up on the Wednesday evening. I almost missed him because I was dreaming about a house being demolished, the tiles from its roof falling into the sea, and his knocking got amalgamated into that. Or maybe caused it. Anyway, I staggered up to wakefulness and let him in. He had a pot with him. I didn't realise how miserable I was until I nearly cried when I saw his big, round, I-had-a-moustache-before-it-was-fashionable face. His smile went from ear to ear but he had a concerned look in his eyes.

'You look atrocious, my darling,' he said. He put the pot on the hob and opened the leather Gladstone bag he's carried every- where for as long as I've known him. He took out a loaf of bread and a navy-and- white striped apron, which he put on; it barely fastened at the back. He opened the window. It was freezing but I didn't com- plain. I'd been breathing the same air since Saturday and even I could tell it was getting a bit rank.

'I think I feel a bit better,' I said. It was true — I'd been sitting up in bed for a bit that morning, and thought about having a shower, though I'd gone back to sleep before I could do anything about it.

'I've brought some chicken soup,' he said. 'Go have a shower while I heat it up. Make it as hot as you can stand. It'll help your chest.'

'I was just about to,' I said. I was going to tell him off for marching in uninvited and overstepping the boss-mark by about fifteen employment laws but, to be fair, he is my only real friend, as well as my boss, and I hadn't bothered to charge my phone. And anyway, just the prospect of his chicken soup was enough to make me feel better, or at least mellow me a bit.

Don't go thinking I eat cold baked beans

out of a can, because I don't, but I'm your basic assembly cook: pasta and a sauce, cheese on toast. Archie claims that he learned his chicken soup from a Swiss cook in the merchant navy in the seventies. I'd happily eat the soup every day for the rest of my life. He starts with a whole chicken and puts a whole load of other stuff in the pot with it: rice, carrots, peas, sherry, thyme, parsnip. The finished result is something else.

When I came out of the shower he'd set two places at my tiny table, washed up the stuff in the sink, and sorted out the sofa so it looked less like a nest for tramps.

'Thanks, Archie,' I said.

'Eat,' he said. 'Chicken soup for my little chicken.'

Afterwards he washed up and talked while I sat on the sofa and listened, or rather, let his commentary wash over me. I heard Melodie's name, and Rob's, and I pricked up my ears: apparently they were 'an item'. I hoped Rob would treat Melodie better than he had treated me. She has a bit more sass than me, on the outside, at least, and I hoped he'd learned something from what happened between us about managing himself better. The fact that he let my tyre down didn't bode well, admittedly. But my brain was too tired to think about it.

And the Archie conversational circus had moved on. He was telling me how he'd sold the umpteen-volume partial *Complete Works of Shakespeare* that's been gathering dust for as long as I've worked in the shop. *Romeo and Juliet* was missing, which I desperately wanted to say something witty about, but my wits were still too ill to bother, and just waved a metaphorical white handkerchief in defeat. Before I could ask whether he'd told the customer about the missing volume, he was on to the next thing: Ben had brought in 'a couple of boxes, mostly rubbish but there might be something worth finding'. That's Archie code for 'I can't be bothered but you might enjoy sifting through them.' I liked Ben. He didn't say a lot but when he brought boxes in he put them down carefully, and the books inside them had been stacked so that they wouldn't get damaged in transit.

'Nathan Avebury came in today,' Archie said, as he started on the drying-up. I was annoyed with my stomach for tensing up at the sound of his name. 'He said to tell you to remember that you're paying for your own ticket next time.'

I didn't say anything but I did think it was quite funny. Cocky git.

■ ■ ■ ■

I went back to work on Saturday. I arrived mid-morning and the shop was full. Sue, Kate and Izzy from Book Group were sitting at the table with Archie. They sometimes brought him a cake, to say thank you for letting them use the shop. Technically it should have been my cake, but if you work on being invisible, you can't really be annoyed when people don't take any notice of you.

'Ah, my little straywaif returns,' Archie said, and wrapped me in a hug.

'Hey,' I said, and tried to sidle away.

I wasn't quick enough to avoid the inevitable: 'Straywaif?' Kate asked, looking at me with a half smile.

Archie's laughter followed me as I walked away. I didn't need to listen, I knew the script.

'I met her when she was fifteen. She came in with a school trip from Ripon and thought she could walk out with *Possession* without me noticing. I was standing outside smoking my pipe, so I collared her. Told her she could come with me to the police station or she could work for me for the afternoon. I kept an eye on her,' pause for laughter, 'and I told her she could come back and work, for money and books, if she so desired. Now,' he did a sort of flourish, 'ta-daa! Here she is, honest as the day is long. That, my friends, is the power of literature for you.'

More laughter, a murmur of approbation that I knew wouldn't stop Book Group from keeping an eye on their handbags the next time they saw me. I got busy among the maps and the poetry books and cringed.

There were times when I heard the story and wanted to go out and give my version: I was on a school trip, an end-of-term no-agenda jolly, and I'd decided to go because the alternative was to stay in school with the kids who had been banned from going and weren't exactly going to give me an easy time of it.

I had set off to York, planning to buy more books, but my purse was nicked out of my bag on the bus. One of the girls who usually snubbed me had sat next to me, briefly, asking about homework. Her friend had slid into the seat behind and, presumably, taken my money then. When I realised I was half furious, half relieved that they hadn't taken anything else. Being hungry is one thing. Being ritually humiliated by the sharing of the loneliest bits of your diary is something else.

Possession was my obsession at the time. There wasn't a copy in the school library and I'd been barred from taking it out of the public library again because there was a waiting list. I could live without the other things I wanted to buy — it's not like having a new jumper would make me any more popular in the sixth form — but I needed a copy of that. Once my purse was gone I had a pound in my pocket. The book was two pounds. I left my pound on the table as I went. So I'm not saying what I did was okay, but there were extenuating circumstances. Archie leaves that bit out. To be fair to him, he also tends to leave out the bit about how after he'd torn me off a strip and put me to work, he brought me tea and a tuna sandwich and I did the full Oliver Twist, eating mine and then asking if he was going to finish his. I wasn't constantly starving. But I hadn't had any lunch because I didn't have any money.

The boxes of books he'd left for me to sort through were taller than me. Ben had brought some of the boxes and others had been left on the step.

Most of the books in the boxes were rubbish, straight for the recycling. We don't tell people that we get rid of excess books that way — even though they might ditch books, they wouldn't put them in the bin and they don't like to think that we do. But think about it. Five million paperback copies of *The Da Vinci Code* were published in 2003. How many of them does the world still need fifteen years later? A lot less than five million. The same goes for pretty much every book that's been massive: *Who Moved My Cheese?, Eat Pray Love,* anything with a vampire. There's an eternal surfeit of the things unless someone somewhere is taking them out of circulation when they get the chance. One of those someones is me. You should be thanking me. And yes, it does break my heart a little bit, even if it is James Patterson.

In among the once-bestsellers, though, one book caught my eye, partly because it was a bit different to the books it was boxed with, but also because we had had it at home. It had been my dad's when he was a kid; it's a really odd thing for a 1970s child to have owned. It's a collection of rhymes for children called *Kate Greenaway's Mother Goose* and it's all 1880s-style illustrations and references to petticoats and spinning. But he'd been attached enough to it to put it in the single suitcase of things he brought from his parents' house in Cornwall after they died.

I turned it over in my hands. Photographs I'd seen of my father as a boy suggested that he was a grubby, tree-climbing little urchin. I was amused by the idea of him opening up this book and reading 'Little Miss Muffet' to himself. And then, in the next second, I wanted to cry.

I suppose I was still in that not-quite-better place where everything gets to you. I was thinking about how I didn't have anyone to ask how, exactly, a copy of this book had come to belong to my dad. Who had bought it? Why had he kept it? I checked and saw that it was a 1978 American reprint of an 1881 original. I would have thought it would have been bought by adults who were Kate Greenaway fans, or older people who remembered it from their childhoods and wanted to show it to their own grandchildren. So there was no obvious reason for my dad, who had no American relatives that I knew of, to have been given it.

When your family explodes (implodes?) it's the big stuff that hurts, for a while, like the impact of a slap, but that fades, quite quickly, because you have to get used to it, and the way to get used to it is, basically, not to think about it. It's the little things like this that get you, forever as far as I can tell.

I turned the pages, carefully — they weren't brittle, but soft, almost bruisable, and they felt as though they could have come off in my fingers, like petals tugged from a daisy. I suppose it's the fact that these small memories come from the kind of tiny reminders that you simply can't predict, and so can't protect yourself from, and they catch you, paper cuts across the heart.

I don't know whether Archie noticed that I was having a hard time with this particular book as I sat at the breakfast bar. I'm always amazed by what he can tell from the back of people's heads: he can look at someone who's browsing and predict with about ninety per cent accuracy both whether they are going to buy and whether they are going to try to haggle if they do. He claims he learned to read body language when he 'got in with some grifters' in London in the seventies.

Anyway, he appeared at my elbow. 'Hot chocolate,' he said. When I get drinks from next door they come in take-out cups. When Archie goes into the cafe he comes out with their best china. 'Take a break, Loveday. I don't want to see you for half an hour.'

Although I was, in principle, annoyed with him for (a) assuming that I wanted a hot chocolate (b) making me take a break as though he knew better than me what I needed, I still went and sat in the chair in front of the fire exit and watched the cream melt and the marshmallows float on top of the milky-brown chocolate. I fished out the marshmallows, sucked the outsides off them where they had been softened by the heat, and then dropped them back in, to melt some more. I was on my own — obviously. I wouldn't have done it in company. I drank the chocolate, washed my hands, and took a good look through *Mother Goose.*

I turned to 'Jumping Joan' and ran my hand across the page. 'Here am I, little jumping Joan, when nobody's with me, I'm always alone'. She was suspended in mid-air, dress ribbons flying, eyes closed. There was a mark on the corner of the page, a smudge of a thumbprint. My mum was always telling my dad off for leaving dirty fingerprints around the place. 'Well, you check the oil in the car then,' he used to say, at least before everything they said to each other was the start of a competition to see who could take most offence, most quickly.

That thumbprint had to be a coincidence.

I didn't think about where my dad's book might have been for the last twenty years, because there's danger in trying to make everything fit with the story that you want to tell. (Nathan's poem flashed into my mind, again.) You only need to look at Jane Austen's *Emma* to see that — she decides what's going on around her and arranges the facts in her head to suit, and look at what happens. Well, she lives happily ever after in the end, yes, but only after a nineteenth-century equivalent of having her head flushed down the toilet. And our book — mine and my dad's still had a dust jacket, even if it was in a fairly crappy state, and that was where he'd written his name, and I'd written mine underneath, on the inside of the front flap.

I remembered how much I'd liked my dad's copy of this book, as a girl. I could read it, easily, from when I was quite small. There are about sixteen words to a page and I liked spelling out the ones I didn't recognise — tuffet, latch, swine — and asking Mum or Dad what they meant. And, oh, the pictures. Nobody was too pretty, too happy. The girls looked pinched and the dogs looked as though they would bite you. It was like no other book that I'd seen. My mother didn't like it — 'I don't know how that doesn't give you nightmares', she would say — and no matter how often I took it to my bedroom, it would always end up back on the shelf downstairs. My dad said she was being soft. 'We're not soft, are we, kiddo?', he would ask, and I would shake my head, solemnly, because I knew from other things he said that being soft was bad. He would read the book with me, growling and exaggerating, 'We're all jolly boys, and we're coming with a noise' and I would laugh.

I wondered about taking the book as part of my allowance, but I decided against it. When I held it I was back on my father's lap, back in our little house, my mother laugh-tutting, me giggling, my dad's voice coming at me not just through my ears but through the front of his big chest and vibrating the tines of my ribs. And although that was sort of nice, it was also sort of unbearable, and I can do without that.

I don't know whether it was having been more isolated than usual because of the cold, or the way looking at the book made me feel, but I was actually looking forward to poetry night. I'd been living in my own head too much, and the books I'd been reading — *Heart of Darkness*, *The Colour Purple* — were basically trapping me in other people's heads. So I didn't debate with myself about going along, I just did it. If I was a chimney sweep I would have been whistling as I locked up the shop. It was the first evening I'd felt properly like myself in ages, despite Mother Goose and her funny sour-faced minions shaking me up.

Rob accompanied me, uninvited, to poetry night again, popping out from the cafe doorway as if by magic just as I came out from around the back of the shop with my bike. I hadn't seen much of him since I got back from being ill, or given him a thought, really, so I jumped when he appeared, and he laughed, which annoyed me, so instead of ignoring him, I said, 'You shouldn't have let my tyre down, Rob. That was a really mean thing to do.'

'I don't know what you're talking about, Loveday,' he said. Too fast.

'We both know that you do, Rob,' I said. I looked him in the face, something I don't often do with anyone. Those brown eyes. He blinked first. 'Are you looking after yourself properly?'

He snorted. 'I'm not about to start losing it with people, if that's what you mean.'

I felt myself go cold, even though it was a warm evening, and I started walking. 'I didn't say you were,' I said. 'I just meant . . .'

I gave up. I'm no good at kindness.

He was quiet for a bit, and then he said, 'I'm alright. I had an . . . episode . . . over Christmas but I'm better now. I have help and I know when to ask for it.'

'Good,' I said. 'And you and Melodie?'

'It's not really serious,' he said. I realised he might interpret that as me giving a damn — all this is so bloody complicated — so I said, 'I don't really like it when you put flowers through the door.'

'Okay,' he said. I was going to ask whether that was 'Okay, I won't do it any more' or 'Okay, but I don't care and I'll keep doing it.' Or even 'I'll stop it with the flowers and do something else, which you will also dislike, because whether you dislike it or not is not really the point'.

We walked on in silence.

It was just before 7.30 when we reached the George and Dragon and I was chaining up my bike when Nathan appeared in the doorway.

'Feeling better, Loveday?' he asked.

'It was only a cold,' I said. Nathan nodded, smiled. He has a good smile — it looks as though he means it, even if he does overuse it a bit. I couldn't help but smile back. Rob had stopped with me. He looked between us.

'What's this thing you're going to, Loveday?' he said.

I thought, look at me. Two men in a stand-off over my evening plans. One has some fairly serious mental health issues and lectures in Early Renaissance Studies and the other one's wearing a cravat. You couldn't make it up.

'It's a poetry night,' I said. 'Melodie sometimes comes.'

'I saved you a seat,' Nathan said. He looked at me, then Rob, and got a funny look in his eye. I suppose Nathan clocked that all of my body language was telling Rob he wasn't wanted. Which was more than Rob could see, obviously.

Either that or he saw an opportunity for showing off. He stuck out his hand to shake Rob's hand. 'Nathan Avebury,' he said. 'Will you be joining Loveday and me?' Then he put his other hand, very lightly, on the small of my back — it made me wonder if men went to finishing school. It was a genius move.

Rob took a step back and shook his head.

'Don't touch my bike,' I said.

Nathan and I walked up the steps and into the pub. Rob hadn't moved. He was looking from Nathan to the chocolate coin in his hand.

'Thanks,' I said to Nathan when we stood at the bar. 'You didn't have to.'

'I know,' he said. Then, 'My sister's beautiful too, and she gets a lot of hassle. I've seen it for years. I just like to help out when I can.'

I think I must have imagined the 'too'. Nathan ordered a pint of Guinness and a gimlet. When the barman brought them I handed Nathan a fiver and said, 'That's for mine, thanks.'

He said, 'Why don't you get drinks after the first half, then we'll be quits.'

Nathan was fourth again, which I thought was a shame. I thought about my poems and wondered what would happen to them here, if I said them out loud. Miss Buckley used to talk about the oral tradition — not in so many words (haha!), but she'd say, 'Remember, in the olden days, before people could read and write, we used to tell each other stories, and remember them. If you write a story you should read it out, to see how it sounds.' I never forgot that; I used to whisper my English homework to myself, under my breath, if the library was quiet.

Words do sound different in the air. One time a teacher read something I'd written out to the class. It was a description of the sea and the way it's always the same but never the same. Hearing my words aloud made me feel proud, exposed. I loved school plays, at least until being looked at started to have other implications, and meant whispers and rumours. So, up to and including my critically acclaimed (by my parents) performance as Blousey Brown in *Bugsy Malone.* But other people's words are safe and easy. Speaking what you've written is something else: your own words can eviscerate you as they come out.

My favourite poem that night, apart from Nathan's, was one about how complicated it is to choose wine in a supermarket.

Melodie came to sit with us during the break: 'Archie tell me you still sick, Loveday, but here you be, with handsome Nathan.' I was tempted to ask her why Rob wasn't with her, but I don't gossip.

I think it was the prospect of escaping Melodie that made Nathan come down with me when I left. Or maybe because I'd told him about Rob and the tyre. Anyway, my bike was fine, and we stood on the pavement, talking, while the other poetry fans had another drink, and couples full of conversations about their evenings wended past.

'I've been meaning to ask you where

you're from,' he said. 'You sound like York-shire, but not exactly York.'

I went with the letter of the question, rather the spirit. 'I'm only about twenty minutes from the shop,' I said. 'It's a new-ish development. It's nice.'

Nathan smiled, gently, as though he knew I was trying to dodge the question, as though I was flirting. 'And where are you from?'

'Ripon,' I said, which was not untrue.

'I grew up in Bridlington,' Nathan said.

I tried to think of something to say about Bridlington. I'd never been there. 'It's on the coast, right?'

That smile again. 'Yes. I miss being beside the sea. I miss it. Even the North Sea.' His voice filled with laughter. 'When we were kids we used to go to Cornwall. My parents had a friend who lived there. It was the first time I'd realised that you could actually play in the sea.'

I didn't want to talk about Cornwall. 'You should have got a better result tonight,' I said.

'I know,' he said, and his smile changed, from something soft to something showy. If I was one of those people who gave away touches, I'd have play-punched him on the arm as a way of saying, 'Don't be an arse'.

'Are you always this sure of yourself?'

He looked at me then and his face changed back, from the public version to the one I saw when it felt as though we were the only people that there were. 'Not everyone pays attention, like you,' he said, 'and because I've been around for a while, I'm like part of the furniture. People know my schtick.' He didn't say it the way Rob would say it, self-pitying; he just stated a fact.

We were looking at each other. We weren't stopping. It was turning into gazing. I don't gaze.

'Well, I'm going to head home,' I said. It was a cold sort of relief to look away from his face.

'It was great to see you, Loveday,' he said. He put his hand on my shoulder and then he kissed me on the cheek, very gently. It wasn't passionate but it was pretty sexy. If I'd been in the market for a boyfriend I might have liked it. I unlocked my bike.

'Where have you put the chocolate coin?' I said.

He laughed. 'I only do that the first time I meet someone,' he said. 'It gets old. I make an exception for the under-tens.'

The next Tuesday night, Book Group got quite emotional. They were reading *After*

You'd Gone by Maggie O'Farrell, though they didn't really have a proper discussion about it, just said whether they'd liked it (five to two in favour, six to two if you count me). She, the divorced one, has taken a lover. The rest of them are agog, and jealous. I can only see trouble, especially as the divorce isn't finalised yet.

Izzy spilled a glass of red wine all over the carpet. They were all really apologetic about it. I told them it didn't matter and when they'd gone I nipped to the corner shop a couple of streets away and bought two drums of salt, one to pour over the wine and one to keep in the back for the next time.

'Morning, Loveday,' Archie said when I came in at eleven the next day, and then he charged out of the door. His pipe was already primed and ready to go. I soon saw why he was in such a hurry. I'd left a note asking him to hoover up the salt when he got in, but of course he didn't. When he came back from his smoke and stroll around the neighbourhood, having bought a bottle of port and a bag of Chinese pears, he claimed not to have seen the note. I'd taped it to the till, and I'd left the hoover out, so he must have climbed over it to hang up his coat, but Archie's Archie.

124

So, there was the pile of salt under the table, which had got scuffed and kicked around all over the place, and I was quite pissed off by the time I'd got it all cleaned up. When lunchtime came, I ate my cereal and banana and I hadn't done a single book-related thing except show someone where the cookery books were and tried not to glaze over (haha! Archie joke!) while listening to a no-pause-for-breath monologue about the evils of wheat. Or maybe sugar. Okay, I wasn't listening.

After lunch I told Archie to disturb me at his peril and I went to the breakfast bar to do some valuations. He bowed and smiled, and brought me tea and a jam doughnut an hour later. Doughnuts are the natural enemy of the book — even if you don't squirt the jam on the pages, you end up with sugar everywhere but I appreciated the implied apology.

Post-doughnut I went through two boxes of sheet music — nothing rare but everything well kept. A lot of people ask for sheet music and I like selling it. I think I like the thought of houses with pianos in them; they feel like the sort of places where things don't really go wrong. Sorting it cheered me up a bit, anyway. I was wondering about a music tattoo but I couldn't think of the opening of any piece of music that I could live with forever. Whereas first lines of books are a different matter. I don't regret any of mine, not even *Jane Eyre* and *The Railway Children* on my shoulder blades, which hurt like hell. The first one (*Anna Karenina*) seems predictable, now. But when I was seventeen and had only just discovered Russian literature I felt as though Tolstoy was speaking to my soul with: 'All happy families are alike; each unhappy family is unhappy in its own way'. So I had it inked on my hip. The font is delicate and fine. And yes, it will go saggy with my skin one day, but I really don't care.

As I sorted I recited some of my poems to myself, in my head. Poetry night was making me think about them in a different way, as things that might belong out in the air, instead of written and re-written on a page until my careful handwriting and consideration of every syllable had made them stiff as boards. One Sunday evening, when I'd been thinking about Nathan, I got the whole lot out, from my late teens to now, and read them all aloud. Some of them were awful. But the more recent ones aren't so bad. I started working on another one, and before I knew it it was gone midnight and I still hadn't eaten my reduced-to-clear microwave tuna pasta thing. I almost texted Nathan to say hello, but it was too late and, anyway, it's not like I'm his girlfriend or anything. He'll have a girlfriend called Trixie or Mc-Kenna, who uses pure essential oil instead of perfume and also has a magician-type non-job, like making hats or dressing up as a princess for children's parties.

This is why I try to go to bed before midnight. I get ratty and stupid if I don't.

I skipped the next poetry night. It's not like I'm legally obliged to go. Whenever I thought about the first poem I heard Nathan perform, and whether I could tell a different story about myself — although it's a moot point because I don't really talk about myself anyway — I felt antsy and I didn't like it.

I next saw Nathan when he came into the shop the following Wednesday. I realised I didn't know where he lived, but I was starting to assume it was out of town somewhere, between York and Bridlington, maybe, as he usually tipped up on poetry-slam day, which would suggest that he wasn't exactly around the corner. I always meant to ask when I saw him, but we ended up talking about other things: poetry and York, Archie and magic. And if I asked him where he lived we might get a bit more autobiographical than I wanted to.

Nathan's summer coat is khaki canvas and smells of outdoor things, as though it's been stored in a hay bale over winter. It's a good smell. It's not a bad coat, though I like the leather one better. Today he stood and talked to Archie for about twenty minutes. They started on York and wandered into politics, global warming, theatre and football. I liked listening to them. It's not often that Archie has much of a conversation: it's usually a performance with an audience of one or two. Here's how it ended:

Archie: Well, my good man, you didn't come in here to talk to old Archie.
Nathan: It's always good to see you.
Archie: Too kind, too kind. Nevertheless, you'll find Loveday doing some valuations, at the breakfast bar.
Nathan: Thank you.

Archie's assumption that Nathan was here to see me made me feel mildly flattered, and slightly annoyed, and I wasn't doing valuations, anyway, I was reshelving the show-business biography and autobiography sections into one, because people don't necessarily differentiate; they just want 'that book about David Beckham/Michael Caine/

thingy from *Coronation Street*'. I reckoned that combining the two would buy me a shelf of space, which I was going to need because Ben had just brought in two boxes of nice first editions of actor biographies from the seventies. I heard Nathan walk to where he thought I was, stop, pause. I decided that if he went back to Archie to report my absence and ask where else I might be, I would never go to poetry night again. I'm not a wayward chicken who isn't where you left her and I can't be arsed with people with no initiative. I found that I was holding my breath.

He must have stood there for a minute, and then I heard his footsteps again — the shop doubles as a museum of squeaky floorboards — and he came straight to where I was.

'Hello, Ripon Girl,' he said. 'I saw the books on the bench and I figured you'd be making space for them. I was hoping you would come to poetry night tonight.'

I went.

On the Buses

*As performed by Nathan Avebury at the
George and Dragon
York, April 2016*

I've only ever lost one thing on a bus.
Well, getting off a bus.
It was a book.
I know, I'm a terrible person.
Since then I've been watching for the things
    that get left on buses.
I think pockets have a lot to do with it.
Things slip out and down into nooks of
    cushion-joins, onto the floor, without
    making a loud enough sound of falling to
    be missed.
Pound coins.
I bet if you turned all the buses in York
    upside down and shook them, you'd
    have enough loose change to pay a
    nurse's salary.
Bus passes.
Obviously.
I suppose they could find their way home if
    anyone bothered to look the owner up.
I wonder if they do.
Cinema tickets.
There's a well-planned first date up in
    smoke.
House keys.

Here's hoping you're on good terms with
　　your neighbours, and they have a spare
　　set.
And then there are the bigger things, that in
　　a moment of panic or tiredness or
　　my-stop-alreadyness get forgotten.

Today, a Debenhams bag with a pair of
　　satin pyjamas inside, silver-grey, size 14.
Maybe leaving that behind has ruined
　　someone's evening.
Or maybe it's changed it.
Changing and ruining are not the same.
Without the pyjamas someone might be
　　lying between a cotton sheet and their
　　lover's skin.
Nakedness might be better.
Next time you leave something behind, you
　　might have just begun a whole new
　　adventure.

HISTORY

2013
SLIGHTLY CROOKED

The second time I saw Rob it was three weeks after he first dropped off his list of books and his hair was long enough for him to need to brush it out of his eyes. I'd put aside an exhibition catalogue I'd found with a few more of the books from his list. As he looked through them I watched his face. He looked down at the titles and up at me, and his eyes were wide and bright.

'Quick work,' he said, 'thank you,' and he smiled.

Already his eyes were drawing back down to the books. I don't think I fancied him. Maybe a bit. I'm not much of a fancier, more of a take-it-or-leave-it sort of a girl. But I did like that he liked books. I think I quite fancied that. I was still young enough to think/hope that love of books equalled fundamental decency. Librarians had always been good to me.

'There's something else,' I said, 'but it

wasn't on your list.'

The book I had found was a vanity-printed travel diary from the 1890s. I only remembered it because the author was called Florence and so I'd been amused by the fact that she'd gone to Florence, and written about it ('Florence's Italy'), and wondered whether there was a special sort of nominative determinism in people with place names that compelled them to be interested in the places they were named after.

Florence Bicknell's prose was florid at best, and she didn't feel the need to be constrained by anything as helpful as chapters or even topic. I realised, after hopping from art gallery to Roman ruin to country walk and then back to another gallery, that she had probably just written about things in the order in which she had seen them. If she had a motto, it was 'more is more', and she recorded everything, from what she was wearing to the possible character of waitresses and guides. She obviously prided herself in being Interested with a capital I. So it took me another week to plough through the book and find the section I was looking for. It wasn't a huge book, but the print quality was poor, and the style meant that a little went a long way, like Joyce.

I had marked the page with a slip of paper, and a couple of other places where there were things that might be relevant.

'Something else?' Rob said, and he grinned, and rubbed his hands together, like a hungry man in a cartoon. And then I remembered that he was working towards a PhD and I'd left school after my A Levels, and I hadn't even known Renaissance Engineering was a thing until three weeks previously. I was clever enough for university — in fact, it was talked about, by teachers and Annabel and social workers. But it meant three more years of being in the system, three more years of being unable to start the only real life I could have — one where I would be totally self-reliant. Plus, even if I had a degree I'd probably still want to work in a bookshop.

I looked at Rob's face and realised the longer I left it the more he was going to think I'd found something really spectacular, like a lost notebook from Brunelleschi with a letter from Leonardo da Vinci inside, as though we were actually characters in *Possession*. So I held out the book and said, quickly, 'It's probably nothing. It wasn't on your list. I don't know anything about this really. I just thought — this is from a short-run of a vanity press — there's quite a detailed description, and the author went to some lectures about Florentine architecture — that's all —'

Rob was already looking through the pages I'd marked. He looked up at me and grinned. 'Have you ever considered a career in research?' he asked. 'You could teach some of the people I work with a thing or two.'

'Loveday already has a job, and she isn't looking to go anywhere,' Archie's voice came from behind a shelf-stack. He had said he was going to do some sorting out but from the lack of noise I'd assumed he was napping.

Rob pixie-laughed, a little nervously. 'I wasn't trying to poach her, Archie,' he said. And then, to me, 'Thanks. Really. This is — thanks.'

'It's half an hour until we close,' I said, 'if you want to see if they are going to be any good to you.'

'Right.' He sat at the table and I went back to the breakfast bar and sorted what I'd done that afternoon. There was a first edition of *Ulysses* and a signed copy of *Midnight's Children* to go on the website, a box of overs, and another three boxes ready for my attention in the morning. I did the website update and put the overs box at the bottom of the stairs. When I went back to the front of the shop Rob was standing at the desk, talking to Archie. They both turned to me as I approached.

'. . . really helpful,' Rob was saying. He was holding the travel journal. Archie, cool as a cucumber, was ringing up forty-five pounds for it on the till, bringing Rob's total to £60. Archie's a great believer in market forces. He says that if there's a book that no one is likely to want, you may as well price it high because if the person who does want it finds it, they won't care about what it costs. Even so, I made a mental note to tell him off about taking the mickey, at the same time as I asked him not to talk about me in the third person when I was actually three feet away and he was butting into my conversation.

'Rob's just saying what an outstanding job you did, Loveday.'

'Thanks,' I said. Rob handed over sixty pounds. I shook my head at Archie. I knew what he'd say: 'supply and demand dictates the price'. True up to a point, I argued, in that if you ran a restaurant of course you would charge more for the rare things. But you wouldn't up the price of a fishcake depending on how hungry people were.

'Would you like to come and have a drink

with me?' Rob asked.

I assumed he was talking to Archie, who has the knack of making you feel as though you're his best friend, and really special, and so people always want to spend time with him. To begin with I thought it was an act but I soon realised that it's how he really is. He's interested in people, and they pick that up, whereas from me they pick up that I, generally, couldn't give a toss.

I'd probably been working at the bookshop for a year before I realised that Archie was bothered about me. I think it was when I was going to miss the bus — he'd asked me to check over the first editions in the locked cabinet behind the desk, and I was so absorbed that I forgot the time — and he insisted on driving me home, even though it was way out of his way, and when I got out of the car, he said, 'You're a real asset to me, Loveday. I hope you know that,' in a serious, quiet way that made me feel as safe as if I was pressed in the pages of an encyclopaedia.

But Rob was talking to me, not Archie. I was trying to think of how to say 'no' to the drink without sounding too rude when he said, 'I'd love to know more about these books, and how you came to think of them,' and because that was exactly what I wanted to explain, I said yes.

'Off you go, then,' Archie said. 'Don't do anything I wouldn't do,' and I laughed because I couldn't think of a single thing Archie wouldn't do, at least once. I went to get my coat and he followed me out to the back and gave me the three twenty-pound notes that Rob had just given him. 'You earned these,' he said.

'You're right, I did,' I said, but I smiled too, because I appreciated the gesture, and the fact that I had money in my pocket. I could pay my way tonight, and save the rest.

When I went back out to the shop to meet Rob, he said, 'I don't want to take up your whole evening if you have plans, but shall we go and have something to eat?' He looked really nervous — he kept pushing his hair out of his eyes — so I smiled and said that would be lovely. Two breakfasts don't sustain you very far beyond 6 p.m., and I didn't want to drink on an empty stomach.

We went to an Italian place and we both had meatballs, which were hot and spicy, with parmesan grated over them at the table by a waitress who looked as though she had many better things to be doing this evening.

Rob started with, 'Tell me about you, Loveday.'

I had to take avoiding action. 'I work in a bookshop, as you may have noticed,' I said, and I smiled, and so did he, spaghetti between his teeth. 'I started there part-time when I was fifteen. I really like it, most days. Tell me about you.'

'When I was fifteen,' Rob said, 'I was desperate to get a job, but my brother and I lived with my grandmother and she was really strict about homework. I would have loved to have worked in a bookshop.'

'You lived with your grandmother?' I said, and I could have bitten off my tongue, because I of all people should know not to pry. But he seemed happy to talk. And, though I had had what could be conservatively described as a crappy start in life, his wasn't great either. He and his brother had been brought up by his grandmother after his parents got on the wrong end of the Manchester bombings when he was seven. His grandmother died when he was nineteen; he wasn't in touch with his brother any more. He said he'd been 'ill' quite a lot. I didn't ask questions about that; he could tell me more if he wanted to, but I kind of hoped he wouldn't. He'd worked his way through sixth form and university with evening and part-time jobs, one of which was reshelving books in the university library, which he described as 'sneaky research time'. I laughed and told him about Archie finding me reading Annie Proulx when I was supposed to be tidying up, and letting me get away with it.

Rob had managed to get grants and juggle things so that he could keep studying; even so, his first degree had taken him six years. I felt bad about the money Archie had just taken off him and tried to pay for dinner for both of us but he refused. In the end we split the bill, because I wasn't going to be paid for, which had nothing to do with my earnings on the books.

It was after ten when we left and although I wouldn't let him walk me home I did say I would go over to his place for dinner on the Saturday night. He typed his address into my phone, asked me if I liked fish (yes, as long as it doesn't still have the head on), and attempted to kiss me, which I saw coming from far enough away to sidestep without looking like I was avoiding him. I like to think about these things.

I knew that if I went on the Saturday it would be a date. I didn't know if I would stay, but I took my toothbrush just in case, along with a bottle of white wine that Archie brought in for me when I asked him what would go with fish. Rob's flat was small and

what you might describe as excessively neat
— the pens on his desk were all the same
brand, lined up with a precision that was
clearly not accidental, and his bookshelves
were more orderly than the ones in the
shop. He asked a lot of questions about me
— I hate that that's the officially sanctioned
way to get laid — but I talked about the
shop, mostly, and asked more about university life. I'd always thought about university
in terms of its impracticalities: the cost, the
debt, the enforced sociability. I hadn't
thought about how you could pick a tiny
part of the world — out of all its possibili-
ties, its places and times and histories —
you are going to spend the rest of your days
digging around in. I liked to hear Rob talk
about it.

I stayed. It was nice enough. I didn't stop
to carve our initials in a tree-trunk on the
way home the next morning, but I wasn't
surprised when he dropped into the shop
on Monday and we did go out, to the
cinema this time, that week. He invited me
over on Saturday night again, and I went,
but the questions were getting to be a bit
much, and when I went to put my trusty
black leather Mary-Jane shoes on before I
left in the morning they had been not only
lined up with their toes a perfect right-angle

to the wall, but also polished. There was a big flashing 'Emergency Exit' sign in my head, and a fluorescent arrow pointing me in that direction.

'What's this?' I said, when I saw the polished shoes. I don't think they were that clean on the day I bought them.

He shrugged. 'I woke up early.'

I laughed. 'And you've finished your PhD already so cleaning my shoes was all there was to do? Not that I don't appreciate it —.'

He was looking at me very seriously, all of a sudden. 'Have you got time to talk?' he asked.

I wanted to say no but he had just cleaned my shoes. And he knew I had to leave soon, so I reckoned if there had to be talking I may as well do it when I had a get-out-of-the-flat-free card in my hand.

'Sure,' I said.

We sat down and he looked at me and I thought, wow, this must be what a woman looks like when she tells a man that their contraception wasn't all it was cracked up to be.

'You know I said I'd been ill, on our first date?'

'Yes,' I said. It would have been churlish to point out that that wasn't really a date.

'Well,' he said, 'it's a sort of — it's a mental illness. I never really got better. I just got better at managing it.'

'Right,' I said.

'One of the big things for me,' he said, 'is control. I don't like it when I feel — out of control.'

I noticed that his hands were on his knees and that their positions were perfect mirror images of each other: the spread of the fingers, the palms on the same place on each kneecap. I was sitting sideways-on, one elbow on the back of the sofa, one leg tucked under me, one leg dangling. I wondered if I should move and make myself symmetrical. I thought about him eating spaghetti, the fork and spoon central on the plate when he had done.

'So I control the things I can.'

He looked at me, and I nodded. I understood that much. Making sure people who might want to find you can't find you is an exercise in control, after all. 'Like your flat,' I said.

'Yes,' he said, and he smiled, so gratefully that I felt bad about the way I felt when I saw my lined-up, polished shoes. 'I know it's too tidy but — it's the best way I have of managing. I'm sorry. I should have realised it would look weird if I cleaned your shoes.'

'That's okay,' I said. I knew I'd never, ever be able to talk about myself the way he was doing it, so I listened.

Rob told me about medication, therapy, his support network. He talked about the difficulty of admitting that the places in your life when you're most productive, most excited, most brilliant are when you're also most ill. He was at great pains to explain that taking anti-psychotics doesn't actually mean you're psychotic if you don't take them.

I listened. I felt for him. There were lots of stops and starts, pauses and deep breaths. I felt miserable and uncomfortable and I thought about how, if I ever told anyone about me, I would look exactly as Rob did right now: frightened, determined, pale. I thought about how he had got lost in his life, like me, and that books had rescued him too. If I had a tribe, Rob was one of my people. Except that he was telling me all this. I would never tell anyone anything, unless I had to. My story was silence, a secret.

When he stuttered to the end, I said, 'Thank you for telling me, Rob,' and I meant it.

He nodded. 'Do you still want to go out

on Thursday?' he asked. We were going to the museum, a talk about architecture.

'Of course,' I said. I didn't exactly mean, 'Of course I want to go out with you again'. It was more, 'Of course what you've said doesn't make a difference to how I feel about you, because I would never judge someone on the grounds of their mental health'. I can see how he took it to be more of a commitment than it was.

■ ■ ■ ■

CRIME

■ ■ ■ ■

1999
TIME IS MEANINGLESS HERE

My father didn't find a job. By the time summer term started, I was having free school meals. I didn't mind. I wasn't the only one. I minded, though, when my half birthday came, on the first of July.

Anyone born between Christmas and New Year will tell you that you may as well not bother with a birthday. You get afterthought presents and the people who come to your party — if anyone is free — look as though they'd rather be at home on the sofa watching cartoons and eating Ricicles straight out of the box. When I was seven, we started celebrating my half birthday. It was my mother's idea. It was still school term so people weren't away, and it was at the beginning of those winding-down weeks full of sports days and school trips, when the holidays are in sight and everyone is excited and happy. That's how I remember it, anyway. I still got a present on New Year's

Day, but the first of July was where the real fun was.

The year before it all went wrong, when I was eight-and-a-half, I'd had a party on the beach. It was a hot day, and there wasn't a lot of wind, which was unusual for Whitby; the stillness of the air made the whole world seem different. I remember the smell of sea and sunblock, as Mum went from child to child, daubing noses and foreheads, the tips of our ears. There was a sandcastle competition and donkey rides and Punch and Judy. There were twelve of us and we carried our picnics to the beach on the end of canes, tied up in big red spotted napkins. People smiled and took photographs as we went past and I felt like the queen of the world. It was a week when my dad was home and he took the photos. Afterwards, looking through them, he'd shaken his head and said, 'I tell you what, kiddo, your mother's got class. If she ever realises she's too good for me then I'll be in trouble.'

This year it was different. I got presents, of course. A Furby (Emma had one, and we all loved it, even though some of the kids at school, the ones who wore lipgloss, said Furbies were for babies) and the first three *Harry Potter* books. I'd read the library copies, but I didn't have my own, and I'd said that I wanted to reread them. There was a receipt with them — the pre-order of *The Prisoner of Azkaban,* which came out a week after my half birthday. I loved my presents but there was no party. Instead, Emma and Matilda were invited back for tea. There was a barbecue, which my dad was in charge of, and he wore a paper hat and made us laugh but it just wasn't a party. It was more like a summer holiday afternoon. Then it rained and we had to bring everything inside. The house felt smaller now my dad was in it all of the time.

My cake was supposed to be a sort of fairytale cottage, covered in sweets, but my mum had hurt her wrist falling down the stairs, so my dad had had to help her with it and, awful kid that I was, all I could see were the places it had gone wrong: the wonky roof and the way the icing didn't go right to the corners. Dad had found some sparklers, so he put all of those in the chimney and lit them, which was funny until one of them fell off and burned a hole in the carpet.

That night I heard my parents arguing again.

I knew what it was about. While they were getting the barbecue ready, Mum had said to Dad that she'd been looking in the newsagent's window and she'd seen that one of the hotels wanted casual help over the summer. Dad had stopped fanning the charcoal and looked at her.

'Casual help?' he'd asked.

'Cleaning, waitressing, I would imagine,' my mother had said.

'We'll talk about it later,' he'd said.

She had sighed and when she turned away from him her eyes were shadows.

Before Dad lost his job I never used to listen to my parents after I'd gone to bed at night. But two things had changed in the post-employment world. One was that their voices were different, these days. They used to be quiet, conversational, making a gentle rumble like the sound of the sea, with only the odd word audible. Now, raised voices, or shouting followed by a 'shush' and my name from my mother, meant that the volume dropped then rose again. And that was difficult to ignore. Dad had given up smoking and Mum said it made him irritable. He said it was his bloody life that made him irritable.

The second thing that changed was how I knew now that the way my parents talked, and the things they said, made the shape of the next day. If they were reconciled then the next morning would be smooth, there would be games after tea and maybe ice cream. Life would feel like it used to feel, before Dad lost his job, or very similar to it. If they didn't make up after their quarrel, though, the next day would be a different story: an excess of love directed at me from my mother, a silence like a sea-fret from my father, impossible to ignore, muffling our little house.

Once I told my mum that she looked 'peaky', which was a word that she used to me sometimes, usually on days when my throat or ears had started to hurt but I wasn't actually ill yet. She smiled and told me she was a little bit tired, then went into the living room where Dad sat hunched over the jobs pages of the local free paper, and said pointedly, 'Your daughter says I look peaky.' A second later there was a bang as his fist slammed onto the table. He got up and dashed all of the framed photographs off the top of the bookshelf on his way to the door. Mum cut her fingers clearing up.

That was, needless to say, the day after an unresolved quarrel. It had got bad again, that night. I think I might have been sent to bed early, because the argument couldn't wait. I never dared to suggest that my mother looked peaky again.

Sometimes I looked at the wedding photo

that hung on the wall in the living room and wondered at how different they looked now. It wasn't a formal photograph, and my mum wasn't wearing a wedding dress, but a pale-blue suit and a straw hat. She was holding a bouquet of white roses and looking at my dad, who was standing next to her in a navy suit, and they were both laughing as they looked at each other, confetti falling down over them. Once, when I was little, I asked Mum what they were laughing about. She said they were bursting with how happy they were, and the smiles were the explosions where the happiness couldn't stay inside any longer. When I asked her where I was, she pointed to her stomach in the photo and said, 'You were there, LJ. All curled up, sleeping, as tiny as a mouse.' They had lived in Whitby, to begin with, because Dad's friend Jim — the one whose wedding my parents had met at — had let them stay in his house when he and his wife moved away to army barracks in Wiltshire. My parents had lived there for a year until the house — my first home — was sold.

I was as beautiful as a peach, according to my mother, and like a funny bawling prawn, if you believed Dad. Mum was in love with Whitby by the time they had to move, and Dad had started working on the oil rigs and could get to and from Leeds to catch his flight easily enough, so they found a place of their own to rent, and there we were. A chance meeting at a wedding, a couple of dates, an unplanned pregnancy, enough love for my parents to think it was worth a shot, and there was LJ, Whitby Girl.

Lying in the dark, the night after my so-called party, I couldn't help listening, even though listening made me feel anxious, as though I'd got on a fairground waltzer and realised I'd made a mistake, but it was too late to get off. I'd been on one once, when we went to a funfair for Matilda's birthday. Up until the last few months it had been the most horrible experience of my little life. I'd felt sick and scared and it had all been made worse because on either side of me Matilda and Emma squealed and laughed, and as soon as it stopped they had wanted to go on again. I'd waited with Matilda's mum the second time and watched them as they shrieked happily, around and around, without me. 'I'm with you,' she'd said. 'You couldn't pay me enough to go on one of those things.' But it hadn't made me feel any better about watching them.

My father was the first to raise his voice. This was the usual pattern. 'You're not going to cook and clean for strangers.'

'I cook and clean for you,' from her, 'and standing at the school gate isn't really the best way for me to use my time at the moment.'

'Because I'm not earning, you mean?'

'Yes,' she said with a sigh, 'that's what I mean. But I don't mean anything by it. I'm just stating a fact, Pat.'

He went quiet for a minute. Then: 'We agreed when LJ was born. You said you wanted a decade to be her mother, that it was the most important thing —'

'I did.' Her voice was calmer than his, and calmer than when she said the cook-and-clean thing, oil on water. 'But look at us. What would be the harm? Three months of summer work would see us through to Christmas, if we're careful. She'll be ten at New Year. And you'll be with her. It's not as though we'd be farming her out to strangers.'

'Oh ye of little faith,' the tideline swell of my father's anger, 'not even my wife thinks I'll be in work by Christmas.'

'That's not what I'm saying. I'm saying, where's the harm? Or, if you don't like that idea then I'll get a real job. Full-time. The call centre is hiring and it pays well. You can stay at home. I wanted her to be looked after by a parent, not sent to breakfast clubs and childminders. That was what I thought was important then, and I still think it's important now. You were making more money, and I wanted to be with her. Don't make this a — don't make it —'

'Don't make it about how you're more employable than me?'

'I did not say that.'

A pause, then my father's voice, in a tone that I would get told off for if I used: 'You'd have to travel to the call centre. You'd be exhausted. I wouldn't have the car all day.'

'I'm not saying I have all the answers.'

'If you're saying it's okay that I wouldn't have the car, then you're saying there's no chance of me getting work.'

'You know it's not. For heaven's sake, Pat.' She didn't sound angry, she sounded tired.

It went quiet, then, and I tried to go to sleep, but sleep wouldn't come fast enough. On my bedside table the Furby snored.

'We agreed,' my father said more gently, so I had to lift my head from the pillow, use both ears, 'that you would have ten years. I promised your mother I'd look after you.'

My mother, a sigh that carried up the stairs, 'That was different. You know it was.'

'Why?' His voice was rising again. He was like this, now: suddenly cross, even with me.

I was learning to think twice before I spoke. The previous week there had been a letter about a school trip to York. I had folded it up, small, and put it in my pocket, then put it in the bin, because I was afraid that it would start another argument about money. I didn't mind. If you didn't go on the trip then you just went to school, as though it was a normal day, but there were no proper lessons. I might be able to help in the library. I liked that.

'When you said that to my mother, what you said was that you'd look after me. You meant keep me safe. You didn't mean make us rich. That was what she needed to hear, at the end.'

I remembered my mum's mum dying. It had been the summer that I got my first school uniform. She had been ill for as long as I could remember. When the funeral was over my mother cried a lot and said 'blessed relief' a lot. She started to cry now, but the sound was different to the way that she mostly cried these days, gentler. I heard my father speak, low, a growl of comfort. I imagined that he was cuddling her.

I was nearly, really asleep, when my mother spoke again. I thought she said 'we're a parsnip' but when I thought about it afterwards I realised the word must have been 'partnership', which was something I'd heard on the news.

'And you have to let me pull my weight,' my father said.

'And you have to let me support you,' my mother said.

My dad's voice rose again, something I didn't catch.

'Now you're wilfully misunderstanding me,' she said. Her voice was the one rising this time, in frustration. 'You're your own worst enemy.'

'That's right, judge me. That will help.'

I knew from his tone that it could go either way.

It went the bad way.

You'd think, because it's a significant thing, that I'd remember the moment I first sussed out that my dad was hitting my mum. But I don't. When I think back to that time, I remember, most of all, the feeling of wariness, of making myself small. After that, I remember how our family was tossed in the shallows where my father's moods met likelihood of work.

Things improved, briefly, after he got a job labouring on a building site that August. 'I'm not proud,' he would say, carrying fish and chips into the house, the hot, sharp smell filling the living room so that we would breathe it in, deeply, the way we would breathe the clear air when we got out of the car after a long drive. But the job didn't last — I don't think it was his fault, I think it was always going to be short-term — and soon we were back to toast and Marmite with Philadelphia cheese spread on top at teatime, although my mother didn't have the heart to pretend it was a treat any more.

I read *The Railway Children,* and was struck when the children were only allowed jam or butter, not both. Bobbie's version of poor, which involved having servants and benefactors sending hampers, didn't really read across to my life. I still loved the book, though. Especially the bit when her dad came back, at the end.

But there was no single moment when it hit me that he hit her. I just went through the days, in my shrinking way, and although, when I was interviewed later, I did say that I thought my father had hit my mother, I really couldn't remember when it started, or give any examples of times or places when it had happened. I wasn't there when my mother fell down the stairs and sprained her wrist. Yes, it does look a bit suspicious in retrospect, but if you're nine I think it's reasonable to assume that your parents are telling the truth.

My mum's black eye did mean a lot of questions at school, and Miss Buckley kept me in one break time, gave me a biscuit, and asked me if there was anything that was making me unhappy. I knew it was wrong to talk about money so I said that there wasn't. When I was invited to Matilda's or Emma's houses for tea, there were often hugs from their mothers, and whispered goodbyes that included something along the lines of: 'You can come for a sleepover any time, just tell your mum that you're always welcome here.' I smiled and said thank you but there was something comforting about home still. I certainly don't remember wanting to get away. I suppose that — and I know I sound like every victim of domestic violence that there's ever been — when things were okay, it was hard to believe that they would go bad again.

And I do believe that, despite everything that happened afterwards, my parents were good people, and they had loved each other, and they did love me, and they wanted to protect me from the worst of themselves. So although it seems that they didn't have the self-control to stop hurting each other, they did their damnedest not to hurt me, and however badly that turned out, I like that they tried.

This, by the way, is my official line. It works and I'm sticking to it. It's how I sleep at night. I suppose Nathan would say it's my story.

POETRY

2016
TURN PAGES

I bit the proverbial bullet. When I got home from Book Group the next Tuesday I looked at my phone and there was a text from Nathan:

Shall I keep you a seat tomorrow night?

Cheeky git. I was tempted to ignore it but I wasn't going to cut off my nose to spite my face. And I had thought that one of these days I might ask him about what led him to write the one about writing a different story for yourself. It was a weird idea. I didn't know if I liked it.

Anyway. I took a deep breath and texted:

You can if you like. And can you put me down on the list?

I waited, then *'Done!'* came back. I didn't analyse what he might have meant by that exclamation mark because I've got better things to do.

I spent most of Wednesday wondering whether I'd really perform my poem. It's not like I was legally obliged — Nathan's the only one with the list, so no one except him knows if you put your name down and bottle it — and exposure isn't really my thing. I hadn't been on a stage since *Bugsy Malone,* and all the stuff that came later really put me off the limelight. But Wednesdays were reminding me that poetry's a living thing and I was just wondering what it would be like to put my poems out there, in shared air, and see what they did. Don't get me wrong, I know the world doesn't need another wannabe poet. It was just going to be interesting.

Nathan put me up third. I was so preoccupied by his poem that I didn't care that much about mine. Every time he stood up on that stage he said something that threw me for a loop. The idea that people might want to relax in a relationship, that it wasn't all for show, or about not being found out — bits of my brain were dying at the effort of thinking about how that might be true.

I'd picked a silly poem to perform: I thought it would be a crowd-pleaser. I've noticed that people laugh at rhymes. I think spotting them, or maybe anticipating then, makes them feel clever.

When I stepped up, my guts were in my boots and my heart was in my throat.

I came sixth out of nine. Honour was satisfied, as Archie says. But I didn't like it. Everyone was looking at me, judging, and my voice sounded feeble, a far-off seagull-cry. I was pretty awful, wobbly, and my votes were sympathy votes, I'm sure. I'd been to the other poetry nights and thought about how the performers weren't very good: they were compensating for something, they were lonely, they wanted to think they were a poet because it was better than accepting their lives as they were. Once I'd stood up there I had a lot more respect for them. And five of them were better than me. That was fair. Suck it up, Loveday, you deserved it.

I watched the last round thinking about whether I should try harder or pack it in. I do like the shelves and the shadows. But I don't want to be a coward.

Nathan walked me home. On the way, he said, 'I liked that your poem went in a circle, and ended where it began.'

I said, 'I like that you noticed. And I liked yours.' Because I did, on both counts. I wasn't flirting.

I asked him in.

Yes, he stayed. Just because I don't like most people doesn't make me a nun, you know. A bit of discernment doesn't hurt. And I'd like to think that, after Rob, I learned to be very discerning.

Chase
As performed by Nathan Avebury at the
George and Dragon
York, April 2016

I know I'm supposed to like the thrill of the
    chase, but — personally —
I like it when the chase is over.
I like the bit where no one has to go and
    get croissants for breakfast, or pretend
    they always have them in the fridge, and
    we just have toast, or Weetabix.
I like unmatching underwear, and fuzzy
    armpits.
I like being able to wear my old Hootie and
    The Blowfish T-shirt with reasonable
    confidence that no one is going to call a
    cab for me.
I like the things that say: relax. We have
    arrived somewhere where we can both
    rest.
Don't get me wrong: I like a bit of tension, a
    bit of fizz. I might not enjoy the chaise
    longue but that doesn't make me ready

for the rocking chair.
But I'll be relieved when you've seen my
weird-shaped toes and that potential
deal-breaker is done with.
So maybe we could skip the chase, and
relax?

Books Behave
As performed by Loveday Cardew at the
George and Dragon
York, April 2016

I like books cause they don't care
If your knickers match your bra
If you've washed your hair.
I like books cause they don't invade your
space
They sit on your shelf
They don't get in your face.
I like books cause they don't mind
What your heart contains
Who you've left behind.
I like a book cause it doesn't give a shit
When you get to the end what you think of
it.
Books don't care if you've got a degree
What you watch on TV.
Books don't judge if you've got tattoos
If your friends are few.
I like books cause they don't care.

I don't mind admitting (well, I sort of do) that I spent the next few days in a mildly happy fug. The night with Nathan was — not to over-share — pretty good, sex-wise, but more importantly, he behaved like a normal person. He had bad breath in the morning and he looked like an idiot when he was half out of his trousers and, well, it was just nice. Better than nice. Basically, he was as good as his poem. No one was holding in their stomach and his two smallest toes are really weird — sort of folded over. It wouldn't last — I wasn't sure it was even going to be more than one night — but I did find myself a little bit cat-got-the-cream.

Archie asked if I was 'in such a good mood because of Mr Avebury', which annoyed me because (a) I don't see why women still have to be happy because of a man in the twenty-first century, as though we're not capable of our own, dick-free, joy and (b) he was right. I stuck my tongue out at him and bought him a cream bun from next door, even though his doctor says he isn't supposed to eat them. (Well, not cream buns specifically, just general artery-furring crap. He takes no notice, of course. He says he's been portly all his life and he'll go out in a portly coffin.)

Nathan started coming around to see me

in the evenings. Not every evening; I didn't always let him stay. He asked me to go to his place — he lived in Malton, a market town between York and the sea — but I just said, 'Not yet'. I didn't want to get myself into a situation I couldn't get out of. Malton was a bus-every-half-hour place, and it took an hour to get from there to York. That's okay for commuting if your day job is close-up magic, because not a lot of those gigs start at 9 a.m. I'd have to leave Nathan's at seven o'clock to get in to work on time, which is, frankly, a little more than I would be prepared to do for love. Not that it was love. It was definitely more than I was prepared to do for sex. And that's beside all of the self-preservation, make-sure-you-can-always-see-the-exit stuff. Also, if his place was like his cravat — the corollary of which, in home decor terms, would be boar heads on the walls and improbably huge armchairs — I thought I'd enjoy things for a bit before his flat put me off him. Nobody needs a boyfriend who lives in the endpapers of a first edition of *The Picture Of Dorian Gray.* Not that he was my boyfriend.

When he came around he did magic for me and I tried to see how it worked. Sometimes I could. He did things with coins and variations on find-the-lady, and once I'd worked something out he'd show me the details of how to do it. To give him credit, he never once made a joke about if he told me he'd have to kill me. I think I liked him because he was basically classy, underneath the cocky.

A couple of weeks in, Nathan invited me to go with him to a kid's party where he was doing magic. I hadn't thought of it as a real job, but it turned out he charged £250 for a party, £400 if there were more than twenty kids. I work most of a week for that, and nobody applauds me and gives me cake to take home. I thought I'd go because — well, why not? He'd seen me at work.

I started early because I was taking the afternoon off. Archie said I could have the whole day if I wanted, but the boxes of unsorted books were piling up under the breakfast bar again and I wanted to try to get through them before we got into summer. Students clearing out their rooms always led to loads of books coming in. That morning I hadn't been able to get to the door to unlock it for boxes piled in the doorway. Archie doesn't accept textbooks but he buys other things by the box, without even looking, sometimes, and I knew for a fact that I would be trying to find space for more poetry, Russian classics in translation, and mass-market mildly anarchic comedy novels. I'm not stereotyping. There would be other stuff too. But this was my tenth summer in the bookshop and I had a sense of what to expect.

Stupidly, I'd thought that because I wasn't normally in on a Wednesday morning, I would be, somehow, invisible, and be able to 'get on', as my mother used to say. The first hour was quiet, in terms of customers at least, but when there aren't any customers to talk to Archie talks to me.

'Have you thought about a holiday, Loveday?' he asked.

'Why?' I asked. Last time Archie asked me if I was planning a holiday it was so that he could make sure I was okay to look after the shop for a month because he'd been offered a bit part in a spy film set in Vienna. I was shattered by the time he got back.

'Well, there's no harm in planning ahead,' Archie said. And then, 'Where have you been on holiday? Where would you go?'

'Cornwall,' I said, then, 'I don't really like holidays.'

'Then you just haven't found the right one,' Archie said. 'It's like cocktails. Or card games.'

'Okay, you need to stop talking,' I said.

'I've just had to go back three letters in the alphabet.'

He was quiet for about five seconds and then: 'If you could go anywhere,' he asked, 'where would it be?'

'I don't know,' I said, 'I haven't got a passport.'

'I have several,' Archie said with a twinkle. 'You never know when you'll need to make a quick getaway.'

I sat back on my heels and laughed. 'What, if the second-hand-bookshop mafia comes after you because they've finally realised you were the one who stole the missing first folio *Complete Works of Shakespeare*, accidentally murdering Lord Mountbatten in the process?'

Archie was laughing too, but then he looked as though he was going to cry. He eased himself up to standing. 'I'm sorry, Loveday,' he said.

'What for?'

'Everything. Nothing. It doesn't matter.' I wondered if he was hungover: that could make him maudlin. He didn't usually mind that he was interrupting me. Maybe I'd sounded rude. I hadn't meant to.

He had turned away. I didn't know what was going on, but I didn't want to leave it like this. I took a breath. 'Archie,' I said, 'I'd go to Whitby. If I was going on holiday.' I didn't realise until I said it that it was true.

I was still pondering what Archie might be sorry for, and what would happen if I did go back to Whitby, when Melodie arrived.

'Loveday,' she said. It always amuses me to hear her say my name because she can't play with it. Almost every name she says she elongates, a sort of flirtation. 'Archeeeee', 'Naaaay-than'; she even manages to roll the 'r' in Rob. But 'Loveday' she can't do anything with. Today she tried elongating the first 'o' but it just made her sound mad(der), and she knew it.

'Melodie,' I said. 'Hello.' I was tempted to stretch out the final 'e' a bit but I didn't. I am many lousy things but petty isn't one of them. I know how much petty shit there is in the world and if I have an aim in life — apart from keeping my head down — it's not to add to it.

'You going to poetry night tonight, with you handsome boy, Nathan?'

'I'm not sure yet,' I said. 'I haven't decided.'

I had, as a matter of fact, but I wasn't going to tell her that. I had a poem that I'd been running in my head, thinking about how I could perform it. Nathan had helped

177

me to practise. I knew it inside out. I don't like being rubbish at things and I was rubbish on my first go. I still wasn't sure that I was going to like performing but I thought if I was prepared, I was at least giving myself the chance to make a fair judgement.

'I will be there,' she said, 'with my boy Rob.'

'Oh, okay,' I said. I thought she looked pissed off, but she was wearing a bowler hat so I couldn't really see her eyes.

I thought afterwards that maybe she wanted me to care about her love life, which I had failed to do, apart from to be (slightly) grateful to anyone who was going to take the roses out of my letterbox, so to speak. Maybe she had got wind of him following me, and thought it was all my fault, with my well-known temptress qualities of ignoring people I didn't like and generally not giving a toss.

Then I thought about what Rob could be like, and whether, if I liked Melodie more, I would try to warn her. I probably would.

'Are you and Rob getting on okay?'

'He a clever one,' she said, with a smile, 'and good eyes.'

'I know,' I said, and then I paused, thinking carefully about how to say it. 'But, Melodie, is he — is he kind? Because —'

She held up a hand. 'I will not discuss my love with you,' she said. 'We see you later.' She walked off. As soon as she'd rounded the corner I wondered if I should go after her. But what would I say? 'Your boyfriend sometimes comes out of the cafe when I come out of the shop'? 'Rob sometimes walks behind me when I'm going home'? Very easily explained away. Unless I told her everything it was going to come over like sour grapes.

I snuck to the breakfast bar before Archie could start on about whitebait-before-it-was-fashionable and lobster-cooked-on-the-beach, his current favourite topics of conversation after a weekend in Devon somewhere.

There was a box of cookery books waiting for me. Well, there were lots of boxes waiting for me, but cookery books was the biggest box with the smallest number of books in it. I'd clocked them when I hauled them in off the step with the other donations that morning. Archie won't let me put a 'We are not a charity shop. Do not fly-tip books here' sign on the door, because he says it won't do any good. He's probably right.

I emptied the box and put them into piles by author. There were a few good finds. No treasure, but books from the 1990s by authors who are still popular, which means that people will actually buy them.

Whoever the books in the box had belonged to, their cookery had been ambition rather than practicality. There were very few signs of use — no pages stuck together, no bits of paper marking often-used recipes, no marginalia about pastry quantities. They must have largely been bought for display purposes on a shelf in a smart kitchen. I thought I might stack them up on the main table, a 'just in — get them while they're hot' type thing. Archie likes a quick win too, though he doesn't really need to think about money. He's not relying on the bookshop to make a living; he doesn't even take a salary, he only pays the rent and the bills and me, and we cover those, most months.

But I knew that selling a dozen cookery books at £8 a go, or two for £15, would put a smile on his face. I started carrying them to the main table, stacking them up in a staggered column so they looked interesting from every angle. As I put them out I double-checked for signs of wear that I might have missed. Archie haggles, but I don't, so if the price is fair to begin with, I stick to my guns.

I realised that *Delia's Complete Cookery Course* wasn't in especially good nick. It still had its dust jacket, which was why I'd assumed it was of a piece with the other books in the box. But even before I'd opened it I realised it was different to the others. It had been used. It had character. Not only that — it had a character recognised. It had a character I recognised.

The dust jacket was torn across the front, for a start. The tear made a jagged line from top left to mid-right, like a cartoon graph of a business making a loss, and it had been inexpertly repaired with Sellotape, short pieces criss-crossing the rip and then a long strip across the top. When I picked it up it was that feeling again, the one I'd had with the Penguin Classics and the Kate Greenaway. I'd assumed they had been chances, coincidences, because what are the odds, really, of those books ending up in my hands?

But now, the past reared up in front of me as though it was going to attack. It was all I could do not to drop the book and run, the way I would if it had just burst into flames.

I closed my eyes, took some deep breaths, and told myself I was being ridiculous.

It couldn't be ours. It couldn't be.

When I opened my eyes again I made sure all I was seeing was one of the bestselling cookery books of all time, which of course my mother had, because almost every other household in the country had one. I looked through the pages and remembered. There was the squidgy chocolate log that we loved, my mother laughing and sometimes doing her version of swearing ('Oh, flipping Nora') as she tried to roll it up without the sponge cracking. She never managed it. As soon as I was old enough to read the recipe I pointed out that Delia said it would crack, but that wasn't good enough for my mother: 'I wanted it to be perfect this time, LJ.'

Then there was the pan-fried pizza that we sometimes had at weekends, though without the olives and anchovies. I suppose it was an odd thing but, to me, it's still what a pizza tastes like, and you can keep your authentic sourdough hand-stretched wood-fired numbers. Whoever had owned this book had liked that recipe too; the corners of the pages were stuck together with what looked like tomato purée.

As I flicked through I could almost taste the Whitby sea again, the kitchen door open to let the heat out, the smell of the beach blowing in with the cooler air. Whoever had owned this book had liked the things we liked. The pages fell open at the scones, the pork chops with sage and apple, the brownies and the parkin.

I looked for the lemon meringue pie,

because I remembered how much I liked helping to make it — there was a lot of 'doing', with the pastry then the filling then the meringue, and when we ate it, usually on a special occasion, I could never quite believe how lovely it was. Archie's birthday was coming. He was impossible to buy for because he had everything he wanted, except for things I couldn't afford, like crazy-expensive cigars and unpronounce-able wine. But if I made him something, he'd know I appreciated him, without me having to say so. I hate saying stuff. That's why I like poetry, I think. Minimum words. You can't argue with a poem. And it's rude to interrupt it.

It was easy to find the lemon meringue pie page because it was already marked. There was a postcard of Whitby in it: a photograph of the crags, taken along from the place where we used to sit on the beach on a warm summer day, although I always thought the crags looked best when it was raining and the skies were grey. They sort of shone, and at the same time they were sinister. I felt as though they were on my side. I looked at the postcard and I swear my heart actually skipped a beat, which I'd always thought was a stupid phrase. I felt it move in my chest, though, up and back for a second, before it went back to doing its usual thing.

I turned the postcard over.

Four words: 'Wish you were here', written in a black ink faded to French navy where the strokes were less forceful. A wonky heart drawn around them.

If my heart had skipped before, it bounced this time.

Or maybe dropped down dead.

It just wasn't there. Neither was the air that had been in my lungs. My eyes still worked and they saw that my hands were shaking.

My mother's writing.

It was plump, like her, all curves, most of the letters almost as broad as they were tall. I'd know it anywhere. On birthday cards, she always drew a heart around my name, and 'Mum' and 'Dad'. I'm not saying she had the copyright on that particular flourish, I'm saying that when I added it up — the postcard, the handwriting, the book . . .

It was her book. Our book.

Just to make sure — my lungs had started working again, except they'd turned up the volume, so I could hardly hear the shop noise for the sound of air heaving in and out of me — I went to the front of the book and started to leaf through the pages.

Our kitchen was small and when Mum and I baked we laid the book flat on the table and put the ingredients around and, invariably, over it; Dad used to joke that if he liked what we'd made and fancied a bit more he could go and lick the recipe page. So we had left an evidence trail of everything we'd baked. And the evidence was here, in front of me, now.

'My mother has that book,' said Nathan, from behind me. I jumped, and wobbled on the stool. 'Hey, steady.' He put his hands on either side of my waist, left them there, stood behind me, his nose in my hair, his lips on the back of my neck. He's very touchy, is Nathan, but not in an annoying way. He puts his hands on you and leaves them there. He doesn't stroke or pinch or ruffle you. I like that. I'm not a chihuahua.

'Mine too,' I said. My voice sounded odd, as though it had got wrapped up in a cough on the way out of my mouth.

I was trying to add everything up, when I hadn't even realised it was a sum. The Penguin Classics. The Kate Greenaway. Now this. It couldn't be coincidence — but if it wasn't coincidence, what was it?

My breath was coming fast. I felt Nathan feel it. He held a little tighter.

'Hey, Ripon Girl,' he said, 'you need a

little doorbell, or something, so people can warn you that they're here. I always make you jump.'

I just couldn't think of anything to say. I was worried if I opened my mouth again the whole thing would blurt out, and everything I'd worked so hard to get away from would chase me down.

'Are you ready?' he asked. He was wearing his full magician monty: frock-coat, winkle-picker shoes, smart black trousers and lurid pink-and-green socks underneath — they weren't visible unless he wanted them to be, but they made a flash of colour when he squatted or stretched and, I supposed, distracted people in the way his wrongly laced Doc Martens did. He was carrying a leather satchel and the night before he'd taken me through everything that was in it, showing me the tricks he was going to do. Even though I knew they were tricks, I still had no idea how he did most of them. It was frustrating and a little bit sexy. It had been a good night.

My mother would put postcards in my father's holdall when he went off to work on the oil rigs. I would draw pictures or write notes, and the two of us would tuck our missives into his bag, between the clothes that smelled of cold, hard work, and we would laugh as we thought about how surprised he would be when he found them. Which he wouldn't have been, of course — he'd have been more surprised if we hadn't bothered — but that never occurred to me. When he came home he would stick the postcards on the fridge, but I never saw the notes I'd written him again — not then, anyway, although they came back to me later when the house was cleared.

I looked back to the book, my mother's writing on the postcard. I felt as though my whole body was filled with tar. Just the thought of moving made me want to cry, and I don't really cry any more. The thought of going to a party and watching Nathan pull chocolate coins out from behind little kids' ears made the tar solidify.

And, suddenly, I was frightened.

Who could know about me? Who was watching? It was too much of a coincidence for my mother's book to end up here in my hands — the hands with the same shaped nail-beds as hers — without someone having deliberately made a connection, wasn't it? I'd assumed all of these momentoes had been lost when everything went wrong. I was afraid to move, or even look around, like someone from an Edgar Allen Poe story. I didn't know what was going to happen but I felt sure it would be bad. All those years I'd believed I'd escaped from my past. Really it had just been a question of time before it found me.

I made my head twist on my neck so I could look at Nathan.

'I can't come. I'm sorry.'

'What's wrong?'

'I just — I can't. There's too much to do here.' I looked at the boxes on the floor, piled up, the ones on the bench, waiting.

'Loveday,' he said, 'we shook hands.'

We had, too, at the weekend.

We'd been talking, in bed. We had stayed up late, drinking wine, and Nathan was telling me about growing up, summer holidays in Cornwall, camping at his mum's friend's house, and I was listening and thinking of my few memories of the Cornish sea and the things my dad had told me. When Nathan asked me what I remembered about holidays, I kissed him and said we should go to bed. Like I've said, I wasn't a virgin when I met Nathan, but this was the longest time I had ever spent with one person, and I was learning what it was like to — well, to really get to know someone. Books are mostly about the falling in love and the longing, the first kisses and the first nights spent together. So I hadn't really thought about how there might be a sweeter spot, one where knowing someone, being familiar with them, meant that everything was, actually, better than it was in the beginning.

No, I wasn't in love. I was just — enjoying the intimacy.

The next morning, Nathan woke up first. I was flat out on my stomach on the bed. The night was hot: the duvet was on the floor. I woke to the feeling of a kiss on the back of my neck. Time was that would have freaked me out, but I just stretched and stayed where I was. Nathan sat back, and his finger traced the words on my back, first one shoulder blade and then the other.

'I like your tattoos,' he said. His voice was as warm as the morning. His own skin was unmarked, pale, like Edam cheese when you pull the wax off.

'You don't have any,' I said.

'No,' he said. 'I'm too scared it would hurt, and I'd end up with half of something. And I wouldn't know how to decide.'

'Mmmm,' I said. I wasn't getting into the whole 'but you're stuck with it for the rest of your life' conversation. You could say the same about having a baby, but you don't.

'Why these ones?' he asked.

My skin stopped tingling and went cold.

That was one conversation that could lead anywhere. And mustn't go there. And yet there was part of me — a whisper from the back of my brain, the hidden place — that asked, why not just tell him? Tell him all of it. I ignored it, obviously, because nothing good would come of that confession. Nathan was a holiday from being me. I was going to enjoy it while it lasted.

'I'll tell you what,' I said, 'you tell me which books they are from and I'll tell you why I got them.'

'Deal,' he said. He kissed my left shoulder blade. My skin tingled. Then he read the words: ' "They were not railway children to begin with." I'm going to go crazy and I say: that's from *The Railway Children*. Do I have to know the author?'

I pulled myself up onto my elbows so I could talk more easily. He kept on running his fingers up and down my shoulder blades, my spine. I felt as though my skin was rising up to meet him. I arched my back a little. He spread his hands wider, started to caress the sides of my ribcage. This Sunday morning I wasn't going anywhere fast.

'No,' I said. 'Just the book. It's because I like that her dad comes back in the end.' If he heard the beginning of tears in my voice he didn't show it. His palms were flat on my back now, rubbing, massaging. I'd told him that my dad was dead. I suppose a teary voice was acceptable, 'Nesbit,' I said. 'I thought you were educated.'

He gave his attention to my other shoulder blade, first with a kiss, then tracing the letters. ' "There was no possibility of taking a walk that day." I feel as though I ought to know that one. Can I have a clue?'

I thought about Jane Eyre, how trapped she was, how my mother had no possibility of taking a walk. I thought of the Penguin Classics on the shelf in Whitby. I didn't think I liked this game, after all, and I wished I hadn't started it. I reminded myself that a beginning and an ending are two different places and, in real life, you might be able to make your own ending, whatever had gone before. Yes, I had thought of that before Nathan's poem. That's partly why it got under my skin, I think.

'No clues,' I said.

Nathan laughed. 'I thought there might not be. Why are all the fonts different?'

'Oh,' I said, 'because I let the people who do the tattoos choose them. I just care about the words, really.'

I turned over and lay back down, my hands behind my head. Nathan had showered before I woke up, and his skin was a little damp still. He'd used my shower gel, so he smelled of grapefruit, sharp with a sweet undertone. The towel around his waist had come undone. He wasn't exactly broad but he wasn't skinny, either, just the perfect width of chest, scattering of hair in the centre. I put the sole of my foot against his sternum and his hands went around my ankle and started to stroke their way up my leg. I knew he didn't know the origins of my collarbone tattoos. On my left side was: 'The book was thick and black and covered with dust' from *Possession*. I loved that book because it showed that love was complicated, and even when it didn't go to plan, it could still be real. Also, it had poetry at its heart. The fact that it was partly set in Whitby brought both comfort and pain. Which is what a good book should do. On my right clavicle sat: 'The primroses were over' from *Watership Down*. I'd read that when I was probably too young to, while I lived at Elspeth Phipps's house, and it frightened me but it also told me that things changed. When I re-read it, when I was eighteen, I got the tattoo as a sort of salute to that scared kid who kept turning the pages even though she was afraid.

Nathan was giving some attention to my right thigh. ' "Some things start before other things",' he read. 'Nietzsche?'

I laughed. 'Cheeky git,' I said. 'That's profound.'

And then he started to trace the words on my hips. ' "Happy families are all alike; every unhappy family is unhappy in its own way" — everyone knows that,' he said.

'Including you?'

'Now who's cheeky?' he laughed. '*Anna Karenina*. By Leo Tolstoy.'

I took my hands out from behind my head and applauded. 'I think that one speaks for itself.' Now that my hands were free, I reached up for his face, and I pulled him to me and kissed him. Kissing Nathan was something I always wanted to do these days. Also, I didn't really want to have to explain the first line of *The English Patient,* which was inked on my other hip. 'She stands up in the garden where she has been working and looks into the distance.' I didn't know whether Nathan would get that a book about people hiding gave me comfort. I didn't want to let him know that the idea of looking into the distance was something that I would never dare to do.

Fortunately, the kissing escalated. Half an hour later, we were lying in the sunshine that was coming through the window and pooling on our skin.

'I think we're getting the hang of each other, Loveday,' Nathan said, with a smile. I nodded.

Then his face got serious and I braced. 'You don't say much about yourself, though,' he said. 'All I really know is that you work in a bookshop. You come from Ripon. Your father died. You don't see your mother. And you've read seven books. Or at least the first lines of them.'

I laughed. Nathan made me laugh because he teased me. Archie teased me a bit, sometimes, but it was teasing-with-a-point, like teasing me about the state of my flat or dying my hair, so I took no notice of it.

'That's all you need to know,' I said. 'That's about it, really.' And if you boiled it down, it was. If you substituted 'Whitby' for 'Ripon' anyway.

He looked at me, then he took a breath and I thought, here come the conditions, and I was right. Except it was one condition and I liked it.

He said, 'I don't care if you don't want to tell me things. But I do care that what we do tell each other is the truth.'

'Okay,' I said, and I had the kind of feeling that I used to get as a kid, on the beach, when there was hardly anyone else there, and I could do one of my rubbish, arse-sticking-out cartwheels with no one noticing. 'Any other deal-breakers?'

'I don't think so,' he said. He stuck out his hand and I shook it. It's weird, shaking hands with someone when you're both naked — inappropriate, in the context. He just about got away with it, like the hat-tip.

'We shook hands,' he said again, now. Tell me the truth.'

I looked at the Delia book and I looked at him, his seaside eyes, and I said, 'Something's happened that's made me feel — shaky. Nothing bad. I just don't feel as though I want to go out anywhere. I couldn't smile and meet new people. I need some time to think about — the thing.'

He nodded. 'Have I upset you?' he asked.

'No, because you're not the centre of the world.'

He laughed, just a light touch of sound. 'Will you tell me about it?'

'I don't know yet,' I said. That might be what's technically known as a white lie.

'Is it anything I can help you with?'

'I don't think so.'

The shop was quiet. Archie was standing just outside the doorway, glad-handing passers-by like he'd won an Oscar for 'Best Character Actor (Bookshop Owners)'.

'Are you going to be okay here? Will you still take the afternoon off?'

'I'll be fine,' I said. 'I think I'll work. I really have got a lot to do.' It's never-ending, and that's what I like about it: the circle of book-life. People come in to find them, other people bring in the ones that have outlived their usefulness in that life, but can be reincarnated into another one. I make the whole system work, like a Saint Peter of books, or . . . oh, I don't know. Sheep, goats, wheat, chaff. Choose your biblical metaphor for getting rid of the crap.

'Okay,' he said. He kissed me, like he meant it, and then he went. He got to the door and then he came back. 'Will you call me?' he said.

'Yes,' I said. 'Piss off and stop asking me questions.'

He laughed and did the hat-tip. I was starting to find it endearing. Despite myself I was actively looking forward to spending time with Nathan. I loved that we could spend an evening together, just reading. When he came to meet me from the shop at the end of the day it seemed like he brought his own light. I know I was being ridiculous. As I watched Nathan leave I saw Rob pass the window, heading towards the cafe. He raised a hand. I pretended that I hadn't seen him. Fringes are brilliant when you're fussy about who you talk to. I could see the sense in Melodie's bowler hat, sometimes. I wondered whether Rob had planted the cookery book — whether he, somehow, knew. He said I talked in my sleep. People came and went through the bookshop all the time and the books waiting to be sorted are on the floor or the bench. I don't know how he would have got hold of my mother's cookery book, though. And if Rob wanted to freak me out he'd be more likely to put a dead rat through the letterbox.

I was sitting with my back to the quiet shop, no one was visible in the mirror, but I felt watched. I really didn't like it.

I took an early lunch, and I took Delia Smith, and I sat in the chair in front of the fire escape for a long time. I looked at the postcard and when I concentrated on the front I could convince myself that what was on the back was the writing of a different hand. But when I flipped it over I knew that I was wrong and there was only one person who would have written that message on that postcard. The words, the letters, the ink, the heart were irrefutable forensic evidence and I knew it. Well, circumstantial evidence maybe, but overwhelming still.

I put the postcard on the shelf beside the chair and I started to turn the pages, slowly, no longer pretending to myself that the book wasn't ours.

I jumped when Archie came through to the back of the shop. 'Are you well, Loveday?' he asked when he saw my face. I suppose I might have been crying. The thought of tidying shelves and talking to customers made me want to cry even more. Plus, it was one of Melodie's afternoons, and I could do without hearing about her and Rob. All I wanted was to go home.

'Actually, I don't feel great,' I said. I thought about the period pain excuse, but Archie deserves better, and anyway, he would probably start reminiscing about when he was Madonna's gynaecologist, or something. I took a breath. 'This book,' I said, 'I think it was my copy. My mother's, I mean. It made me miss her.'

'Oh, Loveday,' he said, and he stood, quietly, and looked at me.

'I don't know where she is,' I said. And then there was the sound of the bell above the front door, and someone calling Archie's name, and I got up and said, 'Do you mind if I go home?'

'Of course not,' Archie said. 'Let's talk about this another time, Loveday.'

I didn't go to poetry night. Nathan texted me, later, to arrange to go and see a film at the weekend. No questions, no faffing. You might say, too good to be true.

■ ■ ■ ■

HISTORY

■ ■ ■ ■

2013
HERE IS FOOD

I suppose, then, I liked that Rob wasn't perfect, despite all the Mr Rochester he had going on. I think that was why I went out with him again, despite the shoe-polishing. I know, I know. But when you're imperfect yourself and you come across someone more obviously broken than you, it's both heartening and comforting. Heartening because it gives you — well, let's take responsibility, Loveday — it gave me a sense that I could do more if I wanted to. I could get a degree, for starters. I could make a future at odds with my past. I was comforted, too, because I felt as though he was one of my tribe, if I had one — in a way that, let's be honest, Nathan is never going to be. I might not take palmfuls of drugs every day like Rob does, but I knew I would never win any wellness awards. So, there were those things, and he talked about books, and when he got to reading Florence's journal he talked a lot about 'richness' and 'texture' for his PhD and, well, he got me on an ego trip, I guess. I wasn't a shop girl any more. I was doing important research. I cringe when I think about it now.

First, I of all people should know that there's nothing better, more important, than a book, and working for Archie pretty much saved me, so I had no business thinking that it didn't matter. Second, there's nothing wrong with working in a shop. And, statistically, given the kind of life I've had, it's a towering achievement; I should be, at best, unemployed, at worst, drinking fortified wine straight out of the bottle, or shooting up in a railway station entrance while people scurry past me in case I mug them. Or in prison, obviously. I'm not stupid; I know that Archie and his books are the factor that have made the difference. So I'm embarrassed at the thought of myself thinking that Rob, with his endless banging on about da Vinci being the tallest tree in the forest rather than some freak-show out-of-time genius, was somehow making me a better person.

I suppose I wanted to think I was important. I was probably just at the point where I'd stopped scraping through days and was looking up and forward, and I wanted there to be more than forty years of waiting for the A Level reading lists to come out so I could make up little packs with all of the texts in, ready for the stream of parents coming in to look for them. (Heaven forbid a sixteen-year-old should do their own donkey work.) At least Rob helped me to see what I had.

It's tempting to say it went bad because of the new tattoo, but, actually, it was never good, it was just that the badness revealed itself slowly, and the thing with the tattoo was the first time it got into plain sight.

I'd read *The Wee Free Men* three months before, and kept going back to it. So I took myself off to get the first line inked on my right thigh.

It takes about an hour to get a line of text tattooed, in case you're interested, and yes, it hurts, because it's a needle going in and out of your skin like a drill bit. It's chosen pain, of course, which makes it slightly different, but in no way thrilling, whatever E. L. James has to say. It hurts less if it's going into a plump place and the nice thing about a single line is that you can feel the progress; I imagine that with coloured-in tattoos there's no way of knowing how much longer you've got to go. I take Paracetamol beforehand and while I'm having it done I count to a thousand and back to zero, slowly, in my head. It takes a few days before the redness goes.

Rob was the first person who'd seen all of them, and he hadn't really commented. He'd seen me dress in the morning, read some of the words on my body, as though he was reading newspaper headlines, but that was it.

I arrived late for our date the next Saturday night.

I thought I'd left my place on time, but I missed the bus and it was twenty minutes until the next one. Then there was a hold-up on the city ring road. Rob had told me that he was making his special osso bucco, which had to be marinated for two days and then slow-cooked for a third, so I assumed it wasn't going to spoil. I was half an hour later than I said I would be. I hadn't texted because — well, because I didn't think to. I'm not what you'd call an experienced dater and I suppose I thought as Rob knew I was coming by bus he'd also know that buses got held up — we had a sort of running joke about public transport. We must have been on about six dates at this point. Long enough to have a running gag, a confessional conversation about mental health issues and, apparently, a false sense of security.

'I'm sorry I'm late,' I said when he opened the door. I started to explain about the bus but he cut me off with a nod that very clearly did not mean 'I accept your apology'.

'Well, I don't think it's quite ruined, though I can't say the same for the risotto alla Milanese,' he said, and he turned, and I followed him into the flat. I took off my boots at the door — they were metallic DMs, almost falling apart with years of wear, and I'd wiped them clean before I left my place. I lined them up at right angles to the wall, toes not quite touching the skirting board.

Rob had set the table and lit candles and clearly gone to a lot of effort, so I apologised again, and then realised that I'd forgotten the wine, which was sitting in a bag on the worktop in my flat. I'd said that I would bring it. Rob shrugged and said it didn't matter, but I could tell that it did. He huffed around his kitchen, finding wine, and I thought, I don't need this.

I said, 'Rob, I'm sorry I was late and I'm sorry I forgot the wine. Should I go? If the evening's ruined we may as well cut our losses.' I wasn't being bitchy about it, I was just asking because, frankly, I could always be eating a pizza and reading a book. I can't be arsed with people who don't say what they mean and Rob knew that.

I think he got the non-bitchy thing because he came over, gave me a kiss and said, 'I'm sorry, Loveday, it's just that I'd planned everything.'

He seemed twitchy. When I look back, I can see that he was definitely different to his usual self — by which I mean, more different than me being late should have made him. Even with risotto alla Milanese ruining on the hob as my bus struggled through the traffic.

It didn't occur to me that he might not be well. I suppose I thought it was just the inevitable dropping of the other (metaphorical) boot.

'I can see that,' I said. I almost said, I didn't ask you to, but that would have sounded nasty, and anyway, I wasn't sure that anyone had ever lit a candle for me in a non-birthday-cake scenario.

The evening looked as though it was recovering. The osso bucco was amazing and Rob could obviously tell that I appreciated it. He went into a long explanation of its history, but that's academics for you. I didn't much mind. One thing I was realising from seeing Rob was that if you don't talk about your past and you work in a bookshop, then your topics of conversation are, basically:

1. Books I've read and liked and why
2. Books I've read and not liked and why
3. Books I want to read but haven't yet and why
4. Books I have decided not to read and why
5. Customers
6. Archie
7. (Melodie)

All rich seams well worth mining, to be fair, but a limited range, so I wasn't going to object to Rob talking about Italian culinary traditions and osso bucco he had eaten, though they all started to blur into one big meal after a while. Then he started talking about his research, and writing.

'I've been working through the nights,' he said, and his words leapfrogged over each other with excitement. 'I'm almost at the heart of it, I know I am. It will be a breakthrough.'

We went to bed. That was a given. I'd shaved my legs and taken the dressings off my new tattoo; it was a little bit crusty, still, but the redness had gone down and you could see the words.

When Rob's hand ran over my thigh, he stopped and said, 'What's this? Have you hurt yourself?'

I said, 'It's okay. New tattoo.'

'I'd say that was hurting yourself,' he said.

He put the light on. We always had sex in the dark. That was what I'd done on my virginity-losing exploit, too. My relationships had not, as yet, lasted long enough for me to get comfortable with day-sex, morning-sex, all-day-Sunday-in-bed sex of the sort that films and TV suggested were the norm. He rolled me towards the lamp — it was really a shove — and had a look.

'I can't read it,' he said.

' "Some things start before other things",' I said. 'It's the first line of *The Wee Free Men*.'

'Uh-huh,' he said.

'I like it,' I said. 'I like that the book's full of strong women, for one thing, and the thing with Pratchett is —'

'Oh, you've got a PhD in Pratchett, have you?' Rob's voice was one hundred per cent sneer.

That was it. I got off the bed — he reached for me but he was too slow — and I started to put my clothes on.

'What do you think you're doing?'

'You're the one who's nearly got a PhD — you tell me,' I said. He got up — he still had his boxer shorts on — and left the room. I dressed as fast as I could and went back into the living room.

I thought maybe he was putting the kettle on, or something — I'd like to think that adults could have conversations, even about things that had started with childish tattoo overreactions, and if he'd offered tea or an apology, I would have accepted. But he was just standing, leaning on the door frame, with the smirk that I would later come to know so very well. His mouth was handsome at rest, but he pulled it into ugly shapes. It seemed to appear around the ends of bookcases before he did, like the Cheshire cat's grin. I'd like to think this was the first time I encountered it, because I'd like to think that I'd have had more sense than waste my time on a smirker.

'Are you leaving?' he asked.

'I was going to ask you what the hell all that was about,' I said, 'but I'm easy.'

'I just thought,' Rob said, 'that getting a tattoo would have been something you might have mentioned to me.'

'Why?' I said, and I laughed, because even then I hadn't completely got what he was like. 'Was I supposed to ask your permission?'

I saw from his face that was exactly what I was supposed to have done. He didn't say that, of course. He said, 'I just thought you would have talked to me about it. If we — like each other, I would think that was what we would do.'

'We'd talked about tattoos,' I said. It had been when we had dinner after the talk on architecture. Rob had started by saying he'd never felt the need for one and asked what my criteria were. I'd said: things that mean something to me. I didn't say the other bit, about reminding myself that first lines did not define last pages in real life the way they did in books. That felt like too much information, like none of his business. And if I'd thought about that a bit sooner I wouldn't be standing in a flat on the outskirts of York with my bra in my pocket, thinking about the hour I was about to spend with the drunks on the bus on the way home.

'You remember?'

'Well, yes,' I said. Suddenly I felt shaky. It was like being questioned by the police, or lawyers; it all looked civil enough, they were gentle as anything, but a part of you knew that if you slipped up, you'd get someone into real trouble. In this case, with Rob, the someone was me. His eyes were too bright. I picked up my bag.

'I said,' Rob said, pretend-patiently, 'that I didn't really like tattoos.'

I swallowed the 'oh for fuck's sake, I haven't got time for this' that was in my mouth and instead I said, 'And you don't have any. That's up to you. What I do is up to me.'

He made a 'well, if that's how you see it' face and I walked towards the door. I thought he was going to block me but he didn't. I stepped out into the hallway and realised why he was letting me go so easily. I turned back to him.

'Where are my boots, Rob?'

The smirk again. 'I don't know, Loveday.'

'Oh, for fuck's sake,' I said, 'what are you, twelve? Give me my boots.'

And his face went from pretend-amused to dark, and he hit me.

Well, slapped, really, across my cheek, with his palm; it sent me sideways, but it didn't knock me over, and as I returned to standing, the skin of my cheek stung. My perfectly balanced opposing instincts were to hit him back — my hand was already a fist — and to run. The net result was paralysis. It was the first time anyone had raised a violent hand to me. It hurt in more ways than one.

I looked at him. I suppose I thought there would be agitated apology; in my world, violence is a flare followed, instantly, by regret. But: 'Come back to bed,' he said, 'and we'll say no more about it.'

'Fuck you,' I said. Archie says I'm Anglo-Saxon under stress.

Rob shrugged and turned away, going back into the bedroom. I think he thought I had no option but to follow him. Apparently he knew me as little as I knew him.

I left the flat, without my boots. I had my socks on and I didn't have to wait too long for a bus, but even the walk to the bus stop and then onwards to home cut my feet in three places and made me feel filthy. When I got back — it was after one the next morning — I took a shower and then I soaked my feet in the washing-up bowl with salt because they still didn't feel clean. I held a cold flannel to my face.

I laid low the next day. I half expected Rob to show and I wasn't going to let him in. I hadn't given him my address but I'd told him I lived in a flat above a new Tesco and there was precisely one place in York that fitted that description, so he could find me easily enough. He'd said he knew where I meant.

I was beyond pissed off. He'd hit me; he

hadn't cared that he'd hit me; and there wasn't so much as a bruise to show for it. If I decided to go to the police I'd have no evidence.

I did think about the police. I thought about it a lot. I wasn't under any illusions that Rob would be charged with anything — it was the classic my-word-against-yours scenario, and we all know how that ends — but I didn't want him to think it was okay, either. And then I thought about him being ill, and got myself in a knot about responsibility. He had said things got weird if he didn't take his medication. I'd assumed he'd meant double vision, or something, but maybe it was the sort of weird he'd been last night. And that's where I got tangled up. Because surely it's not as simple as: you take a pill to stop you from hitting people? My head ached, in a way that was nothing to do with the slap.

I thought about telling Archie, but that would have been another drama altogether, and not one that I was really up for. Though I would have liked to see Rob's face when he opened his front door to Archie and the rabble he'd have roused from the bridge players, book lovers and restaurateurs of York.

Mostly, that Sunday, I thought about my

mother, and how much my father must have hurt her. And I'm not even talking about the whole betrayed-by-the-one-you-love hurt. I mean the pure and simple physical pain of being struck, being bruised, having the parts of you that are supposed to keep you strong, break. Rob gave me, frankly, a nasty, domineering little-girl slap. He's about ten stone wet through and any strength he has comes from getting heavy books from high shelves. And that slap still hurt. It really did. I suppose it's partly the shock of the impact, then every nerve-end standing up and howling at once. Followed by the humiliation. I don't know why I was so ashamed. I felt as bad as if I had been the one doing the hitting.

My dad was a big bloke, and he was made of muscle. He once grabbed my arm when he thought I was going to run into the road, and yes, it was a panicky ill-thought-out move on his part but I still don't think he would have used more force than he had to. He was standing next to me; really all he did was put out his arm and hold. That bruised to blue, and my mother laughed and joked about keeping it away from social services. That, obviously, was long before the social services came.

So when Dad did the things he did, with

force and anger, they must have really hurt her. Of course, I knew that, in my head. Now I'd experienced it in my flesh and I felt a sort of retrospective pity for my mother. Not forgiveness. But — I felt.

I sat in my flat that Sunday, with a bag of frozen peas held against my face and *A Suitable Boy* by Vikram Seth balanced on my knees, and although I was supposed to be reading, I kept on thinking of my mother, hurting, and my father, hurting her, and how none of it was as straightforward as I wanted it to be. And I decided that relationships weren't really ever going to be for me. I wouldn't be staying over at anyone's flat again any time soon, no matter how much they liked my research methods.

Rob came into the bookshop on the Tuesday. My face had recovered and the scrapes on my feet were healing. Archie hadn't noticed anything, which I was surprised by, because I felt more shaky than I would have guessed, and I couldn't believe it didn't show.

Rob brought flowers. I could smell them before I could see him. The bouquet was mainly lilies. The scent of them was too much; it made me want to cry. I wasn't going to, though. I wasn't going to do anything to make him think I gave a fuck, because I really didn't, except that I don't know where idiots like him get off thinking that what he did was okay.

'Loveday,' he said. He wasn't smirking, at least. He held out the flowers.

'I don't want them, thanks,' I said. I tried to say it without edge, a statement of fact. Whatever the message of the flowers was intended to be, I didn't want my flat to smell like an Angela Carter novel for the next three weeks.

'Don't be like that,' he said. 'I'm trying to say sorry.'

I'd thought he would probably come in and I'd thought a lot about what I was going to say. My possible scripts veered from furious put-downs to gentle conversations about what was acceptable and subtle enquiries as to whether he was seeing his doctor and taking his medication properly.

Looking at him, though, I realised I hadn't decided on the line I was going to take. It turned out to be the line of least words. No surprises there, Loveday.

Rob shoved the flowers at me. He looked sorry, but when it came down to it, he'd picked the wrong girl to hit.

I took a step backwards. 'I accept your apology but I don't think what you did was okay,' I said, 'and I don't want the flowers, thanks.'

He looked at the flowers, and at me. 'That's not very nice of you, Loveday.'

'Let's not get started on not very nice,' I said, and I took a deep breath, and another step away.

'At least have a coffee with me,' he said. 'I can wait next door until you finish.'

'No,' I said. 'Really. I've nothing to say.'

He sighed. His sighing was as bad as the smirk. I stood there wondering why I'd bothered at all.

'Are you really going to throw everything away because of one tiny mistake?' he said.

I stood and looked at him, with his flowers and what I thought he probably considered to be an appealing expression. I thought he probably was ashamed of himself. If I had a coffee with him he would probably say so. But there was no 'everything' — we were barely dating — and as for 'tiny mistake', well, sisters, it made me want to spit teeth.

'Yes,' I said, finding a bit of one of my pre-prepared speeches that fitted. 'I am going to throw it all away, because like I said, what you did is not okay. It was not a "tiny mistake". If you think it was you're in trouble.' I tried to make my voice gentle.

219

'Maybe you should talk to someone about what happened.'

He wasn't listening. 'I thought better of you, Loveday. I told you I was ill. I thought you'd be more understanding.'

'In fairness,' I said, and I really was trying to be fair, 'if you'd had the flu, or a broken hip, and slapped me, we'd still be having this conversation.'

We looked at each other, properly, for a minute, and then I turned away and went through the door marked 'private', and for the first time in a long time I wondered where my mother was.

When I left the shop that night the flowers were on the pavement by the door. I was going to put them in the bin by the cafe, but it was full, so I laid them down beside it. I thought about asking him to bring my boots back but I decided against it. They were getting hard up anyway, and some things really aren't worth the grief.

Rob disappeared for a while: he'd told me that he was going to spend some time in Italy and I assumed that was where he'd gone. When he came back he'd show up every now and then, shove flowers through the letterbox, let my tyre down, though that was only the once. In the three years since he'd slapped me, sometimes I hadn't see him for weeks or months, and then he'd be in bad penny mode for a bit.

Maybe Nathan being around made him worse.

I hate to admit it, but I was scared of him.

■ ■ ■ ■

CRIME

■ ■ ■ ■

1999
NO BOOK IS WITHOUT WORTH

I suppose the social services must have planned the timing of their visit carefully, although I didn't think about it then. It was the October half term. I would be ten when the year turned. I wasn't keen on my new teacher and I spent a lot of time in the library. We didn't go to the bookshop any more.

My dad was at the job centre. My mum was in the kitchen. She didn't do as much baking these days — the price of butter was, apparently, 'criminal'. She used to say, 'I don't believe in margarine', as though she was talking about yogic flying, or ghosts. But, for whatever reason, she was making a cake. Perhaps because it was the holiday, or maybe it was to sweeten Dad up when he came back from the job centre. I was going to Matilda's later, for a sleepover, and I was too excited to settle to anything. Anyway, there was a knock on the front door, and I went to open it. There were two women standing there, one tall, one short, both wearing trousers and smart jackets. The shorter one looked a bit pink, as though she'd climbed a hill.

'Hello,' the taller lady said. 'Is Mum in?'

Of course, because the front door was about six feet from the kitchen, my mother's face was already in the kitchen doorway, looking around to see who was there. Since she'd had a second black eye a few weeks ago she'd been keeping herself to herself a bit more, sending me on errands to the shop, letting me be collected by my friends' mothers if I was going to their houses, asking my dad to pick me up.

'Hello,' she said. She came through to stand next to me, and put her hand on my shoulder for a moment, leaving a floury ghost-hand behind.

The women said their names and checked my mother's, and asked if they could come in. I heard them say they were from social services. They didn't look as though they were going to be any fun, although they kept looking at me and smiling, as though it was their first day at school and they wanted to be my friend. It was creepy.

I was glad to be sent upstairs. I didn't try to listen — I'd discovered *Sweet Valley High* in the school library and was reading more than ever. But I did hear my mother raise her voice in a complicated, garbled sentence that had my name and the words 'perfectly safe' and 'no right' in it. Shortly afterwards, the front door closed. I went to the window. As the women walked to the end of the path they turned back and looked at the house; they saw me and waved.

My mother called me downstairs. She looked as though she had been crying. She said that she didn't want us to tell Dad that the women had been to visit. 'It's a bit like when politicians come around,' she said. 'You know how cross they make him.'

I did. My father had been, briefly, a star of local TV news when the Tory candidate knocked on our door in the run-up to a by-election, with a film crew in tow. He'd been asked if he would vote Conservative. 'Absolutely,' he said, and the candidate had smiled, too soon, 'when hell freezes over. Get off my lawn.' Before he said lawn there was a moment where his mouth was moving but all you could hear was a beep. Then there was a close-up of his fist clenching at his side.

'Okay,' I said. I didn't point out the whole 'secrets are wrong' mantra that my mother used to have. I was learning that there were new rules in this new world, and I just went along with whatever made everyone's life easier.

'And there's another thing,' she said. 'Your friends, LJ. And their mothers. Just — be careful about what you say to them.' My mother spoke slowly, as though her words were picking their way across stepping stones, 'Families are all different, and sometimes people whose families are different to yours think they know things about you, but they don't.' She looked at me, stroked my hair. 'People get the wrong idea. Because Dad and I sometimes argue, then some people might think we are unhappy or — or that we hurt each other.' I nodded, because she'd just described exactly what I thought. 'So we need to be careful that no one thinks the wrong thing about our family. If any of your teachers or the other mums ask you if everything is okay at home, I want you to tell them that everything's fine, but Dad is still working hard to find a job. Okay?'

I nodded, although I wanted to shake my head. I wondered what the women in the jackets had said to her to make her talk like this. I knew I was a child and that meant I didn't always understand everything, even when I thought I did. But I also knew, belly-deep, that what my mother was saying was wrong. I think she knew it too, because her eyes looked sad, and they wouldn't look at my face.

'Do you understand?' She put her hand on my head, and looked at my hair as she stroked it.

'Yes,' I said, 'but —'

'That's enough, LJ,' she said, not crossly, but not kindly either, and even though I caught at her hand, she turned away.

And I did as I was told, although I sobbed my heart out at Matilda's later. Her mum came up to the bedroom to see what the noise was about. She hugged me and told me everything would be all right. Her sweater was scratchy against my face and I thought about my mother's softness and sobbed harder.

Our life went to a flat, dead calm for a while. My parents didn't talk much but they didn't shout either. I spent a lot of time in my room, sorting out my shells, re-reading *The Railway Children*.

Then my dad got trained as a forklift truck driver. He grumbled about having to go on the course, but when he came home he was full of chat about it. He got a couple of weeks' trial in a warehouse. He said he might start smoking again, and when Mum glared at him he laughed and called her a 'dow', which he said was Cornish for 'cross old lady'. Mum said, 'Less of the old', and then they smiled at each other the way that they used to.

They gave him a full-time job at the warehouse and there was talk of Christmas presents and there being life in the old dog yet. I hoped that might mean we were getting a puppy. I would call it Bobbie if we did. My mum started baking again and they laughed a lot, in the evenings, when I'd gone to bed. It felt as though the house breathed out.

We ate fish and chips on the beach, even though it was November and the wind was freezing cold. It was just us and a couple of dog walkers, and the sky the colour of a school shirt that had been washed with Mum's black dress. When we got home we lit the electric fire and played Scrabble. I won. I don't think they let me.

I think that Saturday was the last happy day.

The next evening, I was going to go to Emma's for tea and to watch the video of *Toy Story*. The afternoon was dragging. Dad was watching a war film and I was pretending to watch it with him, just because it was nice to sit with him, and I liked it when he explained something about the history. Mum and I had baked scones; she had gone to the shop, and said that she wouldn't be long.

It wasn't an interesting film, or Dad wasn't talking as much as usual, or maybe after months of him being at home the novelty of him being there every Sunday afternoon was wearing thin. I went to the bookshelf. We hadn't started up the book-shop trips again, and I hadn't been to the library that week, so I looked through the pile of my books that were starting to seem too childish for me, or had been reread so often that I wasn't interested in picking them up again. *The Secret Seven* had lost their charm, and so had *Captain Underpants*.

The adverts came on, and Dad's attention switched from the screen to me. 'Maybe you should try one of your mother's,' he said, and he reached into the top shelf, pulling out *Jane Eyre,* the easiest one for him to reach, although I suppose it could have been any of them. 'There's a lot of words in here, kiddo. Rather you than me,' he said, ruffling through the pages. And then he paused. He flicked back through the book, and pulled a ten-pound note from between the pages. Flicked again, found another. He looked at the money in his hand, his whole body still. And then he looked up at me, and he smiled a not-smile. 'Well, well,' he said, 'there's gold in them there hills.' He put the money in my hand, the book by his feet, and took another book from the shelf, flicked through. A twenty-pound note, a five-pound note, a ten-pound note. *Madame Bovary* joined *Jane Eyre* on the floor. And so we went, through the books, more and more notes in my hands. I had never seen so much money.

When the shelf was empty, Dad looked at me. 'Well,' he said, 'that's a lot of arghans.'

I nodded. Usually I liked it when he used Cornish words but this time it made me feel cold. I had been keeping count. I was holding almost three hundred pounds, which was more money than I had ever seen, and seemed an unfeasible sum to be contained on one small bookshelf in our pinched living room. There had been a lot of talk about money while Dad wasn't working; pound coins rescued from handbags and coat pockets on a Sunday evening when my parents did their planning; lists of sums on backs of envelopes. Such a great pile of notes — hundreds of pounds! — should have been a great thing, but I knew that it wasn't.

Dad was looking from the books to the money to me. 'Did you know this was here?' he asked.

'No,' I said. I'd wonder, later, whether I should have said yes. For a long time it was one of the places where I thought I might have influenced the outcome. If I'd said that I did know, then this hidden money would have been a game, a harmless secret, nothing more. But I said no, because it was true, and I had learned the habit and the value of truth all my life. I had been thinking about the women in jackets a lot and every time I did I felt certain that bad things were coming, as though I was reading a ghost story. Up until that knock on the door, I thought that truth was fixed, simple, a harbour wall rather than a tide.

The door clicked open and closed. 'Clotted cream!' my mother called. 'I had to go to two places. But I thought we deserved a treat.' There were the everyday noises of her putting down a shopping bag on the kitchen bench, hanging up her coat on the back of the door. 'It's very quiet in here,' she said as she put her head around the door, then, when she saw the two of us, the books, the money still in my hands, 'oh.' Her eyes were round and fixed on the money. Dad and I were looking at her face. Her mouth wasn't quite closed.

'There's quite a lot of money hidden here,' my father said. 'We were surprised. We didn't know what to say. Did we, Loveday?'

I was mute. I only got my proper name on proper occasions, like at parent-teacher evenings or the doctor. My parents called me LJ, short for Loveday Jenna, and my dad called my mum SJ, short for Sarah-Jane, unless he was angry with her. So even without the ghost-story feeling, I'd have known that it was serious.

I shook my head, looked at my mother, hoping she would say the simple thing — because surely there was one — that would put it alright.

But she had sat down, opposite us, on the sofa. She looked at her hands, drew a breath. 'Not now, Pat,' she said. 'Let's talk about it later.'

'Actually,' my dad said, 'I think, now.' His voice was quiet and that was more frightening than if he had shouted.

'Wait until she's gone out,' my mother said. She was almost whispering, looking at her hands, still.

'Don't use her as an excuse.' Dad's fingers were tapping against his leg, a *rat-a-tat* of flesh and denim. I felt more scared than I was when they were arguing.

'She wants to know, too. Why she's been eating scrag-end stews and her arms growing out of her sleeves when you have enough money to make things easier around here?'

'Now who's using her?' my mother said. She put out her hand to me. I tried to move but Dad had his other arm around my waist, a solid bond that I couldn't easily get myself out of. I couldn't get up. I don't think he noticed he was holding on to me.

'I want to go upstairs,' I said.

'You heard her,' my mother said.

The pressure on my waist increased as my father squeezed and then slackened his hold. I went to the stairs, although suddenly I wasn't sure whether I should leave the room. I thought about helping my dad to tie his work boots, my finger on the knot, and how if I slid my finger out too soon it would all go wrong.

They weren't looking at me. I went slowly up the staircase.

'Don't try to make me the bad guy.' Now I was out of sight my father's voice was gaining volume. Normally I would have done something to make sure I couldn't hear. My dad had given me his portable CD player when he stopped working away because he said he didn't need it any more, and bought me *Now That's What I Call Music*

43 when he got his forklift job. I could have put my headphones on.

I let myself listen. I suppose I wanted to know where the money had come from too, and what it was for. I didn't know how much a birthday party cost but I was sure it was less than three hundred pounds.

My mother's sigh came right up the stairs and around the side of the door, where I'd left it open. 'I've been working, Pat. Just a little bit, now and then. Since school term began.'

'Doing what?'

'Ironing, mostly,' she said. 'Amanda Carter from the PTA has a business. She saw me ironing the costumes for *Bugsy Malone* and said if I ever wanted a job I should let her know. I thought maybe we could have a nice Christmas. That was all.'

'Why didn't you tell me?'

'I wanted it to be a surprise.'

Upstairs, I exhaled. Of course. That was the obvious explanation. I had learned, over the last few months, that Christmas was one of the things that Cost Money, along with: school trips, cinema tickets, butter, burgers, going to the hairdresser's and new shoes. I had got new shoes for the start of the school year, as usual. When I'd shown them to Dad he'd said his were being held together by polish and the laces.

It had gone quiet downstairs. I wondered if they were kissing.

Then, my dad's voice, low. 'I haven't seen you ironing.'

'I've been doing it at her place.'

'When?' The pauses in between what they said were too long. It was as though they were playing chess, thinking about every move before it was made.

'Some mornings.'

'Which mornings?'

'Just some mornings. There's no fixed —'

My dad, interrupting: 'Do you think I came down in the last shower? You might have thought I was unemployable but I'm not stupid.' He'd got loud. I put my hand on my headphones but I couldn't make myself stop listening to my parents.

The next bit came out in a rush. 'Mornings when I've said I was at PTA meetings or when I've known you'll be out. I go to Amanda's, we stand and iron for a couple of hours, she pays me, I come home, I didn't tell you. All right? I lied about where I was and I hid the money. I'm not going to be cross-examined, Pat. I'll not be put in the wrong for trying to —'

There was a strange sound. It took a minute or two to realise it was my dad, crying. Then: 'To what?'

'It doesn't matter.'

'I think it does. What's it for?'

'You need to ask?'

The chess had turned to draughts, fast, like it is at the end of a game. Click, click, click and then you've lost.

'This is your escape fund?'

'If you like.'

'So everything we've said —'

'Do not,' my mother's voice was suddenly full of fury, 'even think about the moral high ground, Pat. Ironing with a broken rib is not something that anyone would do unless they felt they had to. And if it had got worse, well, I needed to know I could get us away.'

'Get you away?'

'If I'd thought Loveday was at risk —' My mother's words, so quiet. My father made a moan that went through me like winter wind on the pier.

'I'd never hurt her.'

'I don't think you ever thought you'd hurt me.' Their voices had become gentle and I was suddenly aware that I was standing at the door, listening, instead of sitting on the bed. I didn't remember moving.

'You know I didn't mean —' He stopped, mid-sentence. I imagined my mother holding up her hand, like a traffic policeman in a picture book. She did it to me, sometimes, when she was talking to someone and I tried to interrupt.

'I don't want to talk about it,' she said, quietly.

I almost relaxed, but there wasn't quite time before my father's voice, loud: 'Well, it's all about what you want, isn't it, Sarah-Jane? That's all that matters.'

I looked around my bedroom door and down the stairs.

'I wanted to be safe,' she said, 'and Love-day too. That's all.' Mum was sitting on the floor, hands spread out in front of her, palms up, head down. I could hear her crying. I don't think the word 'despair' was in my vocabulary then, but when I come across it now, I think of that sound, I see my mother sitting on the floor, crying, my father pulling on his coat. When he came back towards her, to pick up the money from the sofa, she moved backwards, out of his way, a scuttle of a movement.

'For Christ's sake!' He wasn't shouting, but I could tell that he wanted to. 'I'm not going to hurt you.' He stood still for a minute, and I could see how his shoulders were rising and falling, making his black leather jacket move, catch the light. His voice, when it came again, was quieter, but not calm: it was a bulldog straining at a lead. 'I'm going to buy forty Marlboro and have a pint,' he said. The door banged behind him. I went downstairs.

Normally Mum would have made an excuse, said she was tired or he didn't mean it, but she just looked at me and said, 'Oh, Loveday, I'm so sorry.'

'We should have the scones,' I said. 'They're best when they're still a bit warm.' That was what she always said about scones. I think it was the only thing I could think of: the only action in the power of an almost-ten year old. I couldn't go after my dad, because I didn't know where he would buy cigarettes or have a pint, and anyway, I didn't think Mum would let me go. I didn't know what to say to her about the money. I didn't want to ask why she thought our house wasn't safe. But I did know that scones were best when they were warm.

'Yes,' Mum said, her voice flat, 'the clotted cream is in my bag,' but she didn't move.

I went into the kitchen and I got three of the pretty china plates, one in case Dad came back in time. I didn't know how long having a pint took. I took the plates into the living room and put them on the table, then went back for the cream and the scones, the

240

knives and the jam. Mum got up and put the books back on the shelf, though I noticed they weren't in the right order. I thought about the school trip letter I had hidden from my parents.

When I'd set the table, she said, 'Well, let's make a start, Dad might be a while,' and she gave me a hug, but I stood stiff in her arms. I didn't know what to think. Well, maybe it's more accurate to say that that was the beginning of not knowing what to think; I'm probably much the same now. I mean, I have thought things — a lot of things — about my mother, and my father, since, but nothing really sticks. I wish something would.

■ ■ ■ ■

POETRY

■ ■ ■ ■

2016
NO ONE HAS THE KEY

Trying to work out how a book has got to the bookshop is a fool's game but that didn't stop me from playing it. Whitby to York isn't exactly an epic journey, but it took Delia Smith's *Complete Illustrated Cookery Course* fifteen years to make it, so you had to wonder what had happened in between. Well, I had to. I tried not to. But I did.

I bought a cake tin and mixing bowl, and I made the brownies Mum and I used to make. If you microwave them they go all gooey. If you put vanilla ice cream on them when they're warm and eat them on the sofa with your boyfriend, it turns out there's such a strong memory attached to the taste that you cry like a stupid baby, and you can't even pretend it's to do with the programme you're watching, if it's a documentary about René Descartes.

Nathan put his arm around me, and said,

'Loveday, what can I do?'

'Nothing,' I said, 'it's nothing.'

'It's not nothing.' His voice was so full of worry that I cried harder.

And then I said, 'The brownies made me think about my mother. I miss her.'

He pulled me closer, kissed the top of my head. 'Where is she?' he asked.

And that's the trouble with talking to people. They ask questions and before you know it you're halfway to telling them everything.

'I'm going to wash my face,' I said.

This is what I worked out, about the books. After Dad died, the house was left empty until the landlord took it back. I can't remember whether I was asked if I wanted to go back there, but I never went again. It was more than a year until I ended up at Annabel's. When I got home from school one day, only a couple of weeks after I'd moved in, she met me at the door.

'Your things are here,' she said. I suppose she was intercepting me so that I didn't get a shock. The boxes were stacked at the bottom of the stairs, and she'd moved the hat stand out of the way to fit them in. 'I didn't take them upstairs,' she said, 'in case you wanted to go through them first. If there are things you don't want in your room we can put them in the garage.'

I opened the first box but just the sight of what was in there — my jewellery box of shells, the Furby, a couple of comics — made me want to cry, and I'd decided I was sick of crying.

'I don't want any of it,' I said, and I went upstairs.

Almost eight months later, on my half birthday (which passed unmarked, of course), I spent the day going through the boxes. Annabel was the only person I knew who parked her car in her garage — all the other ones on the estate sat on the drives — but she opened the garage door to let the daylight in, and drove her Fiat Panda out of the way to give me some space. By that time, the grief was no longer a forest fire, but a constant flame, never going out but steady, manageable.

I think I was trying to work out a way to think about my mother; I wanted to find a key that would click in a lock and make it all make sense. But what would have made me forgive her was written on her body, or stored in her heart, and all I found in the boxes was evidence of our happy family life. The plates we all made in the pottery cafe with our handprints on were there — I'd insisted we all do one, and my dad had sat among all the children and chattering women and solemnly painted his hand blue before letting me press it onto a dinner plate. There were loose photographs of us on the beach or piled on the sofa at Christmas, and birthday cards, certificates of this and that, blankets and lavender bags that smelled of dust. There was nothing to help me forgive her. Old happiness plus the new miseries I'd had to navigate on my own — my first period, low-level bullying at school, living in a strange house with a kind woman who had no reason to be kind to me, grief — made me sure that forgiving my mother was more than she deserved. I tried, that weekend. She failed me.

And there were no books of my mother's in the garage. I suppose, hypothetically, during the innocent until proven guilty phase, she could have had the social worker collect them — I remember her wearing her own clothes when I was taken to see her. Before the Whitby Postcard Incident five days previously, I'd assumed they'd been lost, or thrown away by whoever cleared the house, but that didn't seem to be the case.

So let's say, hypothetically, someone had looked after them for her, and she'd cared about them enough, in all that hell she was in, to ask the question about having them put aside for her. I suppose she thought she was going to have more reading time. She didn't ask for photographs. She might have been leaving them for me, or maybe she couldn't look at our faces and remember that we had been happy.

I couldn't even think about my parents' faces, for years and years, and I didn't bring the photographs I had at Annabel's when I moved to York. When I think about them now, I find myself thinking about how Dad didn't like us to spend time with anyone else when he was home, and wonder whether that was not just one little quirk or sign of love, but actually something — I hate to say it — that showed the side of him that made life so difficult for my mum. I might start to wonder if they were ever happy, really.

Someone looked after the books for her, then. Either she was able to collect them from that person, or she wasn't. Here's a fork in the road. If she was able to collect them — why give them to a house clearance company now? And, more to the point, if she was able to collect them, why not collect the other things she'd had to leave behind, like — to pluck an example from the air — her daughter? The last time I saw her, on an arranged prison visit when I was fourteen, she promised she would come for me: shouted it, almost a threat, as I walked away — 'I'll come for you, LJ, whether you want me to or not'.

But if she had collected the books herself then she hadn't made good on that. I may have hidden myself away but there must be a trail of breadcrumbs. She could have found me, when she was ready. And she did promise me that she would, although she didn't know when.

She didn't want me to lose both parents, she said, in one of those missives filled to the perimeters of the paper with her hand-writing, that I read and wept over before I started turning her letters, unopened, aside, a month after that last visit, when I'd decided with all of the sense of power of a fourteen-year-old that I had had enough of my broken, ugly family and I would be better off on my own.

In that last letter that I opened, she wrote that she understood I didn't want to see her right now, but perhaps one day, when things had calmed down, I would understand a bit more about how we had come to be in the situation we were in. She wished she had done things differently, she said. I was living in a foster home, and having my own room was the loneliest thing in the world.

I'd never felt like that before. I'd always had the option of curling up in my parents' bed after bad dreams or on weekend mornings, warm as a pebble on the summer tideline.

Mum couldn't have collected the books, because if she had, she would have collected me. Maybe the person who was keeping them for her had lost touch with her, or moved, or died, and in the melee of house clearance no one had realised who the books belonged to. That made sense. Except, of course, if that was the case, wouldn't they have come in together? Not a box of paperbacks one week, then an old book of my dad's, three weeks later, and then a Delia Smith two months after that. And of all the second-hand bookshops in all the world . . . all of the charity shops within a stone's throw of the bookshop, even: why mine?

I asked Archie who had brought the cookery books in but of course he couldn't remember. He said he thought it might have been someone in a blue coat, or they might have been left on the step. So that narrowed it down. I snapped at him. He looked hurt. I knew that I shouldn't take things out on him. This is why I shouldn't think about the past. Well, one of the many reasons. I asked Ben, too, and he shrugged and said,

'They're all just boxes with books in to me, darling.'

Great.

I was in such a glowering mood that I almost didn't bother to go to poetry night that Wednesday. But Nathan's sister was going to be there, and I might not know a lot about relationships but what I do know is: don't piss off anyone's sister.

So I did what I used to do, although I haven't had to do it for years. I sat in the chair by the fire escape and I closed my eyes and I imagined a dial where my heart should be. The dial was set to how much I was hurting. It could go anywhere from 1 to 10, but I had to be honest about where it was set. Today it was a 6. I took a deep breath and I imagined the dial clicking down, from 6 — breathe; 5 — breathe; 4 — breathe; 3 — breathe. I let it be at 3; that's probably my default. I don't think there could ever be a zero. And yes, I do know it's not really any way of dealing with things properly, but it can get you through the next couple of hours, and sometimes that's all you need.

I hadn't met Nathan's sister. I knew he had a sister, and two parents, who are both alive and have been married for thirty-five years, and still hold hands when they watch

252

TV in the evenings, although they often play backgammon by the Aga or do a cryptic crossword after dinner. Okay, I've made up everything after 'thirty-five years' but you can tell, just looking at Nathan, that he's from the kind of happy family that no one would ever write a book about because nothing ever happens, except picnics and weddings and people having lovely giggly babies with unruly auburn curls and sea-green eyes.

Nathan's sister is twenty-eight, two years younger than him. When he asked me about my family I just said Archie was my family, which is true, if you apply the your-family-is-the-people-who-remember-your-birthday-and-look-after-you-when-you-are-ill filter. He didn't look at me like I was an orphan, or anything, which was good, but he did go on about his sister quite a lot. She sounded nice enough but I hadn't really planned to meet her. Not that I minded, exactly, but the trouble with meeting new people is that they ask you a lot of questions and when it comes to answering those questions, I just don't have many options.

Either you have to be honest, which feels like too much for a 'nice to meet you' conversation, or you tell lies. Lies don't much matter if you're never going to see someone again, but if you are, then you either have to be a really good liar, which I'm not, or you get found out, which leads to the conversation you were trying to avoid in the first place, but with sinister background music.

If I was better at social stuff I would be able to do that chatty, deflecty, 'oh let's talk about you' thing that I've seen others do, but the fact is, I don't like most people, and it shows if I try to do anything clever.

And I was still freaking out about the cookery book, obviously, which wasn't helping my social skills any. Wouldn't you be spooked? If you were in my position — oh, never mind, you wouldn't be in my position. Here's what the book was. If it wasn't a completely coincidental arrival from a house clearance, wasn't it was someone saying, 'I know all about the thing you've been trying to hide, that you've spent the best part of sixteen years running away from. And guess what, Loveday? It's not a secret. Now you just have to wait to see what happens.' I did wonder whether the sending of the books might have a good intention behind them — but surely anyone with good intentions would just walk up to me, introduce themselves, and explain what the hell this was all about?

Now, if it was chance that had brought the books in — but we all know it wasn't. The Penguin Classics — the very books that hid my mother's escape fund — the Kate Greenaway and the Delia with the postcard? Thrice was definitely looking like someone trying to make a point. I felt as though I was being watched. It's not an unfamiliar feeling for a freak-show child, but that didn't mean I had ever got used to it.

When I walked into the room Nathan came straight over and hugged me, and even though I am, in principle, opposed to public displays of affection — they're only displays, after all — I hugged back. He's always warmer than me, and he makes me feel safe, even though before I found that book on the pavement I'd have ripped out my own eyeballs and eaten them rather than go to a poetry night, let alone stand up there and perform myself. Don't think I'm going all 'power of love' — nobody's saying the l-word to me and thinking it means any-thing, or makes a difference — it just felt as though he'd opened a door for me, in his gentle way, and I'd walked through it.

He looked at me, straight into my face, and said, 'Loveday.' He shook his head. 'There's something about you. When you walked in just now.' He put his hand on his chest. 'Just seeing you makes me . . .'

I felt the same way, but I couldn't say so. I had no idea what to say. I put my hand on his cheek and kissed him. Just a peck, but he smiled.

'Come meet my sister,' he said.

'Oh, okay,' I said. She hadn't been un-avoidably detained, then. He had said that she was a hairdresser. I'd re-dyed my hair, burgundy, on the Sunday before so I felt equal to meeting a hairdresser.

Of course she was beautiful, like he'd said. Her eyes were calm-blue like his but her mouth was wider, and she had the smile that people smile when they find exactly the first edition they were looking for, but at half the price they were expecting to pay. Her hair was short and sort of choppy, and the most amazing colours — blonde and red and peach, all tumbled up, so that the light clung to it. I didn't think she'd done it at home over the sink, like me.

'You must be Loveday,' she said. 'I'm jeal-ous of your name! It's so unusual. I'm Vanessa.' She made a sort of 'sorry about that' face, as though there was something wrong with a name that wasn't going to make people ask you to repeat it.

'Hello,' I said.

'Nathan and Ness,' Nathan said, and they

both laughed, and then he said, 'When we were kids that's what we were called, and it drove Vanessa mad. So mad —'

Vanessa rolled her eyes. 'So mad that when I was a teenager I insisted that people called me Van. Which my brother still thinks is funny. But now he's going to get us both a drink and I'm going to tell you things about him when he was a teenager, and that will serve him right.'

'Gimlet?' Nathan asked, and I nodded. He looked at his sister. 'Gin and tonic, one ice cube, two slices of lemon and don't let them pour all the tonic in at once?'

'Correct,' Vanessa said. 'And also, don't let them put it in a jam jar.' When he'd gone she smiled again and I was just reaching the point where I was going to freak out. It was like I had gone to school and Kitty and Scarlett, the twin girls in my secondary school form class who were the queens of everything, didn't ignore me or snigger at me but pulled up a chair at their table for me and asked if I wanted to give them advice about boys. It all just wasn't me.

But then I realised that beautiful, nice Vanessa — with her stunning hair and a tiny gold heart-shaped necklace that I just knew cost more than a week's rent — was wearing a bad bra. The seams made downwards curves and they showed through her blouse, so for all of her expensive loveliness her tits were frowning at me. And I felt better. Not in a judgey way, just because I can cope with non-perfection. Nathan was going to have to work on that, now I thought of it, because he was starting to look a bit too good to be true.

'You work in a bookshop?' Vanessa said. 'I'd love that. Except I'd want to read all day, so I'd get the sack in a week.'

'Where do you work?' I asked. I wasn't really bothered — I cut my own hair, in as much as I put it into a ponytail every six weeks, and whack the bottom inch off — but if I had a brother I'd want to know the far end of everything about his girlfriend and I wasn't having that conversation.

'Oh, I travel,' she said.

'I'm sorry,' I said, 'I thought you were a hairdresser.'

Vanessa laughed. 'I am,' she said, 'but I work for private clients so I go where they are.'

'I see,' I said. I didn't, really. I thought hairdressers stayed in one place, unless they were the sort who went around and did wash-and-set for old ladies, which clearly wasn't going to be Vanessa's thing, unless I'd spectacularly misread her. We've established, I think, that I'm not a brilliant judge of character, but I was fairly confident on this.

She waved her hand, a 'what I'm about to say isn't that important' gesture. 'I'm a colour specialist, so I quite often get booked for films and things.'

Bloody Nathan, I thought. Vanessa's a hairdresser in the same way that Prince Charles is a farmer. My hand went to my own hair. I wanted to cover it up.

'I do my own hair,' I said. 'I always have. Well, my mum cut it when I was a kid.'

She looked at my hair, like she hadn't noticed it before, which I'm sure she had. 'Burgundy Rose, right?' she said.

'Yes,' I said. I braced myself for some sort of pep talk on home colouring and how we amateurs should know better.

But she said, 'It's a good choice. It suits you. You're naturally fawny-brown, right, and it goes reddish in the sun?'

'Yes,' I said again. I was a little bit impressed, and I didn't want to get tricked into talking about my mother again, so I asked, 'How can you tell?'

'Your skin,' she said, as though that was an answer, then, 'I wish I had good skin like yours.' I had no idea what to say to that. There's some god-awful quote that Melodie spouts — dance like nobody's watching, blah blah — but it ends with 'love like you've never been hurt' and I thought, looking at Vanessa and then at Nathan when he came back with the drinks, that's what you two are like. You're like little puppies playing in the sun. Your lives are so easy.

Nathan left the drinks and then went off again, to do the rounds. We both watched him go. He wasn't performing that evening: he said he deserved a night off.

Vanessa said, 'I'm so proud of him when I see him now — when I think about what happened to him at school. Has he told you about that?'

'He's mentioned it,' I said, carefully. Not technically a lie: he probably had, in some oblique way. We talked, of course we did, but it was mostly here-and-now talking, poetry and books and magic and York and, well, chatting. I like the present (mostly) — I've constructed it carefully, like my little home library — and that's where I try to stay.

She looked at her drink, at Nathan, at me. 'He was bullied at school. So badly that our parents talked about taking him out of formal education. That's when he started with the magic. It was a sort of obsession with him. It was quite scary, for a while, to

260

see the way he was. He hardly talked. He spent whole days, at the weekend, shuffling cards.'

He'd tried to teach me how to shuffle — sending cards from hand to hand, making a rainbow of then. I hadn't found the knack. He said all it took was time. He hadn't said how much, or where the time had come from.

'He's trying to teach me,' I said. I felt a bit bad: I'd assumed that the only reason you would end up doing magic was because some lovely old uncle indulged you with trips to see magicians and gifts of magic starter sets that came in a plastic top hat. Nathan had had more of a hard time than he'd let on. But then again, as nobody ever says, it's not how you fall, it's how many people are there to pick you up and clean your knee with disinfectant and tuck you up on the sofa with some hot chocolate and a book until you feel better.

'When I look at my brother now, I feel so proud.'

Ah, I thought, there's my warning. Fuck my brother if you like, but don't fuck with my brother, because he's had one nasty thing happen to him, and he needs to be protected from having anything else bad come his way.

261

I knew then, sitting across from Vanessa, that Nathan and I weren't going to last. Well, I'd always known it. To start with, I'd felt as though I was tricking him, by pretending to be someone who could have a normal relationship. Lately, I'd been tricking myself. I knew we were doomed but I was ignoring it. I'm good at ignoring things. Well, I am during the day. The nightmares can be bad. I'm standing in the churchyard at Whitby, and the sea is rising, and behind me the church is on fire. If I jump, I'll drown. If I stay, I'll burn. So I stand there, and I'm waiting to see what happens first, and I'm screaming for my mother, and she's nowhere.

Nathan and I were just too different. In his world problems came with rescue squads, and solutions were white rabbits and home education. I imagined him, lanky and spotty, sitting in a bay window with a pack of cards, practising his tricks over and over, while every so often his mother put a cup of tea and a slice of homemade lemon cake at his elbow.

He stood at the front and clapped his hands, five sharp claps.

■ ■ ■ ■

POETRY

■ ■ ■ ■

2016
FOUND

Archie always pretends he's not bothered about his birthday but he's worse than a spoilt kid. About a month beforehand he goes around murmuring to all of those friends who treat the shop and the cafe as an extension of their homes that he's going to have 'a few drinks' to 'wave off another year' and it'll be 'nothing special'. Selected customers get the nod too.

Then he goes off to the post office with a carrier bag full of thick cream envelopes, printed invitations inside but handwritten addresses, each name a work of copperplate art. Another reason to love Archie: he has even less interest in the internet than I have. We didn't have so much as an email address between us when we had the shop's website set up.

The first year I actually believed the 'nothing special' schtick and turned up half an hour late in the clothes I'd been wearing for work. Archie lives in a big old house in Bishop-hill, and I passed three men in black tie and a woman dressed as a can-can dancer on the way up the drive. Another woman in a ballgown with sparkly hi-tops on her feet answered the door and I realised my mistake. In fairness, the woman in the ballgown was overdressed, but she was probably nearer the median of the dress code than I was.

Archie gets caterers in and he puts on one of his hideous old brocade waistcoats — I once told him he looked like a fat Oscar Wilde and he roared with laughter and said he didn't know which of them I was insulting — and there's a lot of wine and loads of that food that means you don't stop eating all night but you have to make toast when you get home because you're starving. The first year I stuck to the kitchen and the one after I stuck to Archie. These days I know a few more of his friends so I can usually find someone I can have an okay conversation with, which is made easier by the fact that it's the same conversation every year — I'd love to work in a bookshop, isn't Archie a character? That kind of thing. If all else fails you can always ask people how they met Archie. It's never something ordinary, like, well, like 'in a bookshop'. It's usually: 'we

shared a cell when we were court-martialled'
or 'we've known each other since we were
hunt saboteurs' . . . Also, Archie has a
library where I can hide out if it all gets too
much.

After the first year I started buying something new to wear for the party. Nothing
flash — I don't really do dressed up or
dressed down, it's really just dressed or not
dressed as far as I'm concerned — but I
thought something new would show that
I've made an effort. Nobody notices. However much I try I always buy a black dress,
and though I like my tattoos, I'm not going
to display them more than I have to, because
then any idiot who's had two glasses of wine
thinks it's okay to ask about them. By 'ask
about them' I mean: talk about the tattoos
they have/are too scared to have or ask me
whether I'm worried that people will judge
me, by which they mean they are judging
me but think they somehow cancel that out
by talking about it.

This time, though, I'd seen something I
liked so much I'd deviated from the norm. I
was on the way to the high street in my
lunch hour when I saw a dress in a charity
shop window. It was a dark plummy colour
with a velvet bodice and gauzy sleeves and I
just thought: yes. It's the closest thing to a

retail thrill I've ever had outside a book-shop. I paid twenty quid for it but from the label I'd guess it was two hundred, new.

I took it back to the shop. The afternoon was quiet. The party was the next day. Archie and I were working side-by-side for a change — I was sorting books on the floor, then passing them up to him for shelving — and before I'd thought it through, I asked him the question that, I suppose, had been on my mind since I met him.

'Archie, how do you do it?'

'Do what, my little straywaif?' He looked down at me. I sat back on my heels.

'Tomorrow night,' I said, 'you'll be all — relaxed. Like you are here. You'll be able to talk to anyone. You sort of — glide — through things.'

He put his hands in the small of his back, winced as he stretched his spine. 'I think my gliding days are over,' he said.

'You know what I mean.'

He sat down on the nearest chair — I realised I'd just given him the cue for stopping what he was doing, so I stood up and took over his bit. I could listen and work.

'Be yourself,' he said.

Oh great, I thought. I've been doing that for years and look where it's got me. Oscar-level social awkwardness and no friends. 'If

268

I had a party, my flat will be too big for it,' I said, 'and your house will be too small for yours.'

'And are you saying that that is a measure of our relative worth?' he asked.

'Of course not,' I said.

He was quiet for so long that I assumed he was napping, but then he said, 'I once helped John Gielgud build a bread oven in his garden. Halfway through the second day, he said to me, "Archie, old boy, this is not what one would call a two-minute job". Give yourself time.'

'Time?' I said. I could feel my voice was flat with disappointment. I wanted there to be a better answer.

'And be brave, Loveday. Ask the questions you want to ask. Seek out the people you want in your life. It might not be as hard as you think.'

And then he did go to sleep. I thought about what he'd said. I would never be brave. And then I remembered I'd performed some poetry, and I had what some people would call a relationship, and a year ago both of those things would have been completely out of the question. To borrow one of Archie's phrases, perhaps he wasn't as green as he was cabbage-looking.

■ ■ ■ ■

Nathan was going to the party, but he was going to meet me there, because I was going home to change and collect the lemon meringue pie, which I'd baked during my morning off. He might be my boyfriend, but it doesn't mean we have to go everywhere together. Archie had asked him to do a little bit of magic to warm things up at the start of the evening. He'd offered to pay but Nathan had refused to even discuss money.

Of course I hadn't thought about getting to Archie's with a somewhat fragile pastry creation — not until I was standing in the street next to my bike, with my dress all tucked up, realising that there was no way it would survive the journey, as I couldn't get it flat into my bike basket. I had to get the bus, so I was late. Still, as my mother used to say (still says?), someone always has to be last.

The house is as solid as Archie is, and stone-built. I think it's Georgian: it has big sash windows and big, square, high-ceilinged rooms and a staircase that curves. It's basically a junior stately home. There are four steps up to the front door, which is massive, in case you're wearing your hoopiest dress, I suppose. But once you're in, it's friendly. It smells of pipe-smoke and bread, and there's a hotchpotch of coats and hats by the door, and yesterday's newspaper on the kitchen table.

I went straight to find Archie, who was admiring some odd-looking thing that he'd just unwrapped. When he saw me come in he left the people he was with, came over, and kissed me on the cheek, squeezing the top of my arm nice-tight.

'You look lovely,' he said in my ear. I was pleased to see him, and pleased by the contact; it made me feel safe. All I could feel were eyes on my back. It had occurred to me on the way that the person who'd left me my mother's books might well be here. They needed to know me well enough to know where I worked. And if they knew that, they knew Archie. And if they knew Archie, wasn't there a good chance they'd be at his party too? I took a breath.

'What's that?' I asked, taking the object out of Archie's hand.

'It's a cigar cutter,' he said, as though that was a thing. He didn't make a big fuss or introduce me to anyone; he just stood next to me, with his arm around my shoulder. I gave him the box with the lemon meringue pie it. When he realised I'd made it I thought he was going to cry. 'My little straywaif,' he said. He looked around the kitchen, which was filling up with happy noise. 'You know,' he said, 'there's something to adore in every single person who is here. Everyone.'

I laughed, and looked around for people I recognised to put him to the test. 'Melodie?'

'Confidence. Self-belief. Excellent headwear.'

'Victor from the cafe?'

'Patience. Shapely calves. Exceptionally good at logic. Did you know he's won more than five grand in Sudoku competitions?'

'No,' I said. How would you find that out, during the course of buying a coffee, a tea, and two banana muffins? I saw another familiar face, though I turned my head away before he could see me. 'Rob.'

Archie sucked his teeth. 'I almost didn't invite him, to be honest. There's something about him that's never smelled quite right, but old Archie likes to err on the side of kindness. But: tenacity.'

'I'm not sure tenacity is what I'd call an adorable quality,' I said. Then, 'What about me?'

He laughed. 'Don't fish, Loveday.'

'I'm not fishing,' I said. I really wasn't. I

work hard, but I know that I'm also hard work, and I'm never really sure how I got lucky enough to get my job, and keep it, in this customer service world.

Archie squeezed me again. 'You're clever, you don't compromise, and you seem to genuinely believe you're invisible. And you're quite lovely to look at, if one likes pale-and-interesting. No wonder our good magician is transfixed.'

I didn't know what I thought he was going to say, but I was dumbstruck. Fortunately I didn't need to reply, because I was rescued by the next guests, who were carrying a huge stuffed monkey cuddly toy between them and shouting something about how it had been a long time since Borneo. Archie bellowed with laughter when he saw it. He let go of me and set off to greet them, but not before he'd kissed me on the top of the head and said, 'Adore, Loveday. That's my advice to you.'

I went to find a drink. There was a bar set up in the dining room, and I had a gimlet in my hand before I could remember asking for it. I went to look out of the window, my back to the room, hoping that I really was invisible.

After the poetry night the previous week,

Nathan and Vanessa and I had had another couple of drinks, and then we'd all got into her Mini Cooper — Nathan insisted on folding himself into the back seat, which was probably not as hilarious as it seemed at the time, but there's the curse of alcohol for you. Although, come to think of it, Vanessa had switched to water after her one gin and tonic, so maybe it wasn't just the gimlets laughing.

She'd dropped me off and then driven him home. I hadn't asked him in, and he hadn't assumed, which is one of those really nice things about him that gets on my nerves, because if you're going to have to start disliking someone, or at least letting them out of your life, it's more helpful if they piss you off now and then. I didn't want him to slap me, obviously, but a bit of mild inconsideration would have helped nudge things along.

Since the poetry night I'd been thinking a lot about how he'd sneaked into my life. Well, let's take responsibility, Loveday — how I'd let him. I suppose he'd crept up on me or it wouldn't have got so far. The first night he stayed over, he nipped down to Tesco and bought a toothbrush, and he left it in my bathroom. That was just one of those things. Of course he wanted to clean his teeth. It would have been churlish to chuck the brush away. Me buying porridge oats because he said when he was home he always made himself porridge in the morning, even when it was summer? I can't blame anyone else for that. He's bought more coffees than I have, and that's partly because I'm at work and he's visiting, and being nice, but I could have given him the money, or asked him not to, and I didn't.

I'd let one night a week creep up to two or three. I'd told him that my father was dead, and I missed my mother. I'd met his sister. More than all of those things, though, was the way we looked at each other. How we felt.

If I wasn't careful I was going to be in way too deep. I was going to adore him. I couldn't admit it, to myself or to him. And Archie might have the kind of life where adoration should be the norm, but that wasn't my life. I was in danger of forgetting that there was only one way this thing with Nathan was ever going to end, and it wasn't the one where he spends the weekends building a treehouse for our kids. We were going to have to talk.

I'd never broken up with anyone, unless you count going home at midnight in your socks as an extremely roundabout way of explaining that you just can't see a future in this relationship. Was splitting up at a party wrong? I was too preoccupied to learn all the rules in the bit of your teens when you're supposed to pick this shit up. But I knew I was going to have to do it, and putting it off wasn't going to make it any easier. Tonight might as well be the night.

I went to find Nathan. He was in what I think of as my corner of the library. I'd told him that I'd be there when he'd finished warming up the party by breaking its watches and pulling chocolate coins out of its cleavages. It's a long, thin room, probably cut off from another one at some stage; little more than a corridor, really, but that didn't stop Archie from having floor-to-ceiling shelves put in at both sides. There's a two-seater chesterfield with a lamp on the table at the end furthest from the door; if the lamp isn't on, you're almost invisible, which is handy if that's what you feel like being, less so if you want to read. The evening was warm so most people were outside on the patio. Archie calls it a terrace, and when I say patio, he always corrects me, though I'm not sure I know the difference.

Nathan had got there before me. I practically sat on him. He'd already found the sofa. Even though I knew what I was going to have to talk to him about and he wasn't going to like it, I still laughed when I realised it was him. He laughed too, then shushed me and pulled me down next to him.

'I'm hiding,' he said. 'Everyone wants to know how I do the thing with the onion. There's only so many times you can say that if you tell them you'll have to kill them before it gets old.'

'As in, zero times?' I said, and he poked me.

Then he looked at me properly, touched my dress. 'You look lovely,' he said.

'It's only a dress,' I said.

'I didn't say the dress looked lovely,' he said, 'I said you do. The dress is just — the frame.'

I didn't say anything, because what do you say to that? The neck of the dress was cut slightly wider and lower than anything I would usually wear, so I'd put on the little tear-shaped jet pendant that my dad bought me one Christmas; my mum had said I was too young for grown-up jewellery, and she'd been right, in that I'd put it away and only really started wearing it recently. I'd got it out again after Archie had told me to be brave.

I thought Nathan was scrutinising it, and I was flipping through my options ('Don't know what it's made of'? 'Present from my dad'? 'Bought it in a charity shop'? 'Found it in a book'?), but then I realised that the beginning of one of my collarbone tattoos was visible where the shoulder of my dress had slid away, and that's what Nathan was looking at.

He put his finger on it. ' "The book was thick and black and covered with dust," ' he said. 'I'm still working on that one.'

I leaned against him. He kissed the top of my head.

The house was full of the sounds of people chattering, and every now and again Archie's voice would rise above the general noise, roar out something, and laughter would rise to meet his pitch. It was quiet where we were. I liked it; the hush away from the hubbub, the darkness tucked apart from the end of the high-summer sunlight.

Nathan brought both arms around my waist and I rested the back of my head against the top of his chest. Suddenly I was tired. I didn't want to talk to anyone; I didn't want to go and laugh with people who I was never going to catch up with, drunkenness-wise. I felt myself sigh. Maybe tonight wasn't the night to tell Nathan that

I couldn't see a future and I wasn't his girlfriend.

He kissed the top of my head again. 'I was thinking,' he said, 'we should go on holiday.'

'What?' This was not good. I was upright, staring, trying to work out what I'd said, done, to make him think that was a good idea.

'I guess that's a no?' he said. He was doing his cocky voice. Fair enough, I thought. I can recognise a defence mode when I see one.

'Why would you think —' I said.

He laughed a not-laugh. 'Well,' he said, 'there's all the time we've spent together, and the talking, and the sex, and the way you look at me when I come into the shop. You let me practise poems with you and you put up with my sister for an evening. You sometimes text me texts that are more than four words long and you respond to about forty percent of the texts I send to you. I added all that up and it made me think you might like to — you know — maybe spend a week with me.'

I thought about saying his maths was faulty, decided against it. One thing I like about Nathan: he gives you time to think.

'I haven't even been to your place,' I said.

'I wasn't going to suggest a holiday at my

place,' he said.

'I meant —' I said, but I stopped. He knew what I meant.

'I thought you would come to my place in your own time,' he said. 'I thought if we went on holiday that might help you to —'

'To what?' Dander, hackles, whatever you call them — they were right up. I was interested to hear what kind of help he thought I needed.

'To trust me,' he said, quietly.

I opened my mouth and closed it again. I felt my body go soft and so did Nathan; he pulled me closer. I was trying to work out what to say when he started talking, still quietly. It felt as though his words, rather than heading out into the air, were falling off the edge of his lower lip, dropping into my hair, and sliding down the side of my head and into my ear.

'I'm not stupid, Loveday,' he said. 'I know that there's — something — and I don't think it's me. I thought — I didn't mean to push it. I'm sorry. I can wait.'

I knew what I had to say next. Well, I knew the gist. There was a pick-and-mix of phrases available. 'I don't think it's going to work out . . .' 'I've been thinking, and . . .' 'You're really nice, but . . .' 'I've had a good time, but . . .' 'I feel as though I've got in

280

over my head, so . . .' 'I'm not really in a good place for a relationship, and . . .' 'You're a lovely person, but . . .' 'I think I'm happier when I'm on my own, so . . .' 'It's not you, it's me . . .' (Maybe I should have that as a tattoo next. Right across my forehead.)

I didn't say any of it. I said, 'Thanks.' This was the trouble with Nathan. When I was with him it felt as though anything was possible. I felt like a normal person, as though nothing was insurmountable, and being happy, actively happy, most of the time was a reasonable thing to expect. He did my head in. And at the same time I wondered whether some more time would hurt. Not a holiday, of course, but maybe another week of acting normal.

When I did call it a day — assuming he didn't get sick of me first, which was, in a way, my dream scenario — then his world wouldn't end. He might be a bit low, but then he'd look out of his window and there would be a camper van outside, and all of his friends would pile out of it, and they'd have brought a barbecue and some beer, and someone would cook the organic sausages and someone would get out their guitar, and a girl with skinny cheekbones and a nice arse would pick a flower and tuck it behind Nathan's ear, and he'd smile, a bit sadly, and everyone would know it was going to be All right.

'I don't see what you see in me,' I said. 'What's in this for you?'

'Loveday Jenna Cardew,' he said. 'Are you fishing?' (We'd traded middle names. His was, disappointingly, Andrew.)

'No,' I said. Accused of fishing twice in one night. It seemed a bit unfair: I make a point of never talking about myself if I can help it. 'I'm genuinely curious.'

He went quiet for a bit. 'Well,' he said, 'I don't think there's one word for it. It's just that — when I'm with you — I'm me. I don't feel as though I have to pretend or show off. I feel as though I can trust you. You make me — valid. You make me real.'

'Wow,' I said. There couldn't have been a compliment more beautifully honed to make me feel small and inadequate, unworthy and, well, as though I should never have started this in the first place.

He kissed me, properly, and I let him, because I couldn't think of anything to say. And because kissing Nathan is lovely. I knew there wouldn't be many more kisses like this, so I was making the most of them.

Afterwards: 'I'm shattered,' he said.

'All that magic?' I asked.

He laughed, but then he said, quietly, 'I used to have panic attacks. Sometimes in places like this I can feel them coming again. I have to — sort of — brace against them.'

I held his hands. 'I used to have them. They're horrible.'

I remembered the back of a social worker's car, being taken to see my mother, and how my stomach would squeeze and my breathing would race, how time would stop and my eyes wouldn't open when I told them to. How, later, even the mention of a visit to my mother elicited the same response. I was almost fifteen. Annabel stood up for me: my social worker suggested I was faking it but my foster-mother knew better. I learned to head off the attacks with slow breathing and the control-dial in my mind, or maybe it was the fact that everyone got cautious about mentioning my mother, and when I said I didn't want to see her they took me seriously.

The attacks came back when I was seventeen. The social worker told me that my mother had been released from prison. The panic was so severe that he called an ambulance. Afterwards, I made Annabel promise that no one would try to make me see my mum and that she wouldn't be allowed to just turn up. Annabel promised. She told me that my mother didn't know where I lived, which of course was true, though I'd never thought about the fact that her letters always came with my name on them in her handwriting, and then the address filled out by someone else. I was safe from my mother. And even though, in the nights, on the walks to school and back, on the Saturday afternoons that seemed endless, I tried to find a way to want to see her, I couldn't do it. I couldn't take the step. I was too scared of — well, of something changing. I'd written my version of events, in my head. I'd told my story. Forgiving my mother would make it different, difficult, unsafe. I would have to rewrite, rethink; I would have to erase myself and write a new me, and having done that once I knew how much it would hurt. Better to be whatever I had become; better to be in a place where I knew where the margins were.

Obviously, Nathan didn't need to know any of this. So I kept him talking. 'When?'

I felt him sigh. 'A few years ago. I did a magic show above a pub — a little thing, just for a week — but it got good reviews and I was asked to tour it, as a support act for a comedian. So I went from a sell-out being twenty-five people in a bar to seven

284

hundred in a theatre. It was a dream come true. Really. It's what everyone in a room above a pub is hoping for. A talent scout, a manager, someone with some influence who is going to say your name to someone who's going to pick you out of all the other wannabes. And . . .' He shook his head. 'I just couldn't do it. I got stage fright and my hands got sloppy and I dropped stuff. One night I had a full-blown attack on stage. I looked out over the audience and I didn't know how to begin. I closed my eyes and I couldn't open them. My head was — empty. I couldn't have told you my name. And all the time I was breathing so fast that I was sweating from the effort. One of the stage crew had to come on and lead me off, by the hand.'

'That's awful,' I said. I meant it. I remembered what Archie had said, the first time Nathan came into the shop, about how he 'used to be the next big thing'.

'I started to focus on close-up magic, because then you have an audience of five or six.'

'Makes sense,' I said. Make a world that suits you. Maybe Nathan and I had more in common than I thought.

We sat in the quiet for a minute or two and then he started to move.

'There's food in the kitchen,' he said. 'Let me go and bring us a picnic. Wait for me, Ripon Girl.'

'I will,' I said, 'so long as there's cheese.' It would be churlish to break up with someone at a party.

Nathan pulled himself out of the sofa and I watched him go, wondering whether to put on the light and read a book, but knowing that I was content to just sit and wait. I put my feet up.

'Oh, sorry,' I heard Nathan say as he left the room.

'No worries,' came the reply. The voice sounded familiar, and its owner was making his way through the room towards me. It took a moment for me to place it.

Oh goody. It was Rob.

'Loveday,' he said.

'Hello, Rob,' I said. 'I didn't realise you were coming until I saw you in the kitchen.'

'Well, I'm a friend of Archie,' he said. 'I used to be a friend of yours, but you don't seem to have a lot of time for me any more.'

'Don't be an arse, Rob,' I said. I really couldn't be bothered. It's tempting to make excuses for Rob because of the bipolar thing but, actually, it's possible that he behaves like he does because he's a twat. I think treating Rob the way I'd treat anyone who slapped me is much more appropriate than making allowances.

'Budge up,' he said. My sandals were on the floor, my legs on the sofa, and I was taking up all of the space.

'I don't think I will, if it's all the same to you,' I said. He stood over me. I thought he was looking down my dress, but I was wrong.

'Whitby jet?' he asked, looking at my necklace.

'I don't know,' I said, too late and too fast.

And then he put his fingertip on my shoulder, near the base of my throat, at the end of the words inked there. I resisted the impulse to slap it away. I was scared. I didn't want to be, but I was.

'*Possession,*' he said. ' "The book was thick and black and covered with dust." Just about the only jewellery I've ever seen you wear is that necklace. *Possession* has a lot to do with Whitby. Some people might think the place was important to you.'

'Really,' I said. Part of me was ready to panic but I reminded myself that, to Rob, making connections is an academic exercise, no more. I could be calm. I could try, at least.

'I wonder how many tattoos you have now.' He was half-smiling. I wanted to pull my feet under me, get smaller, but at the same time I didn't want to show him I was uncomfortable and, anyway, if I made space he would consider it an invitation to sit down; he'd decide to see it as a softening.

'Rob,' I said, 'I'm waiting for someone.'

At his side, his hand clenched. I didn't think he'd done it consciously but it made me wonder where he was in the cycle of illness, and whether he was taking his medication. I couldn't ask.

'You and Melodie make a nice couple,' I said. I hoped it would be a safe topic, i.e. Not Me.

'She's not really my type,' he said.

I bit back the obvious question, because I think he'd made it obvious for me on purpose. If I said, why not, he would say, because you're my type. If I said, why are you going out with her, then, he would say, you see, you do still care about me. I knew Rob wasn't really carrying a torch. He just wanted to score a few points.

'I don't think I'm your type, either,' I said, trying to make it light.

'Or I'm not your type. You seem to prefer them . . .'

I was tempted to complete his sentence for him. Sexier? Non-academic? Less creepy? Un-slappy?

'Poetic.'

I shrugged. Don't engage, I told myself.

'Well, it's good that we've both moved on,' I said. 'I'd like you to be happy.' And I did, in a no-effort-on-my-part sort of a way. And preferably a long way from me and Lost For Words.

I was thinking that Nathan couldn't possibly be much longer. Then I remembered how distinctive he is when he's dressed as a magician; how everyone would be stopping him, asking him to show them something or other again, and how he wouldn't forget about me but he couldn't bear to be rude, either.

And then, Rob's expression changed.

He smiled, but it was an odd smile; if it was in the book it would come at the end of a chapter, and canine teeth would be mentioned. I found I was holding my breath.

'I suppose it's harder for people like you,' he said, 'with your past.'

'What do you mean?' As I said it, I heard how I sounded shrill, and was already telling myself: stop. He's the one that's fishing, now, at Archie's sodding fishing party. He's trying to get a rise, and you've just given him one.

Turns out I needn't have worried. He already knew.

'I mean,' he said, 'I know all about you, Loveday. I haven't been sleeping that well, and one night I got to wondering about you. I put together what I knew, which wasn't a lot — it was as though you were trying to keep secrets — but search engines are wonderful things. Cardew, Whitby — that's all you really need —'

'Rob,' I said. I didn't know what I was going to say next, but it didn't matter, because he kept right on talking.

'I can see why you're a bit — warped. What you must have gone through, with your parents. Well, parent, singular, I suppose. And foster care. That really fucks people up. Did you know that kids from your sort of background are more likely to —' he held up his fingers, marked things off, a shopping list of waiting failures — 'have unplanned pregnancies, become addicts, end up in prison?'

I was shaking, fear or anger or both, and the chill of being found out. I managed to get out, 'Do you know that children from my sort of background are more likely to seek out a violent relationship?' but the words went ailing into the air, and didn't live long. I don't know if Rob even heard. We looked at each other.

I had one lucid thought. 'The books,' I

said. 'Was that you?' My body was locked into place — I don't think I could have moved if the settee was on fire — but my mind was spinning around a new idea. What if Rob had got hold of the books? I'd dismissed the idea before, but I hadn't known that he knew my story. Plus, wasn't planting books to creep me out just a natural extension of hiding my boots, or putting roses through letterboxes, or even threatening someone in the dark corner of a party while their boyfriend went to get some food?

Could he somehow have got hold of the books? If he knew who I was, he knew who my mother was, and I don't think she would be that difficult to find. Part of the reason I had never dared look for her was because I knew she would have made herself searchable, findable, on Facebook and in the phone book. All Rob would need to do was to pose as an old boyfriend with a sob story, or a university lecturer wanting to get in touch with a job opportunity, and my mother would welcome him with open arms, let him have anything he wanted. I could have kicked myself. I knew that Rob was cold and manipulative; I knew that he could hold a grudge. I hadn't let him see that he bothered me, with his roses and his hanging-about, and so all I'd done was inspire him to find a more extreme way to make me uncomfortable. I could feel how cold my fingertips were, how the goose-bumps were rising along my collarbones.

There was a noise, detached from the party and close by. Rob looked to see who was coming.

'Does your boyfriend know?' he asked, in a half-whisper that was more frightening than a shout.

'No,' I said, 'he doesn't.'

'Well, I suppose the only question, then, is whether you're going to tell him, or wait for me to do it. No one likes a liar, Loveday. Even people who can cope with your back-ground aren't going to accept the fact that you've lied and lied about it. For months.' Without waiting to see my reaction, he took his smirk and (I assume) his hard-on, and he turned around and walked away.

CRIME

1999
REFRACTED

The flashing lights made patterns in the sky. I saw at least two police cars and an ambulance outside our house when Emma's mum walked me back home that evening. We stopped at the end of the road, looking.

It was dark, although it wasn't late. Sunday was a school night, and our mums had agreed that I would be home by eight, with my mum adding the rider that I would go straight to bed when I got home. So I was worried about not being back on time.

I couldn't tell what was going on. The lights hurt my eyes, and illuminated the faces of the neighbours so they looked like ghosts. I'd never seen an ambulance up this close.

The front of the ambulance was pointing towards the top of the road, so there was no chance of seeing inside. I still imagine my mother, sitting on the steps, wrapped in a blanket, crying and grey, the way people do on TV. I have to remind myself that it's imagination, not reality.

The reality could have been worse, of course. She could have been screaming. There might have been blood on her face, hair, hands, his blood, her blood. She could have been calm. She could have been smiling. I'm not sure which version of my mother I want on those ambulance steps. Later, I saw her in many modes, none of which I considered to be 'her': lazy-lipped with medication, jumping with nerves, lucid but frenetic with love and regret. All different. None of them the mother who baked and laughed and made me believe that I was the only thing that really mattered to her.

There must have been a cordon, or something, or maybe Emma's mother just stopped at the sight of the unexpected. A policeman was there almost straightaway, anyway, and I heard Emma's mum's explanation, the name of my parents, the number of my house. And then her hand got tight, spasm-tight, around mine and she said, 'Yes, of course, I'll wait.'

And that was where my normal ended.

A policewoman came over to join us, and she talked to Emma's mum in an urgent half whisper, so all I could catch were the 's' sounds. The next thing I knew we were walking back up the road, and Mrs Medland was saying, in a funny voice, as though the wind was taking it, although it wasn't windy, 'We're just going to go back home, sweetheart, and then the police lady is going to come to see us.'

'I don't have any pyjamas,' I said.

'Don't worry about that,' Emma's mum said, and she burst into tears. So it was I who led her home, and knocked on the door, and it was she that her husband looked at when he opened it.

He said, 'What's happened?' looking from her to me and back again. From the look on his face — sharp, serious — it was hard to remember that he had pink toenails on one foot, yellow on the other, from where he had let me and Emma loose with her nail varnish.

She cried harder. 'I don't know — exactly . . .' she said, and I remember thinking, how ridiculous, to cry and cry like that when you didn't know why. I presume the policewoman must have given her the gist; I don't know what they let slip. Looking back, I suspect she knew that someone was dead, or dying. She probably thought it was my mother. Well, she would have done. Two and two do make four, most of the time.

The details were fed to me like bread soaked in milk given to a Victorian invalid. A little at a time. Gentle, soft. Like that made a difference.

The job of telling me that my dad was dead was shared between a policewoman, a social worker and Mrs Medland. Emma was at school. I suppose it was the next day. I had been upset that I wasn't allowed to go to school, that I couldn't go home either. Emma's mum was holding my hand. They called him 'your daddy'. I never called him Daddy — he was Dad, he always had been — so it took a moment to work out what they were saying. I felt as though I was trying to eat and the knife and fork were in the wrong hands.

I think I nodded. 'Where's Mum?' I asked.

'We're looking after her,' the policewoman said. 'She can't come home just yet, until we sort everything out. She's all right, though. She isn't hurt.'

I thought about the money, the cigarettes, the pint. Maybe he had got into another fight, like he did on the oil rig when he was sent home. 'Did someone hit him?' I asked. He was dead the way a character in a book is dead: I was sad, but at the same time sure it wasn't real. I hadn't realised that I couldn't close the covers and go back to life the way it used to be.

'Why do you ask that, Loveday?' the social worker asked. She was speaking to me but looking at the policewoman. 'Who do you think might have hit your daddy?'

'I don't know,' I said. I wanted my mum so badly that the pain was chewing me from the inside out. 'When can I go home?'

There's a lot of time around that period I don't recall, as though I went to sleep the day after it happened, and when I woke up a year later I was in my long-term foster home with Annabel. What I do remember has the quality of those moments in the night, at the end of a nightmare or the start of a flu, when you surface for a minute or two and whatever vestige of dream is in your brain is hyper-real.

I remember one of the social workers coming back to Emma's house. It was the thin one. She wore a perfume that was heavy with jasmine. Even now the scent of jasmine takes me back to that house, the TV on to mask the noise of the adults talking at the door, Mrs Medland saying, 'As long as it takes'. When I remember that, I still get a spike of hope along with the jasmine, I think because I assumed that they were talking about me staying there until my mum came home. In retrospect, I can see that they were talking about me staying there until they found a place for me in The System.

I remember being taken to see my mum when she was on remand. I was scared of her: she looked wrong, she smelled different, and she cried. Her face was swollen, thanks to medication or tears or both. When she saw me she put out her arms, and when I didn't walk into them straight away she put her head in her hands and made a low, long 'no'.

I remember Auntie Janey coming to visit; I recall the Cornish hum and sing of her voice. That day was like a holiday, a bright change from the dismal misery of missing my parents, and having interviews with people who were trying to disguise how important the conversation was. I showed her around Whitby — she looked in the windows of the jet shops and counted the steps with me, and we had afternoon tea and she licked cream off her finger and said that she would get fat but she didn't much care. When we met the tall social worker again, back at Emma's house, there was another of those overheard conversations that I didn't understand until much later: Auntie Janey crying, saying, 'I just don't

300

think I can', and the social worker making there-there noises. Now I assume that she was there to see if she would take me. Clearly the answer was no. I don't blame her. By which I mean: I do blame her. I was ten. I had no one. I didn't kill anyone. So what if she and my dad hadn't been in touch much since he left school and joined the army? Who cared that I reminded her of my dad, or looked like my mum, or whatever half-baked thing she said to the social worker? So what if suddenly acquiring a ten-year-old isn't in your life plan? It's not like I was on my first-choice path any more either.

I don't remember a funeral. I found out later that he was buried in Cornwall. I didn't go. I don't know why not. I don't remember being asked. I don't know what I would have said. Now I'd say: dead is dead and it doesn't matter.

I remember my first night in temporary foster care. I was in a room with bunk beds and the little girl on the top bunk got into bed with me in the middle of the night. I lay like a plank as she tried to cuddle me; eventually, she got the message, climbed back up the ladder, and snivelled until it was time to get up.

I remember standing in my room at Annabel's for the first time, and her saying, kindly and calmly, that she and social services had agreed that for as long as I was with her there would be no other foster child. The room was bigger than my room at home, which seemed wrong. There was a bed, a desk under a pretend-Georgian double-glazed window, a noticeboard with drawing-pins in a line at the top, a blue rug on the floor, and the smell of the fresh pale-green paint on the walls. Annabel said that I wasn't to bring food upstairs but apart from that I could do as I wished in my room and, so long as she saw me for meals, she wouldn't disturb me. I suppose she thought that, in time, I would become more sociable, watching TV with her, talking to her about my parents.

When I look back I can see how carefully she was chosen. She was on her own — her husband had died — so the family situation I had come from wasn't replicated. She'd had three children, who had all left home. She must have been in her fifties when I moved in. She'd fostered for years, short-term care when her children were small, dealing with children with more than the usual difficulties as time went on. The social worker told me all this in the car on the way, trying to make it sound as though I'd won a prize. I suppose — I suspect — I had. There was no other child for me to deal with. Annabel was patient, and kind — both things that went unrewarded. Her job was typing up transcripts for an agency; she would tap-tap away at her keyboard in the evenings, after I'd gone upstairs. When I came in from school she was always there, to make a cup of tea and ask questions that I mainly ignored, or sit quietly and listen if I did have anything to say. I almost never did. We would listen to the radio and drink our tea, and then I would go and do homework, and when I was called for supper I would go downstairs and we would eat together. It was my job to wash up and then I would go to my room again.

Eight months at Elspeth's had opened my eyes to all the sorts of damaged I could be. I could fail at everything. I could be angry at everyone and everything. I could set fire to a sofa, I could stop washing, I could eat myself fat or vomit myself thin. One thing was clear: I couldn't be the LJ I had been, taking part in school plays and sure that I was loved. I went straight to Annabel after the sentencing. My name hadn't been released by the courts and I had a cleverly-close-to-the-truth cover story that would allow me a 'fresh start'. 'Fresh start', in case you're wondering, is social worker code for 'your life is now screwed but at least we can do something about the pointing and whispering'. I was to say, if asked, that my mum wasn't well and my dad had died so I'd come to stay with Annabel. I made sure that no one asked, snarling my way between home and school and library. I was bullied — of course I was, I was a new kid who looked like a scared dog that would snap, satisfyingly, when poked with a stick — but it was manageable. Well, I managed. I shut myself in my room when it wasn't a meal-time, I read and I wrote poems and I envied everyone who wasn't me, but especially the ones who were in the drama club.

And while I was struggling through those first months, my mother was struggling too. I was told the facts, carefully, as judged to be suitable for a ten-year-old, by Elspeth Phipps and the thin social worker, whose name was Shanice. For the rest of that school year, before I was moved, I picked up the technicolour details: 'My dad says your mother wants locked up and the key thrown away' from the cruel kids, and titbits of kinder news from Matilda and Emma. Once I moved to Annabel's and my new school, I didn't have the information thrown at me any more, but I did have the computers in the school library at lunchtime, so I found out everything I wanted to, without having to look into someone's concerned face while I absorbed it. Because no one was truly concerned about me now, except for the people who were paid to be, and I didn't want that sort of care.

■ ■ ■ ■

POETRY

■ ■ ■ ■

2016
NOT MAGIC

I arranged to meet Nathan in the George and Dragon, on the evening after Archie's party. I'd bolted as soon as Rob had left the library, texted Nathan to say I wasn't feeling well, and gone home. I had locked the flat door behind me, taken the dress off, got under the duvet in my underwear, and cried until the neighbour had knocked on the wall. Then I'd got in the shower and howled. I howled for losing Nathan. For missing Mum. For not being able to have someone wrap me up in a towel and hold me tight, not caring how wet they got. For the fact that Rob had come to me, in my friend's house — in a library, which should be a safe place — and put pressure on my fault line in the hope that I would break. I couldn't even bear to think about the possibility that he might have found my mother, talked to her, taken the books. He would have made her hope.

I'd gone back to bed and thought about writing Nathan a letter. Instead I sent him the text arranging the drink.

Of course he was worried about me. 'You look pale,' he said, after he'd kissed me, sat me down, and slid my drink in front of me. 'I got your usual but would you rather a soft drink? Have you taken any medication?'

'I'm tired,' I said. 'I didn't sleep very well.'

'It must have come on suddenly,' Nathan said. 'I got back and there was no sign of you. I knew I'd been a while, but you seemed fine when I left you.'

Lying is such a terrible idea. Even the little 'I don't feel well' ones grow fangs and crunch holes in you. I changed the subject to the real subject.

'We need to talk,' I said.

'Wow, you must be ill,' he said, and he laughed, and then he saw my face, and he stopped. 'What?'

'I can't do this,' I said. 'Us.' I'd made a plan but the plan had not, of course, taken into account what happened when I got within touching distance of Nathan. The plan had involved poise and calmness and a considered and simple explanation that a relationship was something that I wasn't ready for, didn't want, and needed to extricate myself from as of now. Nathan should consider himself — with regret — let go from the position of Loveday's boyfriend. The plan had not fully taken into account what it was like to sit with Nathan, to look at his lovely face. Oh, how I wished I was a person who could love him, and that loving me was feasible.

'What?' he said. It wasn't that he hadn't heard. It was that he hadn't believed. So I didn't need to repeat it, at least. My voice wasn't feeling very cooperative.

'I'm sorry,' I said. I took a drink. There wasn't enough gin in it. When I put the glass down, I centred it, exactly, on the beer mat. I took my time. I didn't want to raise my face. Nathan wasn't making any noise.

When I looked up his body was still. The only moving parts of him were his eyelids as he blinked and the inner corners of his collarbones, visible in the V of his open shirt, as he breathed.

'Loveday.' His voice had tears in it, and something rough: determination, or anger. I deserved anger. I was pretty furious with myself, for putting us both in this position. With Rob, for his part in it.

'I'm sorry,' I said again. I tried to sound strong. I don't think it worked.

'Loveday,' Nathan said. And he touched my hand, and I snatched it away, as though he had committed a crime by reaching for me. 'I just don't understand what I've done.'

'I know,' I said. He looked so shocked that I felt seasick with shame.

' "I know?" ' He looked bewildered, as though someone had broken into his house while he was out and rearranged all of the furniture. There were tears in his eyes now but they had gone from his voice. 'Is that all I get?'

'I'm not very good at relationships,' I said, my words quieter than I thought they would be. 'I told you that.'

'I don't think you did,' he said, 'not in so many words, anyway.'

'Exactly,' I said. 'Not in so many words. But you knew.'

He rubbed his hand over his head and back again. I'd done that with my hand, before now, too. My palm itched with the memory of his bristly, close-cropped hair.

'Is it because of what I told you?' he asked.

'What?' I had no idea what he was talking about. Conversations outside books are horrible. The other person doesn't know what they are supposed to say. I wanted another drink but I didn't think it would be right to go and get one.

'At the party,' he said. 'I told you about my not-very-brilliant career, and then I went to get some food, and when I came back you had gone.'

'No,' I said, 'it wasn't that.' I touched his hand, the back of it, just for a second, and he didn't take it away. 'You know how people say "it's not you, it's me"? It really is me.'

'Don't you think I should be the judge of that?'

I looked at him. Those eyes, oh, those eyes, and that brow, and that mouth. Those teeth. All of those things books and poems say about eating up and drinking in and consuming? I got that, then. I wanted Nathan to be part of me. Right inside. Not like that. Well, like that as well. My body had got used to sex, and it wasn't going to take the lack of it very well.

And you know how everyone talks about heartbreak? Now I understood that, too. I had the full cartoon zigzag, right across my bloody heart, and looking at him, I felt every ragged, blazing millimetre of the cut. The fact that I was the one with the scalpel just made it worse.

There was nothing I could say. Where would I start? 'There's something I haven't told you?' I knew — a small part of me did — that Nathan would get it. But that wasn't the point. The point was, him getting it would change everything.

'I thought you were happy with us,' he said, quietly.

'Nathan . . .' I couldn't have this conversation. I just couldn't. If I let this happen now it was going to be worse later. And before you go all 'giving in to bullies' blah on me, remember this. I wasn't giving in to Rob; I could have told Nathan the whole story if I wanted to. It was more that Rob putting his massive boot in reminded me of the whole, vast impossibility of me and a relationship. There were too many hurdles. The main one being: once I'd laid out my past — though I only lie by omission — I would never be sure that Nathan loved me for me. I wouldn't know if it was pity that he felt, or whether he was too afraid of how broken I was to ever be honest. I'd imagine that the whole stupid history of my parents would always be there, and it might be like living in a forest, the trees permanently changing the quality of the light.

I'd enjoyed myself with Nathan. It was never going to last. Rob had just been the reminder. It pissed me off that he had done it, but people piss me off all the time, so I was going to have to live with that. If I hadn't got involved with Rob in the first place, none of this would have happened. A normal person would have nothing to hide. Rob would have nothing to dig up.

I stood up, said, 'I'm sorry,' and walked away.

Not quickly enough, though, because behind me, I heard Nathan say, 'I love you.' I pretended not to hear but I think he probably realised that I had. I suppose my next move, in Nathan-land, was to turn around and burst into tears and tell him everything and he would stroke my hair and we would — you see, that's the problem. I really don't know what comes after that. I can't see any sort of an ending.

So I kept walking, and I went home, and if I'd seen Rob on the way I'd have shown him what a proper slap felt like.

Here's what I know.

Just after six o'clock that night — as Emma and I were choosing nail polish colours — my mother dialled 999 and sob-said, 'I think I've killed my husband.'

He died of traumatic brain injury. What had actually killed him was the impact on his brain of the back of his skull hitting the stone floor, according to the pathologist who conducted the post-mortem. Of course, he wouldn't have hit the floor if my mother hadn't hit him on the temple with the cast-iron lid of the cooking pot. He was declared dead there, at the house, on the kitchen floor.

My mother had tried to resuscitate him. She had to be pulled off his body.

There was a cigarette lying near him on the floor, a box of matches still held in one of his big hands. He was lighting a cigarette, it seemed, when she hit him.

She was arrested at the scene. She fought to stay with him; she scratched at the face of the police officer who was blocking her way, and drew blood.

She was remanded on bail, and sent to a hospital for psychiatric assessment.

She refused to say anything in her own defence. She pleaded guilty to manslaughter. There wasn't a trial, just a sentencing hearing.

She got twelve years. She would be out in six.

When I googled us in the school library I was shocked by the sheer volume of coverage the case got. I'd refused to talk about any details with Annabel or Shanice, so by the time I was twelve I had hardly heard my parents' names for a year and I missed them. A lot had been written about us. I found national newspaper articles, local TV footage, blogs and op-eds. There was I thinking our lives had fallen apart; search engines suggested we had caught the twenty-first century zeitgeist. Sunday supplement magazines interviewed domestic violence survivors and talked to experts. Odd-looking adults, who used to be the kid caught in the middle, were asked to speculate about what I, and my mother, were thinking. There were questions on *Question Time*. The wife of the man who my dad had got into a fight with on the oil rig sold her story. She came out strongly for my mum. It seemed that when my dad said that 'you should see the other guy', he wasn't joking.

A lot of people came out for my mum, as though she was some sort of warrior, or making a point, whereas, as far as I could tell, she was just trying to not get hurt again. Of course, I wasn't there when it happened, something that was made much of by a lot of the people who got to have opinions on our lives (i.e. everybody): had my mother got me out of the way in order to carry out her premeditated crime? Clearly not. Because — apart from the whole finding-the-money-in-the-books-thing, which of course nobody knew about, because I didn't tell anyone and there's nothing in any of the reports to suggest that my mother ever did — a premeditated crime would, presumably, involve something a little more sophisticated than catching someone on the temple with a cast-iron pot lid and hoping for a lucky angle if he fell.

The details in the press gave me the bones that my imagination could hang some flesh on. I reconstructed constantly, barely noticing that I was doing it. At any moment, awake or asleep, it was as though there was a film running against the backdrop of my eyelids. Her crying, him trying to comfort her, her relaxing, admitting that she thought he might hurt me, him going crazy. Him giving her a hard time for depriving me of things, her walking into the kitchen, him following her, her turning. Him hitting her and her hitting back. The scenes in my head had different soundtracks, different paces, as though they had been set as homework in a film school. Sometimes when she hit him it was black-and-white, balletic, almost beautiful as he fell in slow-motion to the floor. Or the scene was gritty, close-up, her crying, him crying, and the blow an accident. There was an out-and-out self-defence edit when my mother was cowering, then flailing, but I had loved my father too much for that to stick. At some point — and I couldn't say when — my version fixed itself. They were both angry. He hit her. She went to the kitchen. Maybe she was on her way out, her hand on her coat by the door. He followed her, apologetic, tearful, the way he always was afterwards. She softened. He said something else, something unkind, then turned to light a cigarette. She, who had taken so much, had had enough. She picked up the lid and, frightened, in pain, she swung.

Looking at what had been written about our family made me feel ill. We were not an example, or a case study, or a sign of the times. We were us.

The thing that really shocked me, though, was not the reporting or the endless manipulation, distortion and magnification of our sad little story. What shocked me was that, while we thought our lives were made up of just the three of us, it was clear that our trio had been circled by concerned people who didn't have the wit or the balls to stop what was coming. My teacher had called social services because I was 'withdrawn'. My father's job centre records showed that he was inclined to be aggressive under pressure. When my mother was examined, traces of bruises and signs of broken teeth and broken ribs made my father a monster and my mother a victim. A report to the court said that my mother was suffering from anxiety and depression but was basically of sound mind, and that made her the monster and him the hapless innocent.

She wouldn't say anything. She wouldn't defend herself, not a word. I'm not an expert but I would have thought that would call her mental health into question.

I reconstructed. I imagined. I tried to forgive, but I couldn't forgive one without blaming the other. Most of all, I wished for the world that had gone, where my dad went to work in a helicopter and my mum and I collected stones and shells on the shore.

The week after I ended things with Nathan was wretched. I couldn't sleep, or concentrate, or do anything vaguely sane. Rob was having the wit to keep out of my way, it seemed, so I didn't even have the satisfaction of taking it out on him. I'd seen him once, when he'd come in to talk to Melodie, but he didn't look for me. I'd got the impression that she was trying to avoid him, but maybe that was wishful thinking on my part. He'd obviously decided to stop dropping off the books, now he'd played his trump freak-Loveday-out card. Or maybe my mother had got wise to him, only let him take a box or two. I wished I could ask him where he'd got them from, but I couldn't bear the thought of even looking at his face.

I hated to admit it, but I missed Nathan. I really, really missed him. Gaze-lost-in-the-middle-distance, can't-sleep-can't-eat gloom. I knew it was ridiculous but I genuinely couldn't seem to help myself. And I hate to make the comparison, but the only thing I'd ever experienced like it was the proper, full-on grief when my dad died and I lost my mum. Not anywhere near as bad, of course, but bad enough. Because nothing else in my life had changed, I realised how much time I'd spent with Nathan, and how used I was to seeing him at work, at home.

I'd decided not to go to poetry night on the Wednesday evening, of course, but that was only a couple of hours a week. It was all of the other things. Him meeting me after work and coming back for supper, staying the night. The way he made it easy to talk about nothing much, for hours, and feel as though we were making a world. Listening to him read poetry, his gravel-and-honey voice making every word alive. Him dropping into the shop with a coffee and the sound of him and Archie laughing. The stupid chocolate coins. Even undressing, looking at my tattoos, remembering him trying to figure out the first lines, where they were from, why I had chosen them. Everything seemed a loss, a miss, and even though I tried to wear myself out with cycling when I wasn't at work, or cleaning and reshelving when I was, I couldn't sleep and I couldn't think, unless I was thinking about Nathan and my mother's books and bloody Rob and the fact that my life is so fucked up that my chances of having a normal relationship are about as likely as a copy of *Pericles* signed by Shakespeare turning up. That is, zero, unless he invented time travel as well as ten per cent of the English language. And I'd put myself in a position where I'd seen what a relationship could be. A different story. Lovely in a poem, a shitty, impossible idea in real life.

Do I sound angry? Well, I wonder why that could be.

I woke at five the next morning, trying not to think about what might have happened at poetry night the night before, and I got ready and was at work by six, because why lie and look at the ceiling when you can be sorting out the Health section. At four in the afternoon, all the saved-up tiredness came over me and the next thing I knew Archie was saying my name, gently, his hand on my arm.

'Loveday,' he said, 'you need to wake up. I

almost locked you in.' It was six o'clock. I had been asleep with my back against the maps. Those two hours had felt like the first real sleep I'd had in weeks.

It took me a while to swim back up to life. When I did, I almost wished I hadn't. My arm was numb, my neck hurt and my legs were stiff. And physical aches were nothing compared to the other stuff.

'I'm going,' Archie said, 'but I'll wait for you.'

'I'll be okay,' I said, and I got to my feet.

'I'm not sure that you will,' he said. When I was standing he pulled me in for a moment, his arm around my shoulder: a side-by-side hug. I let him. He said, 'Take some time off, Loveday. Get away. Think about things.'

'I don't know, Archie,' I said.

I did know. I don't really do holidays — I went to a literary festival, once, and I didn't much like it. Too many people, and I was all wrong — everyone is equal when they're reading a book, but not when they're chatting in a queue to meet an author or knowing which cider to ask for at a bar. I've been saving for as long as I've been working, because I know there won't always be Archie, and I'm not sure that anyone else would give me a break. Holidays seem like a waste of money. Especially when there's nowhere I want to go. Wherever you go, there you are, or whatever the stupid saying is.

'I do,' he said. 'You need some perspective. If you come in next week I'm going to send you away.'

I laughed. My throat hurt.

'I mean it,' he said, then added, 'I can lend you a tent, if you like. Give yourself some time.'

'I'm not sure that I want time,' I said, 'or a tent.'

'Take it from a friend,' he said, and he turned so he was facing me, his hands on my shoulders. 'You need some time. You need to think about what you want. If you don't fancy a tent, I can work with that.'

I sometimes think that because I don't live in a detached Georgian mansion with landscaped grounds, Archie thinks I'm a small step up from an itinerant peasant, selling ribbons and begging for bread. 'Tents don't have bathrooms,' I said, 'and I could have my stuff nicked or be trampled by cows.'

'Campsites have shower blocks,' Archie said, 'and anyway, you could get trampled by cows anywhere.'

I nodded, though I'm not sure why. Archie has this way of making you go along with things, even the possibility of out-of-control cows in an urban setting. 'I don't know about a holiday. I don't know where I'd go,' I said.

'Go to Whitby,' he said. 'Like you said you wanted to. Get some air.'

It had been a heaven of a place to grow up: seagulls, beach, and nooks and crannies; the feeling, when the town was full of tourists, that you were lucky because this place was your home. Archie was looking at me as though he was going to cry, as though me taking time off was some life-or-death scenario, so I nodded, and we left the shop.

When I got in the next day I found that my beloved boss had done the whole nine Archie yards. He chose to misinterpret my nod, which had meant 'I will consider your suggestion, but probably not act on it,' as he well knew. In his version it became a nod that said, 'Please ring up your friend who has a caravan site on the cliffs on the outskirts of Whitby, book a caravan, leave Melodie — Melodie! — in charge of the shop for the morning, and then when Loveday turns up for work, bundle her straight in the car, drive her home, stand over her as she puts some things in a rucksack, and drive her to Whitby whether she wants to go there or not, via a posh supermarket where you buy random food for her without asking what she wants, or even likes.'

The strange/lovely thing was, he was right about me needing a break, and he was also right about Whitby.

I hadn't been back since the day I left temporary foster care — I'd stayed for the rest of the school year there, and moved to Annabel's in Ripon during the first summer without my parents, ready to start my new school, where no one would know my history, in September.

For a long time, going back to Whitby hadn't been an option: I didn't want to see people who would know me and, anyway, when you're in care you don't do things like propose a trip. Everything is too fragile, and too finely balanced. Annabel and I had strict operating procedures: that is, we left each other alone. I went along with most things she suggested and she didn't suggest things too often. I kept to myself because that was the only way I could manage. To start with, I think she thought I would come out of my shell. I didn't have a TV in my room and I think she thought that, eventually, I would be drawn downstairs by the desire to watch what everyone else was watching, or at least understand what everyone else was talking about.

She assumed, of course, that people at school talked to me, and I talked back, although a few parents' evenings soon put paid to that idea of hers. I stayed in my room and read. She waited, arm's length, ready, I'm sure, to give me the emotional support that social workers and psychiatrists and everyone went on and on about. While she waited she made nourishing meals and was scrupulous about pocket money and timetables — she'd obviously decided that I could do without any shocks — and fairness.

Every summer she suggested a holiday and I declined. She offered to take me to Cornwall and I slammed doors. She even offered to take me to Whitby and I told her she was heartless; I felt as though she was taunting me. Every day of my life up until I left Whitby I'd seen the sea, and I had hardly glimpsed it in all the years since, although I often dreamed about it. I went on school trips — London, somewhere in Wales — but that was as much holidaying as I'd done. I managed to get my first tattoo on my London trip, thanks to a brilliantly forged note from one of my fellow pupils. There were three of us who sneaked off from Madame Tussauds and went to Soho. I got my *Anna Karenina* and the other two, who had plans for some Chinese characters and the Kaiser Chiefs logo, bottled it when they saw the tattooing gun. Miraculously, the teachers didn't notice we'd bunked off — or pretended not to — and I just didn't mention it to Annabel. I didn't try to hide it. She didn't say anything about it. All was what passed for well.

It wasn't a long journey, especially not the way Archie drives. Some people might say I was sulking in the car. I might even say it was my plan to sulk. But it was irrelevant, because Archie talked the whole hour we were on the road, and even if I'd been feeling chatty, I couldn't have got a word in. He started (no idea why) on the taste of the dust in the air in Berlin the night the wall came down, veered off into how many of the royal family still sleep with teddy bears, and then he was telling me about Clara, who worked at the bookshop when I first started, then emptied the till one Saturday and did a runner. 'I wouldn't have minded,' he said. 'If she'd have asked I would have given her the money. I was sorry she stole it.' He paused, and then added, as though he was answering a question, 'We met when we were walking the Great Wall of China, you know.'

'Oh, okay,' I said, in a slightly sulkier version of my 'I'm not listening to a word of this' tone. Archie didn't notice.

And then he started talking about me. Which made me want to throw myself out of the car and take my chances on the tarmac. 'I remember the first time you came into the shop,' he said, 'and I thought you were just an average teenager. But when you touched a book you did it as though the book mattered. You looked as though you couldn't believe your luck, my lovely, just the fact that you were allowed to come and browse in my ramshackle domain. You went from Penguin Classics to History and you spent the best part of half an hour looking at a book on regimental insignia. I remember thinking: well, well, Archie, we have a true bibliophile here.'

I'd turned, so I was looking out of the passenger window, rather than watching the road roll forward in front of me. I started to recognise the terrain. The moors don't change, though they're definitely easier to appreciate when you're in a car with good suspension. The sight of the abbey, a skeleton on the skyline, felt more familiar than the sight of my own face in the mirror. The sea on the horizon, the colour of a well-washed pair of jeans, made me queasy with memories.

Archie introduced me to Jackson, who owned the caravan site — they met, allegedly, in a bar in Kentucky — and left me to it. He turned down an invitation to lunch. He was itching to leave, I could see that. I think he'd realised that leaving Melodie in charge of the shop was not his finest hour and he needed to get back and do some damage limitation before she turned it into a performance space.

'Well, my straywaif,' he said, 'I'll be back in a week.' He put his hand on my shoulder. I let him.

'Thank you,' I said. I meant it. Just the sight of the sea made me realise how much I needed to be somewhere else, safe from echoes of Nathan's presence and books my parents had owned.

Archie couldn't resist a double-blast on the horn and a wave of his hat out of the window as he pulled away. I was tired. So tired. It felt as though all the sleep I'd missed since I left Whitby almost fifteen years ago was waiting here for me to collect it.

The caravan was one of those static numbers. It was probably bigger than my flat, but so full of maroon cushions and yellow-gold tassels that I could hardly move. I drew the curtains closed and got into bed. It was

two in the afternoon, but I didn't care. I
went to sleep and I woke at nine, starving
and glad of Archie's cheese and olives.
When I unpacked the shopping I saw that it
wasn't random. Nothing needed to be
cooked. Bread, cheese, cured meat, cereal,
bananas, milk. I couldn't work out whether
he was making life easy for me or trying to
make sure I didn't burn the place down.

■ ■ ■ ■

TRAVEL

■ ■ ■ ■

2016
MEMORY STIRRED THROUGH

The first few days were okay. I went into the town and I ate ice cream on the pier. I walked down the steps onto the beach and I measured myself against the big stone blocks there, where Dad used to take my photo. Guess what? I'm taller than I was when I was ten. As I was standing there I thought I heard my mother laughing. I'd almost forgotten that she ever laughed. In my mind she had become sad and frightened, cornered and incapable. I thought about asking someone to take a photo of me at the steps, but standing there was enough. And who would I show a photo to anyway? (That's a rhetorical question.)

I went to the abbey and looked at all of the tourists, wondering at the whalebone arches of the building. I couldn't remember when this spectacular ruin was new to me. It had always been there. I walked around the shops. Some of them were unchanged, too, still selling postcards and rock, jet beads and gothic ornaments.

I touched my necklace and wondered how my little bit of jet felt to come home. I had assumed I would have known how I felt. I didn't. I wasn't excited, or sad, or full of sudden memories. I was just Loveday, still, and it seemed that I was stuck with me. Coming back to Whitby wasn't magic; it didn't have any answers for me.

Except that I liked being near the sea again. The water was the blue of inkstained fingertips. I felt so small beside it, and there was comfort in being certain of how little I mattered. It made thinking about Nathan a bit easier, for a minute or two. But I couldn't be in love, because that was just a stupid thing to be. My parents had been in love, and look where that led. And no, I don't think that all men are my father (or Rob) or all women are my mother (or me). But I am clever enough to see that anyone who takes me on is going to be either weird or very, very nice and kind and patient. I don't like weird, and as I am not nice, or kind, or patient, so sooner or later, it will crash and burn. That's not cynicism. That's logic.

The bookshop I used to go to with my mum was still there. The sight of it stung. I made myself go in. There were the same wooden bookshelves, tall at the front, short for the children's section at the back. I bought *Dracula*, which I'd never got around to reading, and had a slightly awkward 'don't I recognise you from somewhere' conversation with the (same, but older) woman behind the till. Instead of playing it cool, doing a mildly puzzled face and strolling off, I said 'no' and bolted in a way that would make me much more memorable. I wished I'd asked her what it was like to work in the same bookshop for your whole life. She looked happy enough.

As the days passed I got braver, if it was brave to go back to the old places. I think I'd worked out that nothing was going to hurt more for being in front of me than it had been for being in my mind all of these years. Maybe I needed to face it.

I walked back to the house I grew up in, and I stood outside. There was a child's bike by the door and a newish little Citroën on the drive. There didn't used to be a drive, just a path and a scrubby little garden.

I looked up to what had been my parents' bedroom window and imagined my mother there, looking out, watching me walk to the school that was visible from the front gate, imagining myself independent. Well, be careful what you wish for, LJ. I waited for the slap of emotion to hit me but it didn't. I felt sorry, and sad, but I don't think I was any sorrier or sadder for standing there. It's only a house, after all.

After a while a woman came out, a baby in her arms. 'Can I help you?' she called. Her hand was shading her eyes from the afternoon sun so I couldn't really tell whether she was being genuine, but it seemed that she was. I almost said, 'I grew up in this house,' but I stopped myself just in time. Because either she knew the story or she didn't. If she did, it would be tea and sympathy and her watching my face to see where I looked, what I remembered, poised for a drama; if she didn't, then I sure as hell wasn't going to tell her, and that would make answering any 'when did you live here/ where did you go' questions tricky.

I smiled and shook my head, and walked away. I should have done that with Nathan, earlier, before my heart and his were going to get mashed. I was hurting for myself, and for him. My mind looped around and around the fact that if I did tell him everything he would take it in his stride. But it would change our world and I would never, ever know for sure whether he was loving me, or whether he felt sorry for me. Writing a new ending is all very well in the abstract.

Some plot twists you just don't recover from.

I slept and I read and I tried not to think about Nathan. And on my last day I did the thing I'd been thinking about, and avoiding, ever since I'd arrived in Whitby. I went to church.

I had tea and chocolate cake on mismatched china in a teashop playing Vera Lynn. There was parkin on the menu and I thought about ordering it, but I knew it wouldn't be as good as the one that Mum and I used to make for Dad's homecomings. And then I went to St Mary's Parish Church, up on the cliff. I walked up the hundred and ninety-nine steps to get there. I used to walk up counting them. If I was with Mum she would count along with me. If I was with Dad he would stride ahead, three steps at a time, and I'd lose count while I hurried to catch him up, both of us breathless and laughing at the top. If the three of us were together, Mum and I would walk and count, and Dad would walk beside or behind us, calling out numbers to put us off. I would laugh but Mum would mock-glare and say, 'Patrick, you're not helping. For that, you can buy the ice creams.'

I took the steps slowly, remembering, tasting the brine in the air.

■ ■ ■ ■

The church, of course, was no different to the way it had been fifteen years ago. It looks very traditional from the outside, built of stone with a square tower, tall stained-glass windows in the walls. The churchyard is full of gothicky headstones that look as though they belong in comics, until you remember that they are the originals. I stopped at the memorial to the Marwood family, and looked at the names there. I remembered my mother and I talking about Marmaduke; I knew about family graves and thought at first that the cat was buried with them, as I had a book with a cat called Marmaduke but had never heard of a person with that name. My mother had explained. If she ever thought my questions were funny she never showed it. I read out the dates — Marmaduke didn't live long even by cat standards, born in September 1871, dead in January 1872 — and my mother pointed out the word 'son' that I'd missed and said, gently, that sometimes people did die before they grew up, especially in the olden days, before there was good medicine.

I don't know why I was surprised to see that the Marwoods, and Marmaduke, were still there — it's not as though his baby bones would have moved on. But I stood and looked at his name, and then I walked on, into the church porch, where I smiled at the ladies in the shop full of pamphlets and postcards, put a pound in the donations box, and passed through the doorway into the church itself.

St Mary's is the only church I ever went to as a kid. It has wooden box pews, built at odd angles to each other, so you can't see anyone else and you can only see the vicar if your pew is at the correct angle. I know it's unusual, but it just feels like normal to me. Whenever I see churches on TV, with their orderly rows of bench pews, and all that space between them and above them, they seem all wrong.

I always liked the topsy-turviness of St Mary's, and the names on the sides of the pews, telling you who went where: pews for church maids, stewards, and visitors. At the time when the church was built, you knew your place, and you stayed in it. I know the world is supposed to be better now, but be honest: isn't there something about knowing where you belong, whether it's up in the grand Cholmley Pew looking down, or sitting in the pew 'for strangers only'? Except, I suppose, it wasn't much fun being a stranger, and that's what I was.

I went into the pew that I used to sit in with my parents. We didn't go often, but they used to go to church on the closest Sunday to their anniversary, because the church was where they met and where they married.

Dad would show me the corner, inside one of the pews, where he'd carved a P and an S-J and made a rough-and-ready heart around them, on the day they had their banns read.

'I cut my finger,' he said, 'and your mother had to suck it all through the service to try to make the bleeding stop.' She'd laugh and he'd laugh and I'd laugh, although I never felt I really got the joke, and they would hold hands on the way down the steps again.

So many of my memories are happy ones.

The pew was under a stained-glass window, with a curly-headed saint with a sword and cloak. The light fell in blue and red pieces on my skin when the sun shone. My parents had got married in the summer before I was born, so it was often sunny when we came on the anniversary trips. This was the church they were standing outside, in that laughing wedding photo we had on our living room wall.

Like Marmaduke, the carving of their

initials was still there. I put my hand on it and I felt everything that I had half-expected to feel back at the house. Their initials were etched into pale-brown paint and there were other carvings around it. PR loves JL, KEM 4 SAS. I wondered how many others of those linked initials were still together, still happy.

Everything I'd lost came and sat with me, as I sat in the boxed-in pew. I wasn't the one who'd killed anyone, yet it felt as though I was the one who'd lost most.

I'd always pushed those thoughts away. If there's no one who cares about you then there's not a lot of satisfaction in dwelling on all that you've haven't had, or seen, or done. Once you're in the system, people are paid to care for you, and that's fine when it comes to breakfast and new shoes, but not with feelings. My mother had been someone I'd always been able to talk to; my dad was bursting with unconditional love for me. A quiet foster-mother didn't compare. A counsellor wasn't going to cut it. And there was no point crying over spilled blood anyway.

So I'd kept my eyes forward and not looked too far ahead and so far, so good. Like I've said, I wasn't pregnant, in prison, an addict. I wasn't a fully functioning human being either. But, be honest: are you? Is anyone?

It all got a bit Scottish Play in that pew, that afternoon, the ghosts coming to visit, one by one. There was my father, his kind eyes and big, rough hands. My mother, round and smiling, Dad's arm slung around her shoulder, her hand tiny on one of his thick thighs. There was Aunt Janey, the one who came to spend the day with me and decided she couldn't give me a home. There was my mother's mother, who had been a widow for as long as I had known her: a source of comfort and skilfully-palmed cough drops, as she and I were the only ones who liked them.

And there was the gut-deep thought of Nathan, his poet's words and his slender magician's hands, his patience and confidence and his general too-good-to-be-trueness. The week of sleep and food and sea air might have made me calmer but it hadn't made me miss him any less. This was where my 'I'm broken but I can still stand up' position fell down. I wanted to be with him. But I didn't know how. I couldn't go on the way I was.

And of course thinking of Nathan meant sometimes thinking of Rob, mean and manipulating, and suddenly I could see

344

where I was going wrong. It was as though the mop-headed saint had given me the answer, shaking it out of the light his cloak was holding.

I hadn't seen until now that I had a choice.

Rob didn't get to make my decisions and run my life. He knew what I would do and I'd done it, as sweetly and predictably as a waitress in a white apron bringing tea to the table. But if Rob was going to tell Nathan about me anyway, surely I had nothing to lose by telling him myself. I'd be in the same position. Our relationship would still be screwed. But I would have done the right thing, at least. It's the thing that Nathan would have done, because Nathan didn't think twice about trusting me. I used to watch him sleeping, so soundly, in my bed, and want to be him.

Nathan would have told me everything. He had told me about the stage fright, and he didn't have to. Rob had gambled on me being scared of people finding out who I was, and let me screw up my own life. I didn't believe he wanted me. He just wanted to feel as though he was in control of something. He reminded me of the kids at school who'd steal your books and throw them in the nearest toilet, or river, or fire, or whatever. They didn't want them, they just didn't want you to have them.

I sat in the pew and I shook. I watched my fingers as they vibrated. Then I saw that my feet were planted, solid, firm, on the earth above the buried bones. The church was empty of people, and empty of my ghosts now, too. I didn't know how long I'd been there. The place where my parents' initials were carved felt cold under my fingertips when I reached out to them again. If I didn't tell Nathan about my parents, then I was letting Rob choose my destiny. Fuck that. If Nathan and I went wrong, we'd do it by ourselves. I stood up and stood still, as I saw it: it wasn't Nathan I had no faith in. It was me.

On the way out, in the shop, I bought a polished grey stone heart, with a white fault line running through it, and I put it in my pocket. Walking back down the steps, I lost count, and I had to go back to the top again. I didn't mind.

For the time I had left in Whitby I read and slept and walked and ate, and all the time I was thinking about the poem I was going to write. On my last night, I wrote it. I sat up until three, and I thought and wrote, and in the morning when I woke I had a plan. I packed and I waited for Archie's comedy toot-toot, which came forty-five minutes late.

There was a version of myself that was going to tell Archie everything, in the car, on the way back, and get his advice, and apologise for never telling him all of it before. As soon as I saw him it all came rushing up, not the words but the feelings, and I hugged him, tight. It took him a moment to respond. Presumably he was in shock.

We put my rucksack in the car and set off. I was working out where to start when I realised he was quiet, even by a normal person's standards, which is unheard of for Archie.

'What's wrong?' I asked.

'Nothing,' he said. I didn't believe him.

'You're not closing the shop, are you?' I said it jokingly but it's my third worst nightmare, the first being my mother turning up, the second being never seeing my mother again. Yes, I know.

'No,' he said.

'Archie,' I said. 'Please, you're scaring me. What's happened?'

He sighed, and glanced at me, before looking back to the road. 'I asked Melodie to work on Saturday,' he said, 'and she didn't turn up. No sign of her on Monday either — I thought she might come and at least spin me a yarn about why she hadn't bothered. But not a peep, all week. Then today —'

I knew what was coming, or at least where this was going. I should have tried harder to warn Melodie. I should have told her what Rob did, instead of pussyfooting around telling her to be careful, as though she was ever going to take any advice from me. I thought about Rob at Archie's party, the anger and the malicious glee. It would have come out somehow.

I opened the window, for air. I felt sick. 'Yes?'

'She came in. Half of her face is bruised. All of it, from her temple to her mouth. One of her eyes is swollen shut. She went to hospital, and they said her cheekbone is fractured. There was a story about how it's supposed to happened, but I've phoned Rob and told him that he's not to darken our door again. She offered to work but I've shut for the morning.' Archie shook his head, a sad, slow movement. I put my hand on hir arm. 'I hardly recognised her, Loveday'

'Oh, god,' I said.

'He didn't ever hurt you, did he?' Archie asked.

I thought about Nathan, how he'd tell the

truth, without pause. Not because he's absurdly sheltered but because he's whole.

'He slapped me,' I said. 'He took my boots so I couldn't leave. I walked home in my socks in the middle of the night. I thought about reporting it but he didn't hit me hard enough to make a mark. He has medication, and I don't think he always takes it properly. I don't know enough about it to really understand how it all links up.'

'I'm sorry,' Archie said.

'Don't be sorry,' I said. We were quiet for the rest of the journey.

■ ■ ■ ■

POETRY

■ ■ ■ ■

2016
SALT AND VIOLETS

Melodie took to coming into the shop most days.

I tried to be kind. She was quieter, which was sad, but also made her less annoying, so that helped. She wore her hair styled over half of her face to cover some of the damage, and made up her good eye with dark makeup to disguise the bruising on the no-longer mirror side of her face. Her cheekbone was fractured but not displaced, so it was just a question of waiting for it to heal.

I did ask her, on a quiet afternoon, why he had done it, and then I could have bitten my tongue off because the answer, obviously, was 'because he's a prick'. She said something about him having a bad day. I wondered if that was the sort of thing my mother used to say. The police had interviewed Melodie when she was in A&E, but she stuck to her lame 'fell onto a door' (or whatever it was) story. She told me that she worked cash in hand doing her tours, and Rob knew, and she thought he would report her if she reported him.

That first week after I came back from Whitby, Archie drove Melodie home in the evenings, or I walked with her, pushing my bike. She lived in a big shared house not far away from the city centre, and she always invited me in, and I always said no thank you. We were both lousy company. After that afternoon she didn't say anything else about what had happened with Rob and I didn't say anything about my experience, either. I thought about it, but it would only have been to make me feel better about not saying something earlier. We were mostly silent. In the evenings I went home and worked on my poem. The plan that had seemed so clear, sitting in the box pew at Whitby, had become less certain. I could see the merit of it but I doubted my ability to carry it out.

I was crying less but the pain was exactly the same. I thought about Nathan all the damn time. When I pulled an old, out-of-print book about close-up magic out of a box, I put it to one side for him, and I realised that what was keeping me going was not acceptance, but hope. I didn't know whether that was good or bad.

Whitby Loveday, sitting clear eyed in the

stillness of the church, had known that it was time to move on, and tell a new tale. Everyday Loveday was starting to think she'd just had a bit of a holiday moment. Archie takes a couple of weeks off once a year and when he comes back he's always full of ideas. The most recent one was to start a travelling book-circus with clowns and fire-eaters and books. (Me: books and fire? Really?) The next was to buy an ice cream van and kit it out as a bookshop and sell books in tourist areas in summer. (Me: while disappointing a hundred hot and previously happy children. You and I might think books are better than ice cream but I'm not sure that we're in the majority.) You get the gist. What looks good on holiday sits on the borderline between untenable and stupid when you get back to your life.

So although I worked on the poem I'd written in Whitby, I wasn't sure I was going to do anything with it. There was a version of me who would. She was the best version: she came and went, and couldn't be relied upon.

Nathan was as good as his word, and stayed away. Well, you'd expect that, wouldn't you? He didn't come in to the shop or, if he did, I wasn't there. But Melodie would have grassed him up for sure if she'd seen him.

I'd taken the Delia Smith book back to my flat but I'd pinned the postcard to the 'Found in a Book' noticeboard. Hidden in plain sight, I suppose. I felt odd about taking it home. I have no photographs, no letters, nothing from my old life (except me, unfortunately). Annabel said she would keep the stuff for me that I didn't take when I moved out. I'm sure she has. I don't need it. So I hid my mother's handwriting on the noticeboard, where I could look at it if I wanted to, but where it couldn't find its way into my hand in the middle of a wakeful night.

I came into work at 11 a.m. as usual the next Wednesday. Melodie looked paler than usual. The bruising was yellowing and she couldn't quite disguise the jaundice tinge with makeup, but this was worse than that. She came straight to me when I opened the door, and followed me through to the back.

'Loveday,' she said, 'Rob is next door. In the cafe. He wave at me when I pass by.'

'Are you sure?' I asked, because why say something useful when you can say something stupid. She nodded. I was tempted to tell Archie, but suddenly, looking at Melodie, her scared little heart-face, I was too furious to let a balding old bloke with a pipe get all the kicks. If there was going to be kicking, I was going to be the one doing it. I told her to stay put.

Rob was still there, sitting at one of the tables by the window, smirking as he saw me approach. I don't know why I ever thought he was handsome.

'Well, hello, Loveday,' he said. 'Seen your mum lately? I've heard prison-visiting can be quite a nice way to spend a Sunday, if you haven't got anything else to do with your life.'

'Shut the fuck up,' I said quietly, 'and piss off. And don't say anything about it being a free country. If you don't get up and go, I'm going to call the police. Melodie and I will tell them what you did, and then we'll see how brave you are.'

He crossed his arms, uncrossed them, took a drink of coffee. I thought it was probably cold. I took a gamble on him being more scared than he looked. I was more scared than I looked. All I had to do was hold out for longer than he did.

He looked up. I took a step away, just a half pace back, and his shoulders relaxed for a minute until I opened my mouth.

'I suspect we'll find,' I raised my voice, enough to make people look around and listen, 'that you only hit women. Did you know you fractured Melodie's cheekbone? What did you hit her with?'

Then he looked scared, for a second. I felt thrilled — it could be this simple — and then sick, because how was I different to my dad, if I was getting off on intimidating someone? Then I remembered how my mother did nothing wrong, and I thought of Melodie, trying to sleep, waking up every time she lay on the wrong cheek.

'Have you paid?' I asked. 'I'll walk you out.'

Rob raised his hands in a mock submission, 'have it your way' gesture, and stood up. He'd recovered enough to try and save some face. He stood up, gathered his things, and then stepped close to me, not touching, looking straight into my eyes.

'After you,' he said. 'Lead the way.'

I did, because the space was too small to make him go ahead of me, though I resented doing as he had said. Once we were outside on the pavement I turned. I saw that Melodie and Archie were watching from the window of the bookshop. I nodded to them: I'm okay. Rob had used the few steps of the exit to find his arsey equilibrium and he slouched in the early autumn sunshine, hands in his pockets, looking at me as though I was dinner.

'That was sexy,' he said.

I had thought and thought about asking him about my mother. I knew that I couldn't. I would have no way of knowing if he would tell me the truth, for a start. And my heart froze solid at the thought of saying her name to him. But right then I could have gone down on my knees and grovelled for any crumb. I took a breath and touched the jet pendant at my throat. And focussed on the job in hand. I'm good at that.

'Rob,' I said, 'get yourself some help. Please. I don't know what's going on but I can see that you're not well. I think there's a good person in you. Help them.'

For a second I thought he was going to cry. We looked at each other. Then he blinked the moment away and said, 'Maybe see you at poetry night later?'

'Yes,' I said, 'you will.' I had the satisfaction of seeing the shock on his face — he must have thought this was a masterstroke of intimidation, at once 'you can't stop me from doing what I want to do' and 'don't forget I know that you lied to the people you love'.

He walked off and I stood, committed now to the course of action that only a stronger, better, more courageous me would have taken.

I realised Archie had come out of the bookshop and was standing behind me. He put his big hand on my shoulder. It was steady and my skin hummed against it. That was when I realised I was shaking.

'That was brave,' he said. 'Don't do it again, Loveday.'

'Archie,' I said, 'will you come to poetry night tonight?'

I had a hard time persuading Archie that he mustn't do anything to Rob at the pub, because I wanted him to hear my poem. I had a harder time persuading Melodie not to come — in fact, I failed altogether: 'Melodie cannot be intimidated all her life,' she said, and I thought, *well, fair play to her.* Rob's cameo cafe appearance had rattled us all.

I texted Nathan and asked him to put me on the list of performing poets. It turned out that deleting his number was pointless, as my fingertips still knew it. He texted back immediately, a simple 'It's done,' and at lunchtime I went through the door marked 'Private', sat in the chair, and made sure that I knew my poem by heart. I wanted to be able to look Nathan in the eyes when I spoke it; I didn't want to stumble.

Archie closed the shop early and took Melodie and me for a meal. We went to a

Greek restaurant on a parallel street, about three minutes' walk away. I'd never been there.

'Archie! It must be fifty years since the Odessa Incident!' said the owner. I sometimes think that I am, in fact, in some monstrous piece of performance art, and one day Archie will take a bow and I'll discover that not a single element of my life since I walked into the bookshop the first time is true.

We ate moussaka and salad — I don't think we chose, I think it just came — and Archie talked non-stop about when I first started working for him. I let him get on with it. He did a sort of mini-play where he performed the parts of the customer, me, and himself:

CUSTOMER: Excuse me, do you have a book on cultivating vines?
ME: Probably.
ARCHIE: I think what Loveday meant to say was, let me show you where you might find exactly such a book.

Melodie laughed unnecessarily loudly. I hardly minded. He had a point. And what he doesn't know is that even though he would consider that I'm a lot better at that stuff than I used to be, I still think most people are a pain in the backside. So I win.

I didn't see Archie pay, just like I didn't see him order. I did see him put a foil takeaway carton in his Gladstone bag before we left. I guessed it was baklava: we hadn't had time for dessert. He asked me once or twice if I was all right and I said I was. I wasn't not. He asked Melodie and she said, 'Melodie still Melodie,' which was sort of encouraging as she hadn't been on full whimsy setting since Rob had hit her.

We walked to the pub, and because Archie needed to fill his pipe, and then walk along at his stately pace as he smoked it, and then have a long chat with the homeless man who sleeps in one of the doorways and another with a woman who was having difficulty in finding her friend's house, it was just before eight when we arrived. As we started to walk up the stairs I heard the end of Nathan's five-minute-warning announcement.

The first person I saw when I walked in was Vanessa. She walked over and hugged me. I'm not good at unexpected hugs, but I smiled and said that I was glad to see her, which I was.

'Nathan's at the bar,' she said. 'He's getting you a gimlet.'

'Thanks,' I said. I couldn't think of anything else to say so I introduced her to Melodie. I sat at what I thought of as my usual table and listened to Melodie witter and Vanessa admire her outfit, which consisted of DMs and a 1980s shot-silk dress with a tear in one sleeve, sort of Miss-Havisham-does-the-gardening.

Nathan came over, and the nearer he got the more I wanted to run, and cry, and touch him, and blurt, and hide, and kiss him, and generally behave as though Barbara Cartland had just sneezed me out. Of course I did none of those things, just sat there like — well, like me, wordless without a book to rely on. He put my drink down in front of me and then kissed my cheek, softly, in front of my ear. His eyes — for the second I dared look into them — were asking a thousand questions. I felt myself lean towards him.

'I put you on straight after me,' he said, just the sound of his voice ruffling me all over. 'Is that okay?'

'Yes,' I said. I felt as though my throat was closing. I wasn't sure I could do this.

Then Rob came in. I didn't see him at first but I saw Melodie's face go still mid-word and Archie look at me, ready to move, either to my side or to lob Rob down the spiral staircase, I wasn't sure which. I nodded to him: let it be.

Nathan had watched the looks bounce around. I saw him add it up. It hurt that I could read him so easily, and at the same time it made what I was about to do worth the effort.

He said, so only I could hear, 'Oh god. Melodie's face? Rob?'

'Yes,' I said. 'She knew he was coming.' Nathan looked at me and I looked straight into his eyes, something I'd been avoiding, and said, 'Trust me.'

'I will if you will,' he said, quietly, and I thought, *touché*. I deserved that. Then he looked at his watch. 'Shall we start?' he asked. He got up before I could say anything, and as soon as I saw him standing up there I felt the opposite of nervous, which was the last thing I expected. Three sharp claps and then he started to speak and I started to listen.

Beggars Would Ride
*As performed by Nathan Avebury at the
George and Dragon
York, October 2016*

I don't miss the things I thought I'd miss.
Well, I miss getting laid — who wouldn't —

and I miss the thought of you.
I miss being one of two people who are
    making a couple.
I miss washing up two of things in your
    kitchen and buying two coffees in the
    cafe next to the place where you work.
These things I miss.
These things I could have predicted I would
    miss.
So far, so average break up.
But I miss other things.
If you get a new tattoo I won't get to guess
    which book it comes from,
so I'll never solve the mystery of the
    missing first lines.
I miss the look on your face when you're
    reading,
and the twitches of your body when you
    sleep.
I miss your sarcasm and your sharpness.
I miss your good heart
that you try so hard to hide.
I wish you'd tell me what I did to make you
    go
and how I could undo it.
I wish you would talk to me.
I wish I was still buying two coffees in the
    cafe next to the place where you work.

There was a moment after Nathan finished

when I felt every head in the room swivel-
ling towards me — he hadn't taken his eyes
off me, and I didn't look at anyone except
him. I nodded because I didn't know the
facial expression for: if you still feel like that
when you've heard what I'm going to say,
then we'll talk.

My heart was steady but my legs had
forgotten their job as I got up. I wobbled,
and Nathan's arm was at my elbow.

'Okay?' he asked, and I nodded again and
he smiled.

I didn't feel very stable. I couldn't work
out what to do with my hands. They wanted
to clasp each other but I didn't want to look
as though I was reciting something in assembly. So I put my right hand on the top
of the microphone stand and my left in the
pocket of my jeans, where it found the
heart-shaped stone I'd bought in the church
in Whitby, and which I'd had close to me
ever since, as a reminder of how brave I
thought I could be, that afternoon.

I looked at Melodie's broken face, Archie's
solemn one, Rob's measuring, cut-me-and-
I'll-cut-you eyes, and then I looked at
Nathan, and I kept on looking at his face,
and I began.

I could be brave.

I got the first two words out and I felt how

feeble my voice was.

Nathan put his hand on his belly, a reminder: breathe here. I stopped, inhaled, pulling my breath down as far as it would go, exhaled. And I began.

Confession
As performed by Loveday Cardew at the
George and Dragon
York, October 2016

My mum killed my dad cause my dad used
    to beat her
And that's pretty much where I start and I
    end.
This is my story, so far.
I didn't know how to tell you.
I don't tell anyone.
I don't know where to start
I don't know how to write another ending.
If I tell you when I meet you you might not
    like me
Or you might think I'm damaged and be
    scared
Or you might think I'm damaged and like it.

You might be thinking that he hurt me
He never did
I thought he was brilliant
And he was, to a kid.

You might forgive my mother if you thought
    she was protecting me
I'll tell you this for nothing — she was far
    more wrecked than me
Cracked ribs, broken teeth, black eyes.
Social worker came but Mum did the full
    Tammy
Standing by her man till she didn't

Mum said it was an accident
And I think that's right
Things were bad, but not that bad
It was just another night
The courts and police and the foster care
wasn't a picnic but I didn't much care
I'd lost them both — first Dad, then Mum
Got moved to a new place where no one
    knew my name
Grieved and sulked and waited
Saw my mum in prison but I hated it
Decided I was better off with my books
Tried a boyfriend, he was awful.
Met another, he was you

I had another verse but I couldn't get it out.
It was a sort of 'now you know' stanza, and
I think I'd thought I would say it with an
eye on Rob, but I couldn't take my eyes off
Nathan and he nodded when I said 'he was
you' and I thought he might be crying. So I

stood still. I couldn't do anything else. There were pins dropping all over the place. I'd thought a lot about the poem, and standing up and saying it, and whether I could do it. I hadn't thought about afterwards. I suppose I was jumping off a cliff: it was all about making my feet do the opposite of their instinct for firm ground. I guess I'd assumed that once I was in the air I wouldn't have to make any more decisions.

Then Archie was on his feet, applauding, shouting, 'Brava!' as though he was at the bloody opera.

Rob was on his way down the stairs, so mission accomplished there.

Melodie was crying. Melodie cries at pictures of hedgehogs in teacups that she finds on the internet, but these tears were different. She smiled at me.

Nathan stood up. He nodded and started coming towards me. I thought about how I'd chosen a poem because it's a way of not talking and I wasn't up to the conversation. Not then.

So I bolted off the little stage and past the members of the audience and headed for the loos and I waited. I ran a tap, washed my face, and thought about the sea. I thought I knew what would happen next and, sure enough, the show went on. After a

369

minute or two the next poem was filling up the air I'd left, looking for attention: I heard laughter, applause, and I thought about how weird it was to no longer have a secret.

The door opened. Vanessa.

'Hey,' she said.

'Hi,' I said. I was braced but she didn't come in for a hug.

She just said, 'That was brave.'

'I don't know,' I said.

'I do,' she said. 'I know I have no right to say this, but I'm proud to know you, Loveday. I can't imagine.'

'Thanks,' I said.

'Nathan's waiting,' she said. 'He says the poets can take care of themselves, and you don't need to talk about it, but he wants to see you. He's downstairs.'

'Okay,' I said.

He was standing outside the pub on the pavement. He offered his arm, like an old-fashioned, cravat-wearing gentleman, and I took it. I felt the way you feel when you go out for a walk when it's just been raining: as though everything is different, better, even unremarkable pavements and buildings you walk past every day.

'Where to?' he asked. I knew that in the fairy tale I would say, 'your place', but I wasn't ready for that. And now that I didn't have secrets, I wanted to show him every-thing.

'I left something at the shop,' I said, 'something of my mum's. I want to go and get it.' Suddenly I needed the Whitby postcard to be in my hand. I felt as though I had moved a step closer to my mother tonight.

'Okay,' he said. We walked on, quietly, his hand on my hand where it peeped through the crook of his arm. I had thought I might feel more than this: some sort of great sense of unburdening, relief, giddiness, tears. I suppose I've been reading too many books. I just felt tired.

When we reached the shop he said, 'Why don't I get something to drink? I could come back to your place. I wouldn't expect to stay.' There's a smart, too-expensive-for-me off-licence on the corner.

'Okay,' I said. God, he was so easy to be with. I wondered if I would become easier, now that I wasn't protecting my softest place any more. It was too soon to say. 'I won't be long.'

'You amaze me,' he said. 'You're brave. Not just tonight. Going back to Whitby like that. All those awful memories.' And he kissed the top of my head, and headed for the off-licence.

I locked the door behind me but I didn't put the light on; the streetlight was enough for me to get to the noticeboard. I took the pin out of the postcard and let myself think of all I'd lost. I felt homesick, and angry.

I folded the oblong of card, handwriting in, Whitby Abbey out, and put it in my pocket, next to the heart-stone.

And then I realised.

There had been nothing in my poem about Whitby. Archie might have told Nathan I was on holiday there, but nobody knew why it would be significant to me. As far as Nathan was concerned, I was Ripon Girl.

No wonder he was so calm. He knew.

Now the world really did spin, and not in a good way, in a panicking, please-don't-throw-my-schoolbag-off-the-bus way.

I thought back to when I met him. It was only after that that the books started to come in, first the Penguin Classics, then the book of my dad's, then the cookery book with the postcard in it.

Rob hadn't admitted to having anything to do with the books, and it wasn't like him not to point out how clever he was.

Nathan had always looked too good to be true.

He had spent summers in Cornwall.

His family had stayed with a friend of his mother. She was called Jane.

Okay, it's not an unusual name. But: what if Nathan's mother's friend was my Auntie Janey? If Janey had got hold of my mother's books, in the jumble and panic of the house-clearing . . .

There was a rattle at the door, Nathan's voice: 'Loveday!' I stepped behind the nearest bookcase so he couldn't see me. He tried the door, rattled it, stepped back, looked both ways down the street, tried the door again. He pulled out his phone. I knew mine was off so I watched him wait, looking at the screen.

He walked off again. I suspected he was going to go on to my place. He'd need an hour, there and back. So all I needed to do was wait in the shop for forty minutes, by which time he'd be nearly back here, or he'd have returned to the pub. He'd go the short way, I'd go the long way. Easy.

My head was saying: Well, Loveday, if it looks too good to be true, then it probably is. My heart was different.

Not Nathan. Not Nathan. Not Nathan.

Over and over, my heart chanted those two words, as though they could take the truth back.

Nathan knew more about me than I'd told

him. Whenever my parents' books had showed up, Nathan had been close by.

I sat on the floor, my back against the bookshelf, legs stretched out in front of me so the toes of my boots caught the street-light, and I thought back over everything I could remember him saying, not saying. No bloody wonder he was so laid-back about the fact that I wouldn't tell him anything. He already knew it all. I wondered why he would have done it. And then I tried to think of a man I knew who'd been good to women they supposedly loved. Not my father. Not Rob. Even Archie loved them and left them.

I thought about my father, and the way my mother used to talk about him, before things were disastrous: 'At least with Dad you always know how he feels, Loveday.' I think it was probably after an outburst about work, a job not got. I was scared by his shouting. I didn't understand what she said then but I did now.

So. Here I was. Single, but I was single six months ago. I had a job that I loved and a boss who looked after me and a flat that was fine. I liked my own company well enough, and I still had that. I may have just told a room full of wannabe poets my deep-est, darkest secret but I wasn't stupid enoughly to think that it mattered much to anyone but me. Apart from that, things were the same.

Rob was off my back. Archie would go all touchy-feely for a bit. Melodie would be a nightmare, trying to catch the gossip and what she would perceive as the glamour. But I could wait that out.

And Nathan could piss right off.

I felt around the place where I kept my thoughts about my mother, my father, the massive mess they made of their lives and, by default, mine. Bringing it into the light didn't seem to have done anything new to it. It hadn't grown, or shrunk. If I was Cinderella, then I'd stayed out after midnight and my carriage was still a carriage after all. Except in my story it never really stopped being a pumpkin. Do I sound jaded? Well, let's swap places and we'll see how you do.

I was still shaking. And then, just as I'd rationalised myself into waiting another fifteen minutes, then going home and making beans on toast, the panic attack started.

My breath wouldn't come and my chest hurt. My hands were cold, my throat closing, as though it was trying to strangle me. I thought about standing up but there was no way I could do it; I was as good as nailed to the floor, everything stuck, no power, no agency over my limbs.

I would have cried out if I could, but my mouth wouldn't move and, anyway, there was no one to hear me.

Instead I counted to a thousand, slowly, and then I counted back to zero again. By the time I got there, I was not calm, exactly, but I was in a state where I was able to get myself out of the bookshop and back to my flat. I wanted to think; about Nathan and about my mum, about where I went from here.

Then the door rattled again. Nathan had made it back quicker than I thought. I wasn't going to face him now, when I was frightened and unprepared. I would work out how he'd got the books, why he was messing with my head like this, and then I would deal with him the way I'd dealt with Rob in the cafe earlier. I pulled my knees up so that my feet were out of the light and I held my breath, as though that would make a difference. There was a knock, another rattle, a pause, silence. I closed my eyes. Pictures moved behind my lids: the sea, St Mary's church. I tried to breathe deep. I thought about the postcard in my pocket but I didn't need to get it out to look at it. I could see it in my mind, as clearly as

I could still see my mother's face.

Books burn slowly.

Especially old books.

You get smoke first. The pages are so dense that there isn't that surrounding air that would make loose papers erupt. And the shop always smelled of smoke anyway, because of Archie, who carries pipe tobacco in his pockets and smokes his pipe in the shelter of the shop doorway when it rains.

Maybe that's why I didn't realise straight away that that second person at the door, with their rattle-knock-rattle, wasn't Nathan. It was someone with an alcohol-soaked handkerchief that they pushed through the letterbox, leaving a corner outside, and then lit, allowing the flames to flicker and rush down to the books and papers on the desk below.

No, there will not be a prize for guessing who struck the match.

By the time I worked out, with a jolt of terrified shock, that the smoke was more than eau de bookshop owner, the fire had taken hold. There wasn't a lot of flame but when I came out from behind the bookshelf where I'd hidden from Nathan, there was pretty much a wall of smoke. The pile of books and papers on the desk was on fire, and some of them had fallen on the floor, blocking my way to the door.

I half ran straight through the bookshop to the back where the fire escape was, and of course I couldn't move the bloody armchair.

It was dark and it felt as though the smoke was coming after me; suddenly the place was as unfamiliar as a forest in fog, impenetrable, full of witches.

The chair back was jammed into the space and I just couldn't shift it. I ran back towards the front of the shop — there was a fire extinguisher next to Archie's desk — but I couldn't get to that for the flames. I'd started to cough and couldn't stop. It had been quiet, but now there was a cackling: the wooden table and chairs burning, I thought.

I needed to go back to the back door and make the damn chair move, whether it wanted to or not. Archie always managed to shift it when the fire inspectors came, though when I thought about it I remembered that last time he'd had to get someone to help him with it. He'd joked that it was like the sofa stuck on the stairs in whichever Douglas Adams book that was. Still, I would just have to do it. I wasn't dying in a fire when I had Nathan's lying arse to kick.

When I turned around I saw that the smoke had sneaked in behind me, too, though it wasn't as dense at the back of the shop as it was nearer the front. There was a solid mass of flames where Archie's desk used to be.

I bowed down, lower to the ground, wondered if I should be crawling or if that would make me more vulnerable. My eyes had started watering — not that that made the stinging any less — and I started to grope my way, as good as blind, dizzy and disorientated. Back towards the fire escape.

I made a map in my head, combining what I knew with what I could feel, and wondering what the next best thing to getting out would be, if I couldn't get as far as the door. I thought of the corner at the back. Poetry/plays/maps. If I squeezed in under the bench would I be protecting myself or clambering into my grave?

The smoke was getting thicker. The heat was coming, moving faster than I could in the dark. I thought I could hear the fire alarm but it might have been part of the ringing and roaring in my ears — I couldn't trust my senses. I could feel my back, my calves, getting warmer; my stomach, in contrast, felt granite-cold, my heart salt-white. How long did I have before the ceiling came down? How long did I have? Maybe smoke inhalation would get me first. These were sober, calculated questions, Stephen Hawking thoughts. Curiosity.

And then, panic.

Not ten minutes ago I would have said I didn't much care whether I lived or died. Now I wanted to live. To see Nathan, walk on the beach, read all the books I hadn't read yet. Find my mother. Not necessarily in that order.

My body, suddenly, wanted to hyperventilate and sob and cry and do all of the other things that are really not wise if you're stuck in a burning building. I was having a hard time stopping it. I might not have had much of a life plan but dying in a fire sure as hell wasn't in it.

A crash of glass made me jump; I assumed that one of the windows had broken. A whoop of burning followed the crash, as the evening air cheered the flames on. So this could be it, for me. I might not have been very good at physics but I know that fire is faster than people, especially when they can't get the damn door open.

A rush of noise came in with the air. I heard sirens that seemed like a very long way away, and then shouting, closer. It took me a second or two to pick out my name.

Even the air felt hot. Seeing and hearing hurt.

But there it was, fighting through the smoke to find me. My name. And Archie, calling it.

I turned, even though putting my face towards the heat burned. I could feel the fire drying my tears as fast as the smoke was making them. The thought of Archie turned me into a little girl, desperate for rescue, and I opened my mouth and yelled, although very little sound came out and I got another lungful of smoke. I started to really cough then, and I think that's probably the sound Archie followed, because I'd never coughed like that before: a furball-hack, rasping through the smoke. I dropped to my knees.

He was almost on top of me before I saw him. He was doing a pretty good impression of the Angel of Death, with his Crombie coat over his head. He held his arms open and crouched to me, and I stood into the shape they made, under the shelter of the coat, which was holding a pocket of cooler air. I breathed in, too much, coughed again, fell against him.

He held me — the coat fell over my head, not cool, exactly, but not yet burning — and I felt him turn, pivoting around me. The smoke was coming at us from the side now: the shelves rammed with sci-fi and graphic novels had caught fire. Nathan was behind Archie, leather coat held over his head, and Archie pass-the-parcelled me into Nathan's hands. Archie shouted something, or tried to, but as soon as he opened his mouth he took a lungful of smoke and started coughing. Nathan turned on the spot the way Archie had done, wrapping the coat around me, and there, in front of us, was the broken window above the window seat, and the way back to life.

Nathan shoved me forward and I was halfway through to where Melodie and Vanessa were on the other side, reaching out to coax me through, steadying me as I stepped over the edges of the glass.

Then there was a crash and a cry from the shop. Archie. Nathan let go of me and I sort of fell onto the pavement. I heard the sirens get closer and I felt the heat on my back, making the October air chill in comparison.

I couldn't get up; my arms and legs could do nothing, and all I was was lungs and heart and mouth, as I hacked and howled the smoke and panic out of me. There were hands in my armpits and I was pull-dragged further down the road, away from the fire.

I wanted to call Archie's name, Nathan's, but my throat wouldn't let anything out. I could see that the fire was blazing through the shelves now, eating the books alive, and the street was filling with smoke. My eyes were streaming and it was only now, out in the air, that my body was starting to tell me all of the places where it hurt: eyes, throat, fingertips, the place where my lungs used to be. I coughed and hacked and, as the air burned my nose as I breathed in, I willed my legs to work, to turn me around and get me back in there. I was aware of talk around me — Nathan's name, Archie's — and of more people gathering.

There was too much of the wrong things in the air: coughing, ash, voices calling, the crash of, I assumed, a falling bookshelf, and the sirens and the lights, deafening now. I was thinking of what the crash, the cry might have been. And Nathan was too stupid/good to leave Archie in there. Then I remembered that Nathan wasn't good after all. Still, the thought of him trapped in there made my heart shake.

I saw two shapes emerging from the bookshop window, one tall, one round as a pheasant, and I saw them double over, coughing.

The next thing I knew, there was someone

with a kind face but a grip that wasn't taking no for an answer, holding my arm, guiding me up into the back of an ambulance, putting an oxygen mask on my face. My hands, on my knees, were shaking, cold now, dirty and unfamiliar. The oxygen felt as though it was hurting my throat more than the smoke had; whatever it was doing in my lungs didn't feel as though it was helping, though I knew that if I tried to get the mask off, the steely paramedic would have something to say. Also, I doubted I could lift my hands.

The paramedic was talking but my ears weren't really taking anything in. The blood pressure monitor clenched, released, clenched my upper arm, and there was a clip on the middle finger of my right hand, now, bone-white against my sooty skin. I saw an arc of water, soon joined by another, going in through the shop window.

Books. Fire. Water. I closed my eyes and, as though I had given my permission, the ambulance doors closed and it moved away.

■ ■ ■ ■

POETRY

■ ■ ■ ■

2016
OH, THE PEOPLE

Smoke inhalation doesn't kill you — if you're so-called lucky — but it sure as hell doesn't make you stronger. I was feeble. It hurt to breathe and it hurt to cry, but I couldn't stop crying. Confined to bed in hospital, I pretty much slept and coughed and sobbed for all of the next two days.

The police interviewed me and I managed to choke out Rob's name and the little I knew about his illness. It seemed impossible that he had done what he'd done. My mind couldn't get around it. I hoped he had thought the shop was empty.

Melodie came to see me. The bruise was nastier and yellower, and she hadn't bothered with the makeup. She was wearing a man's striped shirt over jeans and had a scarf around her head, like she was channelling land girl. I told her that she still looked worse than I did, but she didn't laugh.

She said that Nathan had come back to the pub to see if I'd gone back there, and she and Archie and Vanessa had come with him when he'd returned to the bookshop. When they arrived, the fire was just getting hold. Melodie had dialled 999 but there had been no way of stopping Archie and Nathan mounting a rescue mission.

'They like tigers for you, Loveday,' Melodie said.

To give her credit, she wasn't getting off on it. She had told the police what had happened at the poetry night — so much for 'the only people who know Loveday's story are a bunch of poets who will have forgotten it all in a fortnight' — and, when they asked her about her eye, she told them Rob had done it. They were around at his place before you could say 'Leonardo da Vinci'. He'd been arrested for reckless arson, and was being questioned. It looked as though he would go to prison. I'd explained to the police that I was hiding, that the lights were off, and he would have thought that the place was empty. Even so, the fact that he'd used an accelerant damned him. They assured me that he would have a full psychiatric assessment and that would be a factor in sentencing. I was furious with him, yet at the same time, I couldn't help being sad for him, too. One moment. One match. The end of life as you know it.

I couldn't think about the bookshop for long, in the way that I wouldn't hold my fingers in a flame. Our beautiful, ramshackle, peculiar home-from-home was as good as gone. It doesn't take a genius to work out that what the fire hadn't wrecked, the water had. Melodie said that no structural damage had been done and the neighbouring buildings were okay; in terms of a building fire it wasn't, apparently, that bad. In terms of a bookshop fire, obviously, it was a different matter. My experience of Archie was that he did a good job of diffidence, but I was fairly sure that the bookshop had been the most solid place in his life; he'd stayed there longer than he'd stayed anywhere else, and though he said that was simply because he'd run out of miles when he ended up in York, I didn't believe him. He'd chosen the bookshop.

When I asked about Archie and Nathan, I was told that Nathan had been discharged the morning after the fire, having being kept in overnight for observation, and that Archie was 'stable', which I took to mean that he was in the same state as me: temporary physical wreck, hopefully no permanent damage done. I had burns on my forearms and lungs that felt as though they had been sandpapered and then soused in vinegar. My eyes ached and my nose bled.

I felt weak and stupid and angry. I lay, dozing and trying not to think about Nathan, thinking about the bookshop, instead. Archie was insured and so, although most of the stock would be going straight in a skip, we would be able to start again. New everything or, knowing Archie, old everything; we'd be trawling flea markets and antique shops for bookcases and a table, a desk to replace the one in the window where the till and all of the papers were kept.

I decided I would persuade him to have shelves built floor to ceiling all around the sides of the shop, chased to fit against the higgledy-piggledy walls so that we could make the most of the space. Then if he wanted to rescue sad old bookcases from junk shops to fill the central area, we'd both be happy. Well, happy wasn't quite the word. Part of me knew that we just had to get on with it; another part was all about turning my face to the wall, closing my eyes, never walking down that street again.

And I was assuming that Archie would want to rebuild. He might not. He might decide it was time to go and sail the seven seas again, or whatever. I suppose I would just have to do what everyone else without a job did: apply for Jobseeker's Allowance, put together a CV which said, in my case, 'good academic qualifications, not much of a team player, has had one job, which she did pretty well, but only because she was left to her own devices'. Alternatively, I could hang a sign that said 'unemployable' around my neck.

Lying in my too-narrow, too-high hospital bed, I'd think like that for a while and then I'd give myself a kick and remind myself that Archie wouldn't admit defeat and he wouldn't abandon me. Maybe there were other alternatives. A book boutique, where we turned down all the crap and became properly antiquarian. Some sort of subscription library for academics. We could set ourselves up as book detectives. Archie would like that. We could hunt down obscure books and charge people a fortune for the privilege. Well, Archie wouldn't, he'd smoke his pipe and say, 'Loveday, did I ever tell you about the time when . . .' and I would sort of zone out — listen to the sound of his voice but not the actual words — and do the work, and we would both be happy. Yes, he might go for the book detectives idea. We wouldn't have to worry so much about restocking then.

Before I'd been able to talk myself down off this particular daydream, the nurse who I disliked least — she didn't try to talk to me and her hands were gentle — poked her head around the door and said, 'There's a visitor for you. Are you up to it?'

'Yes,' I said, because I was sick of my carousel mind, and I hoped it might be Archie.

It was Nathan.

My head and my heart disagreed about whether to let him stay. He had known about my history and not told me. He had planted the books that freaked me out. He was never on my side, but he encouraged me to think that he was. And he had come into a burning building to save me, and gone back to rescue Archie. The world had shifted. Only a bit. I couldn't decide what to do so I closed my eyes. Maybe he would make my mind up for me. I was still on the wrong side of tired.

His boots squeak-squeaked on the floor as he came towards the bed and touched my hand. I opened my eyelids and looked up at him.

I was used to being the pale one, but I was getting a lot of competition from him and Melodie all of a sudden.

'Loveday,' he said. He kissed my forehead.

I didn't stop him but I didn't react.

'Thanks,' I said, 'for getting me out.'

'It was scary in there,' he said. He sat down, and put his head in his hands. 'The bookshelf that fell just missed Archie.'

'The nurses told me,' I said.

He didn't say anything, just sat with his forehead resting on his palms. I noticed a bandage on his hand. I touched it.

'What's this?' I said. I sat up, swung my legs down over the side of the bed. They dangled, because heaven forbid that anyone in a hospital be allowed to get in or out of bed with anything less than an undignified hop. I felt wobbly, vulnerable.

'Oh, it's nothing,' he said, without raising his head.

'It doesn't look like nothing,' I said.

'It's a burn, that's all.'

'So you're not badly hurt?'

'No.' He smiled. 'I'm fine, Ripon Girl. You gave me a fright, though.'

I hadn't been sure how to start the conversation, but he'd just given me my cue. 'Don't call me that,' I said.

He looked up, puzzlement painted onto his face. 'What?'

I laughed, though it turned into a cough. I couldn't believe his front. 'You bastard,' I started, but then I had to stop to pull in some breath.

'What?' Still the puzzled look. Not even the grace to admit he'd lied to me.

'You know what,' I said. 'You knew about Whitby. I never told you I was from there. You knew. You lied to me and you put the books in the shop for me to find —' I was just about to let go of everything I was holding — the pain, the fury — when something I wasn't expecting happened.

Nathan looked straight at me and his eyes were full of anger. 'For fuck's sake, Loveday,' he said, and his voice was quiet but it was oh, so furious. 'Have you any idea what I've been through? Me. Not you. Just this once. And I don't mean the fire.' He got up, the chair scraping as it rushed back over the floor, and he paced to the window, back again, and stood too far away from me for me to touch. 'I love you. I've loved you since I saw that notice you put up in the window. I've waited and I've put up with all your crap —'

'No one made you,' I said. I could feel that I was going to cry. I wanted to touch him but I was afraid he would shake my touch away.

'You made me,' he said, 'because — because I loved you and I knew there was a reason. And then your poem, Loveday, your poem . . .' He was crying, not moving, standing straight with tears running down his face. 'I heard your poem and I thought, god. I don't know what it's like to have been through what you've been through, I can't imagine, but it made you make sense. And I thought, now we can start. Really start.' The rage went out of him as suddenly as it had filled him.

I hopped down from the bed and took a step towards him, took his hand. He didn't hold it out to me but his fingers curled around mine.

'Nathan,' I said. I was crying too.

He looked at me, reached for my other hand. 'And then you disappeared when I went to get the wine. The fire. I thought you were dead, Loveday. Can you imagine what that was like? We got you out. And now you're accusing me of — of what, exactly?'

'You knew,' I said, 'about Whitby.'

'Not until — after,' he said. He sighed, empty now, and sat down.

'After what?'

'After you —'

I saw that he was searching for the right word. I don't mind that. I waited. He took a breath, looked me in the eye. 'After you dumped me.'

Ouch. Well, probably the right choice of

word. It was my turn to think of something to say, but then Nathan ploughed on, his gaze on his hands. 'I couldn't make sense of it, Loveday. I mean, I knew what you were like, but I was sure that you loved me.'

'Yes,' I said. It came out before I could stop it.

'So I went to see Archie. Melodie had told me that you were in Whitby. I took him out for lunch and we drank a lot and I told him what had happened. He put me on my honour not to say anything to you, and then he told me about your parents.'

'Archie doesn't know about my parents,' I said.

'He does,' Nathan said. 'Oh, Loveday. He saw you put the pound on the table for *Possession*. He decided to give you a chance. Your foster-carer came to check him out.'

'What?' I said. Not very original, I know, but Nathan had just taken my very fragile world out of its protective covering and kicked it all around the floor. 'I don't understand.'

He stood up, and he moved next to me, and he kissed the top of my head, my greasy hair with the smell of smoke forever in it, and he said, 'I know. Come and see Archie. He's waiting for us.'

I had to go in a wheelchair, with something to hold the drip that was keeping me hydrated until my throat could cope with as much water as I needed. Archie was up a floor and I was still a bit shaky on my feet. Nathan's boots squeaked us along the lino floor of the hospital corridor, and he went faster than most of the other patients, so we veered around people with walking frames and crutches. The rhythm of his footsteps calmed me down. He didn't say anything. I'm not sure there was anything either of us could say. I'm not exactly verbose at the best of times but there was a big old shocked space in my head where the thoughts ought to be, and although I knew I must have questions — fury — things to say, there was no evidence of them, yet. Just the sound of the boots and the shape of his kiss on my scalp.

Archie looked wrong in a hospital bed. I know it's said that people look smaller when they are ill, but Archie looked too big. I'd seen his bedroom, wandering around looking for an unoccupied loo at one of his parties. The room itself was vast, and his bed was big enough for at least three — no, I didn't ask why — and pillowed and cushioned to all hell, like beds in country house adverts in magazines. Definitely an Archie bed, unlike the hospital single, with the bars and the plastic-covered mattress.

When we went in he was looking out of the window at the grey sky. He was on a drip, like me, and part of his face and one of his arms was bandaged. His eyes were bloodshot and he did look a little bit deflated.

When he saw me his face brightened. I suppose mine did too. 'Loveday!'

'Archie,' I said. 'How are you?' It was one of the few times in my adult life that I actually felt as though I really, really needed to hug someone. But between the wheelchair and the height of his bed and my wobbliness and his bandaged arm and our two drip stands, I decided against, and reached out to hold his good hand. He raised it to his lips.

'Thank you,' I said.

'I would never have forgiven myself if I'd lost you,' Archie said.

I took a deep breath. I kept on doing that, forgetting how it hurt. 'How are you?' I asked again, when I'd recovered.

'I'll live,' he said.

'Thank you,' I said again. And then I thought I was going to cry, but I didn't, just sat there, so full of tears and questions that not a word or a sound would come out. Archie had tears running down his face and getting lost in his jowls, but he wouldn't let go of my hand.

After what seemed like ages he took his hand back, pulled a handkerchief from the breast pocket of his pyjamas, and wiped his face. 'Mr Avebury,' he said, 'would you be good enough to bring some tea? Then we can talk.'

'Back in a minute,' Nathan said, and Archie went back to looking at me. I felt fidgety under his gaze.

'You knew,' I said. I had to start somewhere, if only to get Archie talking — I don't think he'd ever been quiet for so long, and it was disconcerting.

'Yes,' he said. And then, 'Patience, Loveday.' Which struck me as a bit rich coming from someone who gets bored by the time he's got to Defoe if he's tidying the classics.

'I don't feel very patient,' I said. My voice was rasping; I sounded more annoyed than I meant to. Fortunately Archie is used to me sounding more annoyed than I mean to, and didn't take any notice.

'That was quite a performance,' he said, 'and quite a poem.'

'Yes,' I said.

Poetry night seemed like another age, another person. Being in hospital, the bookshop wrecked, made me feel as though I'd side-stepped into another life. It was a bit like when I went into foster care. I was me, but I wasn't, because my surroundings had changed and my life had taken what a blurb writer might describe as 'an unexpected twist'. And then another one.

'Thanks for being there.' I knew that he'd know I meant more than the poetry.

'I wouldn't have missed it,' Archie said. 'I was very proud of you.'

'Thanks,' I said. And then Nathan came back with three teas and three of those muffins that come in sealed individual plastic bags. I looked at Archie. 'Well?' I said.

Archie sighed. 'Please, Loveday, hear me out.'

He started on the day I had to bring in the permission form to work — I was fifteen — and Annabel had signed it. She'd added 'foster-carer' in brackets. He'd asked me if she was my foster-mother and I'd chewed his head off: she wasn't my mother. I didn't remember, but it sounded in character for me, at the time.

'She came to see me, the next week,' he said, 'and I liked her immediately. She was nicely dressed and she was fierce with me. She was determined to protect you. I took her out to lunch. She gave nothing away.

She was completely professional, although she was pale. I told her she looked like a weary Modigliani. She said she didn't take kindly to flirting.'

I laughed. I couldn't help myself. 'Sounds like Annabel,' I said, and then I was crying. Nathan had a handkerchief, and so did Archie. I had a tissue in my dressing gown pocket and I used that.

'She talked about "safeguarding" and "vulnerability" and I wouldn't have been surprised if she'd asked to look at my teeth. I was tempted to tell her that if you'd got a weekend job in Sainsbury's, the manager probably wouldn't have allowed quite such a thorough investigation. In the end, I said to her, "Old Archie isn't stupid, I can see that there are what you might call issues. There's limited trouble she can get into in a bookshop and I'll look out for her." '

'This was when I first started?' I said. I thought of myself, getting on the train from Ripon to York every Saturday morning, imagining that I was temporarily free of the day-to-day grimness of being The Child Whose Mother Killed Her Father With a Pan Lid. Archie might not be stupid, but I was.

'Yes,' Archie said. 'I told Annabel I wouldn't tell you that she'd been to see me

401

and we agreed to keep in touch. She came to see me when you were seventeen and your mother was going to be released and you were refusing to see her. She broke down in the middle of the shop, and I took her out for a drink, and that's when she told me the whole story.' He reached for his handkerchief.

'Are you okay?' I asked, because I am the queen of the stupid question.

'Yes,' he said. 'I remember thinking of . . . all you must be going through. I almost talked to you about it, but Annabel said she thought the shop was a place of escape for you, so I kept quiet. It wasn't easy.'

'I expect your spy training helped,' I said. If you can't cope, deflect.

'Of course,' he nodded.

I had no idea what to think. I started out angry, as though he and Annabel had tricked me. And then I felt myself deflate, go fuzzy at the edges, as something I had always believed turned out to be a lie. My life at Lost For Words was not my own, not separate to my back story. And therefore not made, as I'd always thought, without pity or allowances.

I should have been angry — I was angry, but I was also tired, so tired of it all. My past, my mother, the ache and pull of missing her, like stitches that never heal. I could feel that I was crying. The tears stung my face.

'What about the books?' I asked. 'Whose bright idea was that? Because it really freaked me out.'

Archie and Nathan looked at each other, at me. 'What books?' Archie asked. His face isn't as good as hiding his feelings as he thinks it is. I could tell he didn't know what I was talking about. Nathan didn't, either.

'So it really wasn't you,' I said to Nathan.

'What?' he asked, then, 'No. I have absolutely no idea what you're talking about, Loveday.'

I looked from one to the other. Archie's face was still, resting after a fit of coughing, and he needed to shave. He looked miserable.

I explained about the Penguin Classics, the Kate Greenaway, Delia Smith, the postcard. How I'd suspected Rob of tracking down my mother to get one over on me, then I'd thought Nathan was on a mission masterminded by Auntie Janey. As I explained, I could hear how crazy my suspicions sounded.

'How did you think I was getting the books to you?' Nathan asked. 'By magic?'

'Um,' I said, because I realised that that

was pretty much what I had thought. Conan Doyle could have had some fun with me. 'The books coincided with you turning up.'

'We don't exactly run a secure system,' Archie said. 'Anyone could have left them. Put them on the step. I don't know what your mother looks like. She could have come in when you weren't there.'

'Well,' I said. I hate it when Archie's right. Except he wasn't.

'My mother isn't allowed to know anything about me. How would she know where I worked?' I asked. I didn't know whether I wanted her to have delivered the books or whether I wanted there to be (yet) another possible explanation.

'I don't have all the answers, Loveday,' Archie said. He closed his eyes.

Nathan, who had been silent through all of this, though at some point had taken my hand, said, 'I didn't know any of this until after you'd gone to Whitby. I promise.'

The idea of them talking about me behind my back made me feel a bit creeped out. I felt ten years old again. I felt the way you do — although you, dear reader, are unlikely to know — when social workers and judges and a whole lot of other people who don't really know you at all are deciding what needs to be done with you, because your parents are suddenly unavailable. I felt sick.

Archie said, 'He pumped me full of Viognier and he wouldn't take no for an answer. Melodie had been in with her black eye. I was all at sixes and sevens.'

'You sent me to Whitby,' I said. He wasn't off the hook yet. 'Even though you knew.'

'You said you wanted to go there,' Archie said. 'If you hadn't, I never would have suggested it. You seemed to be — healing. A year ago wild horses wouldn't have dragged you to a poetry night, and Mr Avebury here wouldn't have stood a chance. I thought you could get some air, and some rest, and a break. I'd know where you were. You'd be safe and I could come to get you if you needed me.'

I still couldn't get my mind around how much they knew about me. 'I'm not a bloody toy,' I said. it was the closest I could come to expressing how I felt: picked up, posed.

'No,' Nathan said, 'you're someone we love.'

I bit back all of the things I could have said to that and so something I hadn't fully considered slipped out of the space. 'Where's my mother now? Do you know?'

'She lives in Leeds,' Archie said.

Leeds. I closed my eyes. It was odd to

think of my mother in a real place, somewhere I'd been to with Annabel, who had
taken me to a Christmas market there. I
was used to thinking of her in the abstract:
'inside' or 'out' but not in a real setting,
somewhere where she might buy milk or
wait for a bus.

'Have you seen her?'

'No, but Annabel has. She's doing well.
She'd love to see you.'

I put up a hand, panic rising, and Archie
stopped talking.

'No,' I said. I didn't need to think about
it. Or want to.

Archie nodded, as though he was agree-
ing. 'A letter came for you, at the shop,
when you were away. It had a return address on the back, so I guessed it was from
your mother. I was waiting for the right moment to give it to you. Maybe after I'd heard
your poetry performance, if it was what I
thought it was going to be. But — events
overtook.'

I smiled at him, though it hurt the burned
skin on my lip. 'Thanks, Archie,' I said. I
held his hand in one of mine, and I was still
clinging to Nathan with the other one. I
looked into one round face with a singed
moustache, one lean one with honest blue
eyes and a mouth I would never get tired of

kissing. 'Thank you,' I said again, and then I had to take my hands back to wipe my tears.

'The letter is in my bag,' Archie said. 'It's under the window. I think there might be some baklava in there as well, if someone would be so good as to pass it.'

When Nathan wheeled me back to my room, I got into bed and closed my eyes. I was doing it because I didn't want to talk any more before I'd had time to think about everything. I didn't intend to fall asleep. But I did. When I woke up it was twilight and Nathan had gone.

I looked at the ceiling and I thought about my life, especially the bit of it since I'd left care, when I was eighteen. I had been so determined that I was on my own: once my parents had gone, I was someone no one wanted. And I made it so.

Our pasts are as unfixed as our futures, Nathan's poem had said, the first time I saw him perform. And then: the freedom to tell a different story.

I thought about Annabel, and instead of seeing her as someone who had been getting on with her life the way that I was getting on with mine, I realised how much she'd done for me. She'd made a safe place for me. Her grown-up children had never come to stay when I was there. She'd gone to them, from time to time, when I was on school trips; I had never thought of how she was making sacrifices for the sake of my wellbeing. She sometimes had friends around in the evening and, more rarely, went to the cinema, once I was in sixth form.

But because Annabel wasn't my mother — because she wasn't the person I chose to have looking after me — I didn't see any care at all. I saw duty. I knew that I was lonely. It didn't occur to me that she might be lonely too. It was only now that I saw how isolated I must have made her, and how much she did care, coming to Archie, checking him out — I'd have loved to be a fly on the wall for that — staying in touch. Finding a way. I'd written her out, but that didn't mean she was gone.

Annabel was there. Archie was there. My mother was there, even when she wasn't.

It was tempting to be angry, and part of me was. Nobody likes being lied to, and I hated the idea of people talking about me, plotting behind my back. But I lay looking at the ceiling and I wondered what other choices I had given them. I think we can agree that there weren't that many. They moved me from Whitby to Ripon, they gave me a cover story and a safe place, and the rest was up to me. They led me to water. I wouldn't drink.

It wasn't bloody-mindedness. Not really. Not to begin with, anyway. It was griefs and losses, piled one on top of another onto a little ten-year-old who didn't know anything outside her cosy home, where her parents tried to protect her even if they didn't know how to protect themselves. All I could do was create silence, because every voice that I heard wasn't one of the two I wanted to hear. Nobody bothers children who read. I read. And when I started to un-numb, I had become the girl who reads, who writes, who likes her own company and doesn't say much. I was the non-participative teenager, the self-sufficient loner. I was Ripon Girl, who went straight to her room. And I was, under all of that, the person who didn't know how to ask anyone to help her.

The nurse came to check on me. It was nearing eight. Not too late to start a different story. I took my phone out of the bedside cabinet and switched it on. Before I could think about it too much, I dialled Annabel's home number, which I'd never forgotten.

'Hello?' she said. Her voice was warm and

soft, as ever.

'It's Loveday,' I said. 'I've missed you.'

'Loveday,' she said, like breathing out. Then, 'Is everything alright?'

Of course, I thought, she would think I was calling because there was a problem. I decided to ignore the question for now. There were more important things to say.

'Archie's told me everything,' I said. 'I'm calling to say thank you, and I'm sorry.'

'You've nothing to apologise for,' Annabel said.

We talked for a little while. I got in first with the questions and she told me about her family, and Ripon, and how she was retired now, from work and fostering, and she was filling her days with gardening and volunteering. I thought about how lovely she was. And then, of course, she wanted to know how I was doing. I told her where Archie and I were.

'Do you want me to come?' she said. 'I could come tomorrow.'

And I said yes.

It was that easy.

I didn't yet think what I would do about my mother, yet. But I knew that I would do something, and for the first time in a long time I felt warmth when I thought about her. *I'll never stop loving you, LJ,* she'd written, in one of the last letters I read. I'd torn it up. But I'd never stopped loving her, either. And there was a new letter, now, when I was ready.

I wasn't stupid; I knew we were a long way away from a Louisa May Alcott ending. But maybe we could have something. I picked up the crumpled Whitby postcard, which was on the bedside table, propped against the water jug, still smelling of smoke. My mother was full of love for her family then. She would still be full of love for me now. She had tried to come for me but something had stopped her. I looked at her handwriting on the envelope Archie had had in his bag. I would open it tomorrow. I'd be ready then.

Somewhere around five in the morning, I drifted off to sleep.

The nurses woke me for painkillers at seven, then let me drift off again.

The next thing I knew, there was mid-morning light filling the room and Nathan was sitting on the straight-backed plastic chair next to my bed. His sleeves were rolled back, his elbows on his thighs, his forehead in his palms. I saw writing along his forearm. He was close enough for me to reach out and touch it.

'What's that?' I said.

'My tattoo.' He stretched out his arm. I read, 'The first primroses were beginning to bloom', the words inked onto his skin in a flowing script. I couldn't speak. It was the end of the last line of *Watership Down*.

I kissed the back of his hand, found my voice. 'Thank you,' I said.

He nodded. 'I worked out *Possession*', he said, 'and *The English Patient*.'

'Thank you,' I said again, 'that's amazing of you.' I meant it. In Nathan's mislaced boots, I wouldn't have been making any commitments to me.

He looked at me and sort of smiled, but it wasn't a real smile, and then he kept on looking at me, as though I was written in a foreign language and he was trying to find a word he recognised. He stood up, then sat down again, suddenly, as though he'd only just remembered he was standing.

'Loveday,' he said, 'I went to see Archie. Just now.'

'Good,' I said. 'I'm going to go back later. I've thought about everything. I'm lucky to have him.'

And then Nathan's eyes made a sort of wince and he was crying, shaking his head. 'Loveday,' he said, 'Archie . . . Archie died.'

'What?' I'd heard wrong, obviously.

'Just now. Just —' He waved a hand,

indicating the area behind his shoulder. 'I went to see him, so I could tell you how he was doing, and one minute he was talking, saying how glad he was that everything was out in the open and how proud he was of you, and the next —' Nathan was sobbing now, struggling to speak.

'What? What happened?' I got off the bed so that I could reach him properly, put my hand on his shoulder instead of touching the back of his hand with my fingertips.

'He died,' Nathan said. He took a deep breath and then he put his good hand over my hand, covering it. There was redness on his knuckles and two of the nails were jagged at the quick, black underneath, where the soot had worked its way into his skin.

Everything stopped, for a second; even, I swear, my heart.

'No,' I said. It was like someone, somewhere had just taken a photograph of Loveday's worst day ever (2) and the world had paused at the shutter-click.

Then, I got it. Then, I really started to hurt. I was standing with my hand on Nathan's shoulder and he cried and I didn't, just listened to the sound of the world collapsing around me. Being trapped in a burning bookshop had nothing on this.

'It was his heart,' Nathan said. He looked

up at me. I felt myself swaying — that 'was' did it, I think — and he put out his arm and I sat on his lap. I couldn't say anything, but I rested my cheek against the top of his head, and I — well, I don't know what I did. It was like someone had taken away my sky.

Nathan's arm went around my waist and I felt the strength go out of me. 'He had a heart attack. Right there in front of me. They did the — everything they do — but he died.'

I opened my mouth to say: 'Stop saying died'. But no words came. I just started to cry and, even though the salt hurt on the outside and the effort hurt on the inside, the physical pain was nothing compared to the way that my feelings were ripping at me, and it was a long, long time until the tears stopped.

■ ■ ■ ■

MEMOIR

■ ■ ■ ■

2016
CHOOSE

My precious Loveday,

It wasn't hard to find you. Annabel and I have written to each other many times. Once she told me that you worked in a second-hand bookshop. Another time she mentioned York. She was scrupulous about protecting you — something that comforted me more than you can imagine — but I had nothing to do but analyse her letters, and I made a connection that might be true. It was worth exploring.

There are eighteen second-hand bookshops in York and so I decided to start with them. If I couldn't find you, I would expand the search to Yorkshire. (Because, of course, if you lived in York it would be easy for you to travel by bus or train. You might have a car, although Annabel hadn't mentioned you learning to drive. I have a lot of time to think about these things.)

I started by ringing the bookshops and

asking for Loveday, but after the first two I thought, what if you answer the phone? I didn't want our first contact to be a shock. I think I owe it to you to be gentle. So I decided to take the train to York on my days off, and look.

Your bookshop was the second one I went to, and when I was standing outside deciding whether to go in or to look through the window, I saw the sign about the lost poetry book, which said 'come in and ask for Loveday'. Suddenly I was terrified. I went to have a cup of tea in the cafe next door and I watched people coming and going in the street, and I wondered what to do. I knew I couldn't just come in, call your name, hug you tight, even though that was all I wanted to do.

And then there were all of the things we had to talk about. Where would we start? How could we plunge in to that conversation when we hadn't spoken for so long? And I know you'd made it clear that you didn't want to talk. But I hoped that there had been enough time apart for us to try.

So I made a plan. I knew you'd remember all the books we chose together. I still had them — they'd all been stored for me, by my social worker — and I'd read the prison library copies of every single one of them. So I thought I could come to see you, catch you after work, and bring them, and then if I did that we would have something to talk about, something easy to begin with.

I arrived not long before the shop closed and I waited opposite and along the way a bit, at the bus stop. I had the books in a box, and it was heavy.

You came out of the shop and locked the door behind you. I just looked at you: your face was serious, the way it used to be when you were colouring in or reading, learning lines or measuring out the ingredients for the parkin — but it was beautiful. Those eyes of yours, as bright as stars. The way you moved, the way you shook your hair back — everything was a memory, and I was pinned down by the shock and the pleasure of seeing you. You went down an alleyway and came back a few minutes later wheeling a bike. I tried to call your name but my mouth wouldn't work. I was crying. A man at the bus stop offered me a tissue. Things like that — unexpected contact — scare me a bit, these days. By the time I'd recovered, you had gone.

So I left the books on the step. I didn't know if you would recognise them but I liked the idea of you handling them, and maybe remembering you and I in the bookshop near the bridge.

Next time I came, I made it into the shop. You weren't there but I talked to a lovely man in a mustard-coloured shirt, who I think must have been the owner. I left the book with some others in a box when he wasn't looking.

I was busy at work for the next month, and short of money, so I couldn't come again for a while. When I did, I brought the Delia Smith and I left the postcard in it. I didn't know whether I was going to dare to talk to you or not. I kept thinking about you, so grown-up, so beautiful, and I didn't know how to approach you. I knew that you had hated me. I thought you might, still. I hoped the books might make things easier. I saw them as messengers. But the day I brought the cookery book, I saw you through the window and I knew I wasn't brave enough to ever tap you on the shoulder or say your name, just like that, the way any of the people that you see every day would. I decided to write a letter. This is the letter. Well, it's what feels like the hundredth version of it.

I'm not going to try to tell you everything now, and I'm not going to try to explain anything away. I just want to try to say enough to tell you what you might need to know, so that you can decide whether you have a place for me in your life, or not.

I'm back in the world now, and I don't think my life will change much. I work in a bakery, and I have a little flat, and I belong to a reading group, and if I could change the past then I would. But I can't. All I can do is tell you where I am, and wait, and hope.

I've written a lot of letters over the years. To you, of course, and to Annabel. When I was first in prison I wrote to your dad's family, and Janey wrote back and asked me not to write again. I didn't, of course. She was quite polite, considering. I don't know what I was thinking. Well, I do. I was thinking; I want people to understand. I want them to forgive me. But I know forgiveness isn't easy.

When you started to miss visits it broke my heart, but I wasn't surprised. It was all explained to me. The rights of the child. The panic attacks, the nightmares. Trauma. Time. Patience. I threw things and I screamed; I was medicated. I imagined them saying, well, there's a temper on her for sure. Six of one, half a dozen of the other in that marriage.

I had counselling. I was seen, at least partly, as a victim of my circumstances. You can read books about domestic violence until they come out of your ears but unless you've been there you never understand that you might love someone who hurts you, because you know that it's the best part of them that loves you and the worst part of them that hurts you and they really, really want to be the best them. Your father was a good man with a good heart and a bad temper. People told me I was in denial. Maybe I was. All I wanted to talk about was you, because that was a new pain, every day. Thinking about your father was a rumble, like the sea when we lived so close to it, but thinking about you was like starting each day to find I'd woken up outside, in a hailstorm. It shocked me, it made me panic, and it hurt.

I thought a lot about what would have happened if he hadn't found the money that day. I had a lot of thinking time, and when wondering what you were doing hurt too much, that was what I thought about. (Were you going straight home from school? Did you have a friend to walk with yet? Had you joined any after-school clubs? Were you going to be in a play? When Annabel started writing, she told me some of the answers, but they weren't the ones I wanted.)

I think if your dad had got a job then things would have got better. Not perfect, but good enough. He knew that he was wrong when he hurt me. He never would have touched you, although I was scared you would get caught up in it, and that was why I thought I might need to get you away. Or maybe I would have left him. Then you would have had a more ordinary broken home. What I wouldn't give now for that to have been your world.

I didn't intend to hurt him. But I did. Which is what he would have said about hurting me: I didn't mean to. Not that that makes it right. But it makes it — grey. Not black and white. So when the police asked me what happened, and when the lawyer and the barrister tried to get me to tell 'my side', as though it was a competition that you and your father hadn't already lost, I didn't say anything. I didn't defend myself. I let things happen. It was what I deserved. Though not, I see now, what you deserved.

I thought you might want to see me when I was released from prison, but my social worker soon put me straight. Severe panic attacks, she said. The rights of the child. Patience.

I was not patient. I was distraught, and I was vengeful, not at you, but at myself. I couldn't sleep, didn't eat, missed a probationary meeting. My social worker came to see me. She coaxed me into her car and drove me to hospital. I spent three months in whatever mental hospitals are called these days. I got a little bit better. There was a counsellor there who helped me to think about my own life, separate from yours, until you were ready to come in to it. I was too tired to fight the idea in the way that I wanted to. Why, I wanted to scream, why should I wait any longer? I didn't ever mean to hurt my daughter. No, said the counsellor, but is not meaning to hurt the same as not hurting?

They helped me to find a little place to live and I remembered how much I liked to bake. I got one of those halfway jobs in a factory and then another in the bakery, where they kept me on. I got fat again. I fed the birds in the park and I joined a reading group and started working at a community garden. I tried finding you online but either you were the only person in their twenties not on Facebook or you'd changed your name.

You are the treasure of my life, Loveday, the best thing I ever did, and knowing that

I'd destroyed all of the things I'd worked so hard to give you — the confidence, the security, the sense of being loved — is what broke me every single day that we've been apart.

I worked. I waited. I never found patience, but eventually, patience found me.

I'm here, sweetheart, and I love you.

Mum x

■ ■ ■ ■

POETRY

■ ■ ■ ■

2016
HEAL YOUR HEART

Archie's funeral was insane. I'd been out of hospital for five days. It was too sunny — the hottest October day on record — and as we waited for the hearse to arrive, the churchyard looked as though a moody circus had moved in. Silver shoes, frock-coats, someone with a rabbit on a lead. A couple of actors and three people important enough to have bodyguards. There'd been a security sweep in advance too. I suppose that was the royal. I'm not sure if the royal was the one who came in the helicopter or if that was some other dignitary. Not that any of it mattered.

There was quite a lot of air-kissing and crying before the service began, and I was afraid it would be awful. I mean, awful as in 'not what Archie wanted' as opposed to the grim, awful goodbye that it was always going to be.

But, of course, it was an Archibald Brodie

production, and it went like clockwork. It seemed as though Archie had given a lot of thought to organising his funeral. Everyone received their instructions from his solicitor in the days after he died. They came in envelopes of thick blue paper, with typed letters inside. It was a bit like being given a part in a play.

Everyone did as they were told on the day. It made me laugh, and cry, because it was so perfectly Archie: unbridled showing-off balanced by a thoughtfulness that meant no one had to do anything that they couldn't cope with. The funeral directors, the caterers and the horse-and-carriages people had all been paid in advance. The church was filled with chrysanthemums — the most showy-offy flowers that there are — and it smelled of those, and of incense, which is very like pipe-smoke if pipe-smoke is the thing you would rather be smelling. There was one instruction common to us all: 'Everyone, but everyone, must go back to my house and eat, drink and be merry for as long as they can manage' when it was over. The plans had last been updated eight months ago. His solicitor told me that Archie went through them every year.

I was the first follower of the coffin. I had Nathan on one side of me, and Annabel on the other, and they both held my hands, tightly. When the coffin got to the front, we sat in the second pew, and those who were reading or singing or doing a burlesque routine — yes, really — sat in the front pews so that they were ready to step up when it was their turn to pay whatever tribute Archie had assigned them. The vicar was another friend of Archie, of course, because there's no way you'd get fire-eaters in a church without some inside help.

Once I sat down I broke my heart with crying, again, the way I had every day since Archie died. I could feel Annabel and Nathan looking at each other over the top of my head. Then Nathan's arm came around my shoulder and Annabel handed me a tissue, and I slowed my breathing down, and imagined the sound of Archie shouting 'Love-DEEEE'.

The organ music — which was 'With a Little Help From My Friends', in case you're interested — stopped. Everyone hushed, a taffeta-and-silk sound. The vicar moved forward and put his hand on the coffin, looked down at it, sighed.

'Well, Archie,' he began, 'what are we going to do without you?'

Although I was dreading the funeral service

and burial, afterwards was worse, because my usual level of social awkwardness was amplified to the power of ten by grief and the absoluteness of the loss of my friend and protector. I was The Girl Who Got the House, so everybody wanted to talk to me. Some of them were less pleased than others by my inheritance, largely because Archie had lost the house in poker games to at least a dozen people over the years, and they'd generously allowed him to live in it until his death. He'd shaken hands with them all, and signed nothing.

My bequest, however — the house, the business, and the money in the business account, which was, I'm sure, many tens of thousands of pounds more than the shop ever made — was legally bomb-proof, and when it came to it, there was something in Archie that made decent people behave decently. So there was the odd jibe about the house — did I fancy a game of cards, double or quits — but nothing to worry about. And Archie had had more than enough to go around: there were a couple of other houses, paintings, many things that looked like tat but turned out to be priceless. Melodie got his hat collection, Annabel a diamond bracelet and an instruction to sell it and go on a cruise. She laughed and said that was what she had always wanted to do. (Why hadn't I known that?) Archie was as generous in death as he had been in his larger-than-life.

I sat on the sofa and either Nathan or Annabel were with me the whole time. After the first hour, everyone was too drunk to bother with me much, any more. After the third hour I slipped away to the library and lay down on the Chesterfield. I was aware of Nathan following me; the next thing I knew, he was waking me, and the house was, if not quiet, at least quieter. The caterers had left and there was a card game going on in the kitchen, with bodyguards at the door, so there was still a royal in residence.

Nathan steered me up the stairs. I stopped. 'I can't stay here,' I said.

'Loveday,' Nathan said, 'Annabel's got one of the guest rooms ready for us. You're going to have to stay here sometime. Anyway, there are still people here. We can't go.'

I was too tired to argue, so I let him propel me upwards. 'I still can't believe this is my house,' I said.

'It's weird,' Nathan agreed. Then, 'Annabel says she'll call you tomorrow evening. The cleaners are coming in about eleven in the morning. They can tidy the poker school away if it's still going.'

'Yes,' I said. Archie, always a fan of Douglas Adams, had stated that the party must go on for as long as it wanted to. I was assuming it would run out of steam somewhere around the twenty-four-hour mark. If it went on any longer, it was going to have to sort out its own food.

Nathan woke me at nine. The room Annabel had put us in was one of the five bedrooms, and it was the smallest, with matching double bed, wardrobe and dressing table. I would say they were 1950s, warm dark wood and smooth curves. The wallpaper was William Morris-ish, or maybe even original William Morris, knowing Archie. In the en-suite shower room, everything except the wooden floor was bright white. The shower was the best one I had ever used, with high pressure and a disc shower-head fixed in the ceiling so you could close your eyes and pretend you were in a good, hot thunderstorm. The windowsill was wide and deep, the perfect place for a collection of shells or stones. I might make it my room. I shook my head. It was too soon to think about any of this.

After I'd dressed, Nathan and I sat in the sunny kitchen, with pork pie and New York cheesecake left over from the wake. The bodyguards were gone. Someone was asleep on a chaise longe in the main living room, someone else sprawled on the floor in the dining room. I hoped that the lurcher wandering around the garden belonged to one of them.

'Do you want me to come to the shop with you tomorrow, for the insurance assessor?' Nathan asked.

'Yes please,' I said. Did you see that? I was getting better at accepting help. Well, let's face it, I'd have been burned to a crisp in a bookshop without it.

Once the insurance company was done, I could hire a skip and start chucking out all the dead, wet, scorched, charred remains of the place that had kept me safe. In an odd way, I was looking forward to it. It was a job of work that had to be done. It wasn't abstract. Whatever I decided about the shop, it would still have to be cleared.

The house was a different matter altogether. I knew I ought to live in it, but it felt ridiculous for me to rattle around in Archie's dear old mansion. Drifting off to sleep, I wondered about making it into something else — a respite home for kids in care, a place where bereaved people could grieve, a halfway house for women clambering back from prison or abuse — but on waking I couldn't imagine ever being up to such a task. Whereas filling a skip, or scrubbing a floor — that was achievable.

'Vanessa says she'll help,' Nathan said. 'So does Melodie.'

'That's kind,' I said. I meant it.

The morning passed quietly. Nathan and I talked about going to Cornwall; he would show me the places I remembered and the ones I didn't, and we would visit my father's grave. I looked at some of the inscriptions in the books in the library while Nathan napped on the sofa. I rubbed my palm over his head as I passed him and he didn't stir. I wandered through all the rooms where Archie wasn't. Part of his 'when I die' plans had included booking a cleaning company to strip his bed and wash the sheets and laundry and throw out the food in the fridge and any partly used toiletries. He really had thought of everything, except the fact that every inch and atom of his home exuded him, and I had no idea how I was going to get past that. I'd said as much to Annabel.

'One foot in front of the other, Loveday,' she'd said, and I'd wished I'd learned to talk to her when I was eleven, instead of wasting all this time.

I read my mother's letter again. It made

me miss her like I had in the beginning, a scared ten-year-old with everyone who was precious gone from her. When I wasn't breaking my heart over Archie, I was thinking about how monumentally alone Mum and I had been, and breaking my heart about that.

Nathan and the stragglers roused when I started cooking bacon and eggs. Once we had all eaten, he offered to open a bottle of champagne, which I thought was a risky strategy, but it worked, because both of our guests went a bit green and called cabs.

It was just the two of us.

For now.

'It's nearly time,' Nathan said. 'Are you going to be okay?'

'Yes, I am,' I said. I meant it. I felt calmer than I had in — well, in forever. The loss of Archie hurt. The change in my circumstances was bewildering. But the fact that I was allowing myself to be me, and reaching out to Nathan and Annabel — it was as though I'd finally found a comfortable way to stand, feet on the ground, eyes forward, no need for anything except taking a breath and deciding what next.

Yesterday, as Archie's coffin went into the ground, I'd made a decision. I'd thought about how Mum had wanted to come and get me. How she'd found me; how her nerve had failed her. Just like mine had, so many times, when I could have reached out to Nathan or I could have reported Rob or I could have made Melodie listen to my warning. I could have told Archie everything, on any of those occasions when he'd shown me how ready he was to listen. I hadn't.

Finally, I understood. There was nothing I wanted more than to see her and nothing that was more frightening than the thought of seeing her. Contacting her didn't mean a quick coffee and a catch-up. It meant the beginning of the future I always should have had.

I knew that my relationship with my mother was in as good a shape as a burned-down bookshop. Nothing had been simple for us. There was no reason to think it was about to get any simpler. As the funeral car had taken us back to the house, I asked Annabel to call my mother and invite her to come to see me. She had said she would come today.

'Do you want me to make myself scarce?' Nathan asked.

'Maybe to start with,' I said.

'I'll be upstairs,' he said. 'Just call me when you need me.' He kissed me, softly;

my lip had only just healed and the skin was shiny and thin.

He took his copy of *Grinning Jack* from his bag and walked up the staircase, to our bedroom.

And I made my way out into the late autumn sunshine to wait for my mother. I imagined her leaving books at the shop, putting them on the step like flowers at the site of a car crash. She had wanted, so much, to talk to me. She had been so scared. I knew what those things felt like.

The thought of her was as warm as ginger parkin, as sweet as finding a perfect shell on the shore.

Choice
As performed by Loveday Cardew at the
George and Dragon
York, January 2017

Nobody else got the life I got.
I was happy, then wretched, and I cried a
    lot.
Then I grieved then I sulked and I got in a
    knot
And I didn't know how to get out of it.

Not a lot of people lose both parents in one
    night

Just like that — the end of the light
No coping strategies, no end in sight.
And I had no way to get out of it.

When you only want your mum and dad
   then no one else will do
When you push other people away they will
   leave you too
I acted like I knew it all but I didn't have a
   clue
And I didn't know how to get back from it.

And then you realise what you've done is
   made yourself a shell
You've shut right off, right out, right down,
   the pussy in the well
And no one close enough to hear the tale
   you've got to tell
How the hell are you meant to get over it?

It turns out if you take a step then someone
   else will match it
It seems that if you drop the ball some
   cocky git will catch it
The past won't fix the future, you have
   power over that shit
And that's how I might get over it.

You are cordially invited to the reopening
of Lost For Words, York
Rare and beautiful books
for book lovers everywhere
Reading refuge upstairs

Proprietor: Loveday Cardew
Event catering: Sarah-Jane Walker
Entertainment: Nathan Avebury
Guided tours: Melodie

A BOOKSHOP

A bell over the door: a brassy, jangling
    clang.
There should be no clock. Time is
    meaningless here.
No book is without worth.
Let there be a marbling of the light,
    refracted through old windows, to remind
    us that nothing is ever true.
Here is all that you do not yet know.
Everything is slightly crooked, except the
    lines of words on pages.
Here is food.
This place is crammed with what is
    unlooked-for.
There should not be music, but there
    should not be silence.
Fingers must not be shy. Touch spines.
    Turn pages.
A door that no one has the key to is in the
    corner.
Giggling. And little cries of 'Oh!' when

something forgotten is found.

A bookshop is not magic, but it can steal away your heart.

The air is not like any other air. It has memory stirred through it.

There is something here for you. All you need to do is choose it.

That smell. You know. Patchouli. Honey. Salt and violets.

And oh, the people. They must be forgiven their sins because they are here.

A bookshop is not magic, but it can slowly heal your heart.

ACKNOWLEDGEMENTS

Many people helped me to understand the detail of Loveday's story:

— Mary Hill, Laura Lane, Rebecca Mason and Marion Robson talked me through social work and long-term foster caring
— Jack Fellowes and Tom Furnell explained to me how a bookshop would burn
— Kirsten Luckins and James Wilkinson answered my many questions about performance poetry
— Barry Speker OBE DL showed me how complex the law around domestic violence is
— Stuart Manby of Barter Books in Alnwick took me behind the scenes and told me the secrets of second-hand bookselling

I'm grateful to you all, and claim any

mistakes and misrepresentations for my own, with apologies.

I'd like to give a special shout-out to Scratch Tyne, a rehearsal group funded by spoken word charity Apples and Snakes. The poets there were patient and encouraging with me as I fumbled my way to understanding what performance poetry is and how it works its magic on both poet and audience. I remain inspired by you all.

My beta-readers were Alan Butland, Rebecca Mason, Emily Medland, Tom Nelson, James Wilkinson and Susan Young, and their feedback was key in helping me to figure out how to tell Loveday's tale. Shelley Harris read the beginning at the beginning, and has cheered me on throughout.

Claire Dyer of Fresh Eyes Consultancy gave intelligent, valuable feedback into what worked, what snagged, and what could be better.

Archie is named for Arch Brodie, who taught me English, along with Mary Adams, Margaret Rogerson and Bev Millman. The school that I went to was unremarkable, but the English teaching was, I believe, exceptional. Bev, in particular, saw a spark of something in my writing; I'll always be grateful.

My agent, Oli Munson at A. M. Heath, is

my champion and my friend. Thank you for keeping the faith.

Eli Dryden is part editor and part creative partner-in-crime, and I love working with her. Her input and insight work wonders. The team at Bonnier Zaffre are a delight to work with — committed, clever and bubbling with ideas. Thanks, all.

The families of writers have much to put up with. Thank you for being there, when I was (sometimes literally, often metaphorically) absent: Alan, Ned, Joy, Mum, Dad, Auntie Susan.

ABOUT THE AUTHOR

Stephanie Butland lives with her family near the sea in the North East of England. She writes in a studio at the bottom of her garden, and when she's not writing, she trains people to think more creatively. For fun, she reads, knits, sews, bakes and spins. She is an occasional performance poet.

www.stephaniebutland.co.uk

Twitter: @under_blue_sky
Instagram: @StephanieButland
Facebook: @StephanieButlandAuthor

The employees of Thorndike Press hope you have enjoyed this Large Print book. All our Thorndike, Wheeler, and Kennebec Large Print titles are designed for easy reading, and all our books are made to last. Other Thorndike Press Large Print books are available at your library, through selected bookstores, or directly from us.

For information about titles, please call:
(800) 223-1244

or visit our website at:
gale.com/thorndike

To share your comments, please write:
Publisher
Thorndike Press
10 Water St., Suite 310
Waterville, ME 04901